THE
BOOKSELLER'S
DAUGHTER

THE BOOKSELLER'S DAUGHTER

A YOUNG WOMAN'S JOURNEY INTO MYSTERY, FANTASY, AND THE FUTURE

Steve Burt

Inquiries should be addressed to:
Steven E. Burt
17101 SE 94th Berrien Court
The Villages, FL 32162
352-391-8293
passtev@aol.com
www.SteveBurtBooks.com

ISBN 978-0-9856188-6-5 (paperback)
ISBN 978-0-9856188-0-3 (mobi)
ISBN 978-0-9856188-1-0 (epub)

Printed in the United States

Interior design by Dotti Albertine
Illustrations by Hanah Cincotta
Cover by SelfPubBookCovers.com/VISIONS

Contents

Acknowledgments

My thanks to the following people who served as first readers, offering corrections and suggestions: Lorraine Grey, Joyce MacMullen, Nancy Goss, Wendy Burt-Thomas, Sandra Wilber, Joyce Gordon, Lee Ireland. And special thanks to my wife Jolyn for her support, editing, major suggestions, and conscientious 25 readings.

I am also grateful to my California team, award-winners in their fields, who have worked on my projects for 20 years: copywriter Laren Bright (www.larenbright.com) and book designer Dotti Albertine (www.dotdesign.net). I highly recommend both of these fine professionals.

The cover was designed by SelfPubBookCovers.com/VISIONS and was purchased from SelfPubBookCovers.com. A few modifications were needed. The cover artist was easy to work with, making them quickly and professionally.

Interior illustrations were done by Hanah Cincotta, a talented art/animation major at Lesley University in Cambridge, MA.

Preface

A Grave Situation in Wells, Maine

In the small town of Wells, Maine—which measures barely seven by eight miles—they say you can't walk a dog without tripping over a grave. Not surprising, considering the 56-square-mile town contains 201 listed cemeteries.

And one that's not listed, which a stranger in town desperately needs to find.

Trouble at Toil & Trouble

It was 10:45 p.m. the last Wednesday in June when Marcy Stonestreet, the Wells police dispatcher, took the call from two dishwashers at the Maine Diner on Route 1.

Zach Burns and Caleb Dwyer were high school juniors working summer jobs there. Marcy knew them both and had no reason to believe the call was a prank. They had been emptying the trash into one of the dumpsters behind the building when they heard something flap by overhead.

"*Whoosh, whoosh, whoosh* is what it sounded like," Zach told her. "So we looked up to see what it was."

"It was backlit by the moon," Caleb said. "Looked like a humongous turkey vulture or a bald eagle, maybe a super goose."

"A super goose?" Marcy asked.

"Had to be three times the size of those big white ones," Caleb replied. "Maybe even bigger than that."

Zach added, "It was like a pterodactyl on steroids—wings more like a bat's than a bird's, with a bulky body."

"Humongous wingspan," Caleb added. He liked the adjective.

"It was tracking south, right above Route 1. When Caleb yelled, 'It's going down,' I'm pretty sure it heard us. It looked back our way. Birds don't do that."

"It looked back?" Marcy asked.

"Yes," Caleb insisted. "Seriously, Mrs. Stonestreet. It did look back. I know it did. I saw these red eyes."

"Me, too," Zach agreed. "Red, like glowing. You could see them, even that far off."

"Thank God it didn't circle around and come back," Caleb said. "If it had looped back, we'd have been inside the diner in two seconds."

Marcy recorded the call but also jotted down what Zach and Caleb told her. "Stay inside. I'll have somebody at the diner in under five minutes. I think Officer Stevenson is close."

"We know Aaron," Zach said. "He's AJ's older brother. Great basketball player. He gives talks at school."

"Figured you knew him," she said. "I'll tell him to meet you by the back door." They disconnected.

Aaron Stevenson was in his third year on the Wells P.D. He was a Wells High grad who had stayed close to home, attending York Community College and earning a criminal justice degree. He knew everybody in Wells, including Zach and Caleb.

He met them behind the diner and took a report that was essentially what they had told Marcy Stonestreet when they called it in. Aaron knew the boys to be decent, honest high school juniors whose story, though it was odd, he couldn't easily dismiss. When he finished, he drove south on Route 1 until he reached the I.G.A. parking lot, where he parked nose-to-tail with Maine State Trooper Alicia "Smitty" Smith's cruiser.

Aaron and Smitty were talking window-to-window when another call came from dispatch. Marcy had gotten a call from a security monitoring company.

"They've got a tripped silent alarm at Toil & Trouble Books," Marcy told Aaron. "They also notified the owner, Geoff Swett, who is on his way. He'll meet you there."

Marcy gave Aaron the address even though he knew the place. It was a half mile back toward the Maine Diner, where he had just taken the dishwashers' report. Smitty called her State Police dispatcher and got permission to assist. The two cars pulled out.

Toil & Trouble wasn't a regular-hours bookstore like Annie's Book Stop on Wells' south end. This was a one-man book fulfilment service Geoff Swett ran out of an old Colonial that had once housed his mother's antiques shop. From his second floor office he dealt in rare and antiquarian books, mostly mysticism, magic, and occult. He generated nearly all of his business through online auctions.

Aaron turned into the driveway, activating the motion-sensor spotlight over the front porch. He parked next to a faded sign: Yesteryear Antiques. Below it hung a smaller rectangular sign with three gold-lettered lines: *Toil & Trouble, Rare Books—Mysticism, Magic, Occult—Appointment Only.* Under that were a phone number and website.

Smitty pulled her car over so it straddled the narrow shoulder and left its light bar flashing to slow drivers and shunt northbound traffic away from the scene.

A Volvo wagon approached from the north and shot across the center line into the driveway, narrowly missing Aaron's car. It bounced up onto the front lawn and braked. The driver's door opened and a trim man in a Red Sox jersey climbed out. He walked over to Aaron and Smitty.

"Geoff Swett. I'm the owner," he declared, and he held up his right hand. "I have the keys." Then he recognized the cop and said, "Oh, hi, Aaron." Aaron introduced Smitty and they exchanged nods.

The house was dark inside.

"How many doors?" Aaron asked.

"Just front and back. No side, no cellar," Swett said.

"Locks?" Smitty asked.

"Padlocks on both, and standard locksets above the handles. Back door also has a wooden timber across the inside. I haven't taken it out of the iron brackets in years."

"How many alarm systems?" Aaron asked. "You still have two business signs: one for antiques, one for rare books. Dispatch sent me to Toil & Trouble."

"The whole building is wired as Toil & Trouble. Yesteryear, my mother's old business, has been dead for years."

"So when we go in," Smitty said, "what'll we see—antiques down and books up?"

"Pretty much, yes. Still a few antiques upstairs with the books, which are mostly in the room that's my office."

"How about cash?" Aaron asked. "Anything that might attract druggies or teens?"

"Nope. I deal in checks and credit. Toil & Trouble is an online business, with payments almost exclusively made by computer, phone, or mail."

"Druggies wouldn't know that," Smitty said. "They just want a business to break into. And while kids wouldn't care about antiques, they might have an interest in your kind of books."

"Okay," Aaron said, "so we have alarms on all windows up and down?" Aaron asked. "And on the two doors?"

"Correct," Swett replied.

"Cameras?" Aaron asked.

"Nope."

"Anything else we need to know?" Smitty asked. "We don't step on a land mine."

"Don't look for wall switches. The only one's at the bottom of the staircase, for the ceiling bulb at the top landing. Everything else is floor or table lamps."

"Okay," Aaron said. "First Smitty and I will check the outside, see if any locks or windows are broken. You stay here until we call you. Then you can let us in the front."

The two cops approached the porch.

"Padlock still in place," Aaron said. "Meet you around back."

They split up and worked their way around the building. The windows and latches were okay. They met by the back door. Still locked. They aimed their lights at the upper back windows: original double-pane six-over-sixes: a half dozen small glass squares of three-over-three in the top half, the same in the bottom half. At first glance everything looked okay. Then Smitty rechecked the upper left window.

"Look at that," she said, and focused on the middle pane just below the thumb latch.

Aaron peered up. "Nothing broken that I can see, if that's what you're asking."

"Exactly," Smitty said. "You don't see any jagged glass. But there's no reflection, either. I think that pane of glass is missing. My flashlight glints off the other five panes, but not that one. I think it's missing."

The room behind the window was pitch black.

Aaron examined the ground near his feet. "No ladder marks in the dirt. And no tree close enough to shinny up."

"What if somebody brought along a little square of plywood," Smitty suggested, "to put under the ladder so it wouldn't leave marks. You go up, you break the window and reach in, and you unlock and open it. You climb inside, pull out the jagged pieces in case anybody looks up there, but it appears intact. You climb out when you're done, close the window, climb down and walk away with your ladder, your square of plywood, and whatever you stole."

"Interesting," Aaron replied. "But it's a little too premeditated for a kid or a druggie looking for cash."

"Yeah, probably," she said. "But still, it appears to be missing. Let's go get Swett to unlock and we'll check it from the inside."

They returned to the front and found Swett already waiting on the porch.

"Any chance there's a missing pane in one of the upper back windows?" Aaron asked. "Left side when you're looking up."

"Not that I know of. Why?"

"We're not getting a reflection," Smitty said.

"Can't be," Swett said.

"What room is that?" Aaron asked, and made a hand motion. "That corner."

"That's my office. I was in this morning and didn't notice any glass missing." Swett entered a number sequence for the alarm system, unlocked, and pushed the front door open.

Aaron stepped in and swept his mag lite around the room. There were dusty loveseats, chairs, and tables with lamps everywhere. But nobody was lurking.

Swett pulled the chain on a floor lamp. The light came on.

"How many rooms?" Aaron asked quietly.

"Four down, two of which we're looking at. This is a double parlor. Two you can't see back there." He pointed. "Four up. Center staircase straight ahead. No back staircase."

"Smitty," Aaron said. "I don't want to go room to room if this is just some scared kid who got stranded when his buddies ran off with the ladder."

"Good point. But it may not be a scared kid. What if it's a bad guy?"

Aaron called loudly, "This is the Wells Police Department and the Maine State Police. There's only one way out, so come out now with your hands where we can see them."

Five long seconds, no response.

Smitty announced, "This is the Maine State Police. Let's not make things any worse. Come out so we can hear your story."

A floorboard creaked upstairs.

"My office, top right," Swett whispered. "One door in and out."

Aaron and Smitty rested their hands on their holstered weapons.

"Listen up, you upstairs. This is Officer Stevenson of the Wells Police Department. Come down now with your hands in plain sight."

No answer. No movement. No second creak.

"Come. Down. Now," Aaron said firmly. "This isn't worth messing up your life."

A different noise, like a chair or table leg scraping the floor. Maybe more than one leg, like someone moving a piece of heavy furniture in the dark.

Aaron spotted the wall switch at the bottom of the stairs. "I'll turn it on," he said softly, "see if we can encourage our friend to come down out of the dark."

Smitty drew her weapon. The two of them crept toward the stairway.

"Upstairs, look, we know you're scared. We're going to turn on the light at the top of the landing, outside your door. Step out with your hands raised and everything will be fine."

No answer. No movement. No noise.

Aaron reached for the switch. Before he could touch it, the board squeaked again and the furniture scraped. Then a crash. Glass shattering. Followed by the creaky floorboard again, and footsteps running. Like a track-and-field long jumper heading down the runway for the takeoff board. Had someone thrown something through the window frame, then backed up and run at the window and dived out?

Aaron flicked the switch and the light over the landing came on. He charged up the stairs with Smitty two steps behind. She held her weapon and flashlight clamped together in a two-handed grip, the beam aligned with the gun barrel. Aaron's lanky body filled the doorway to the right, his own weapon and light in front of him sweeping the room. He took two steps in and turned to the window, Smitty framed by the doorway behind him.

The entire window—both sashes—was gone: the upper six-over-six and the lower six-over-six smashed outward. Both cops stepped close to the gaping hole and shone their mags down at the ground below. But no one was sprawled there, injured or dead of a broken neck.

What they saw was a high-backed deacon's chair, heavy polished oak with rich red upholstery, lying on its side five feet from the building, its feet tangled in splintered pieces of window frame. The piece was massive and heavy. The window and sash had slowed its forward momentum and shortened its trajectory so it dropped almost straight down. Anyone diving or leaping blindly out the opening into the dark after it would surely overshoot it and crash to earth past it, breaking bones if not the spine.

"Where'd he go?" Smitty asked. "A gymnast couldn't stick that landing."

"I don't know," Aaron answered. "Even if he managed a forward somersault on impact, we'd have seen somebody running away."

"Maybe he didn't jump," Smitty said, alarm in her voice, and spun around in a quick about-face. She flashed her light around the room again, this time in the shadows behind the desk and bookcases.

Nobody. No crazed druggie. No lurking bogeyman. No frightened teenager hiding behind the desk.

Swett stepped in and turned on the brass banker's lamp on his desk. When he saw the missing window, he made a quick visual inventory and said, "Crap, not my grandfather's deacon's chair."

☞☞☞

Smitty stayed in the room with Swett while he tried to determine if anything else besides the antique deacon's chair was missing.

Aaron walked downstairs then around back to look around. No injured perpetrator near the deacon's chair. No disturbed earth to suggest a hard landing. No tossed-aside flashlight or knocked-off ball cap. He called Marcy at dispatch and requested a search team and a K9 unit.

Fifteen minutes later the dog and handler arrived. They picked up a scent on the deacon's chair but there was no scent trail leading away from it. They covered an area forty feet past the chair and got nothing, so the handler brought the dog inside. No scent downstairs but upstairs they struck gold. The dog sniffed the little pile of broken glass on the floor below the window sill, which led to Swett's desk and lamp, then to several bookshelves. The dog returned to the window and found a different scent trail leading straight back to an interior wall then back to the window again: the long jumper's runway and takeoff point. Which is where it ended.

Sergeant Elmer "Elly" Stedman arrived shortly after the K9 unit.

He was one of three detectives who made up the Wells Police Department's Criminal Investigation Division or CID. Stedman put the break-in sequence together right away.

"But the perp didn't know the thumb latch broke the circuit," Stedman said, "and set off the silent alarm. Because he didn't hear anything, he thought he had time to get comfortable. Probably turned the desk lamp on so he could see, figuring if anybody saw it they'd think it was Mr. Swett working late. Then Stevenson and Smith pulled up out front, trapping him up here. He snapped off the lamp, hoping they'd see the padlocks in place and the windows secure, and go away. If nobody came inside, he could wait until the coast was clear."

"Smitty figured out the missing pane," Aaron said.

A patrolwoman came in. "No ladder, Sergeant Stedman. We thought maybe the perp grabbed one from a neighbor's barn or something, but there's not even one close by. And no marks on the ground out back."

"Footprints?" Stedman asked her.

"None yet," she answered.

The German shepherd strained at its leash, as if it wanted to climb out the window. The handler gave it a little slack. It put its front paws on the sill and stuck its head out, then sniffed the outside edge of the sill and began to yip. The handler pulled it back.

Aaron went to the window, careful not to step on the pile of broken glass, and poked his head out. He looked down at the ground, then inspected the sill.

"Marks," he said. "Scratches. Like somebody hung on while he broke the pane."

"Are we back to teens?" Smitty wondered aloud. "One comes up the ladder, the others yank it away and leave him hanging?"

"I don't think so," Aaron said, and turned back to Stedman. "Sarge, you're going to want pictures of these. They're wide and deep, like the ones my parents' dog left on the door the day they left him alone all day." He backed away so Stedman could take a look.

"Not fingernails," Stedman said. "Thicker and wider. More like claws from a bearskin rug." Stedman started taking photos.

Aaron thought back to the moments before he charged the stairs. He'd been about to flick the light switch when the crash came—that would have been the deacon's chair exploding through the window—then the creaking board again, and the running footsteps, like a long jumper. That was the sequence, he was sure of it.

The footsteps came after the crash, not with it. So he didn't jump out clutching the chair to his chest. He tossed it out to enlarge the opening. But he didn't have the time or the lighting to see where it hit. The chair landed close to the building, leaving an angle too steep for even the best acrobat. So he couldn't have dived after it and used it to break his fall. Besides, it was too dark to see the chair.

Aaron tried to remember if he'd heard the grunt, oof, or yelp of pain that would have accompanied a hard landing. The memory wasn't there. After the crash he had heard the floorboard. The intruder had backed up and gotten a running start. Seconds later he and Smitty had found the room empty. No sounds and no signs of anyone hitting the ground.

A childhood memory floated to the surface of his mind: two white geese taking off from the narrows in front of his grandfather's camp on Lake Arrowhead. He could see and hear their broad wings cleaving the air in slow motion, their webbed feet seeking traction on the lake's surface, their wingtips kissing the silver blue water—*flap, flap, flap*—a steady battle to gain altitude. Why was his mind hearing the geese's slow ascent now?

He thought back to the dishwashers' story an hour and a half earlier at the Maine Diner. What had they said? *Whoosh, whoosh, whoosh.*

Section I

A Mysterious Visitor in Wells, Maine

CHAPTER 1

Annie's Book Stop in Wells had just opened on Friday morning when a squatty, hunchbacked nun shuffled in. At least that was what it looked like to the bookstore owner Maryann Keegan at the customer counter and her daughter's best friend AJ near the front-room Local Author display.

Maryann glanced up and smiled invitingly as soon she heard the tea bell tinkle over the front door. She warmly offered her usual welcome-to-Annie's-Book-Stop greeting and tried not to look surprised, which she was.

AJ also looked up with a smile, too, but as soon as she spotted the short, black-robed visitor she couldn't help but stare slightly open-mouthed. It was impossible to look away.

The visitor framed in the lower two-thirds of the doorway wasn't simply a person in a robe, not like a choir member in a church's holiday cantata. This visitor was *hidden—buried* inside the robe—with not an inch of skin exposed. The robe's material was obviously heavy, like an old Army blanket, a faded black garment that might have been salvaged from a trunk in a medieval convent. The hood wasn't peaked like a friar's but was rounded. A gauzy black veil hung like a curtain from forehead to chest. Large black gloves covered both hands. The excess fabric along the robe's bottom puddled on the floor, frayed and ragged from rubbing over dirt and blacktop.

AJ had watched the movie *Sister Act* many times and remembered how Whoopi Goldberg had looked after federal witness protection transformed her from lounge-singer-on-the-lam-from-the-mob into an inner-city nun. The outfit was called a *habit*, AJ recalled, and the headpiece was a *wimple*. But this person at the bookstore door now was clothed in something very different from Whoopi's and the other sisters' habits and wimples, which had been black and white. She remembered Whoopi or someone joking about penguin suits. There had been panels of white somewhere around the face, AJ thought—had it been under the chin? And their faces had

shown, framed by the wimples—no veils. The figure entering Annie's now was dressed in something that functioned more like a beekeeper's protective gear or an astronaut's helmet.

Maybe this wasn't a nun. Could it be a Muslim woman whose face was hidden under a *burqa*? No, there was no slit through which to view the world. This was a veil that acted like a heavily tinted car window: the driver could see out but nobody else could see in. Maybe this wasn't even a female—how about a Franciscan friar, a religious brother, or a jokester in a Halloween costume? Or even a robber with a pistol in a waistband under the robe.

"May I help you, Sister?" Maryann called from the register.

The dark-robed visitor leaned into the main room like a weatherman reporting in a nor'easter and shuffled on leaden legs toward the counter.

Heavy boots? Maryann wondered. *Or arthritic knees. Maybe both.* It was impossible to tell. The forward movement was tempered by an off-balance wobble that reminded her of Charlie Chaplin's Little Tramp.

The odd newcomer neared the counter and Maryann could see from her own 5'8" vantage point that the top of the robed head would be a foot lower than that.

She's not hunchbacked after all, not like I first thought. But her shoulders are definitely oversized, like she's got on football shoulder pads.

Whoever was buried inside the robe looked like she'd shrugged too hard and the shrug had frozen in place.

"When I called yesterday, I spoke to someone named Keegan." With the voice and words came puffs of the veil that indicated where the speaker's mouth was.

High-pitched, definitely female, very good English, slight French or French-Canadian accent. I don't recognize it, though, so it wasn't me she talked to on the phone.

"You spoke with Keegan? That would be my daughter. She's in the work room. What was it about, Sister?"

"You needn't call me Sister. I dress this way because my body cannot tolerate sunlight. I blister easily and cannot risk daylight exposure. I have to shield my skin completely." She held up both hands in a gesture of surrender. "That's why I have the gloves. I realize that my dress is unorthodox and makes people uncomfortable—humans fear the unknown—and if they are not uncomfortable, they are at least curious. But I can assure you, I do not suffer leprosy or anything contagious, so you have nothing to fear from me. I and others like me are sometimes called *moon children*."

"I've heard the term," Maryann said, nodding. "Well, I'm very sorry you have to go through this, especially in the heat of the summer. You must be sweating like crazy under there."

"It's not as bad as you imagine," said the voice. "I don't sweat." She said it flatly, like it was a simple biological fact. She was facing the counter and Maryann now, but with her face hidden behind the veil, there was no way to know if she was looking straight ahead or directly up at Maryann. So Maryann simply looked down a little and imagined eye contact, picturing an inquiring face beneath the hood. "So how may we help?"

"Your Keegan said the books I seek are not in stock, but you can order them. I do not use credit cards and was unable to offer a deposit over the telephone. I told Keegan I would come in this morning."

The work room door opened and a tall slim brunette about Maryann's height walked out. She wore prewashed jeans and a Wonder Woman tee shirt. Above her temple, on the right side of her head, was an inch-wide shock of white hair. Her eyes registered no surprise at the customer's outfit. She had cracked the door for a look before walking out.

"Hi. I'm Keegan. I recognized your voice from the phone."

The non-nun made a waddling half-turn to face her, hood and veil tilting slightly as she looked up at the girl.

"Zelda?" she gasped, clearly surprised.

Keegan stopped in her tracks. "Pardon?" She looked confused. She could picture the shock on the face behind the veil. She and her mother had seen it before—especially in Keegan's teenage years—when other people had mistaken her looks or her voice or both for Zelda, Maryann's younger sister. In her teenage years, and especially now at seventeen, Keegan was a dead ringer for her birth mother, the 21-year-old college student who had died of a cerebral hemorrhage while bringing her into the world.

"*Mon Dieu,*" the visitor said in French. "You look just like her—except for the blue eyes, of course, and that streak of white hair." She motioned toward Maryann but continued speaking to the girl. "Zelda's eyes were green, like this lady's. Which means," she said, turning to eye Maryann, "that you must be Zelda's sister."

"I am. I'm Maryann Keegan. And Keegan here—who insists on going by her last name—is both my niece and my adopted daughter. You may not have known this, but Zell died in labor." Before the visitor could respond, Maryann motioned toward the front room and added, "And this is AJ, Keegan's best friend."

After a waddling 180-degree turn, the woman in the robe focused on a slender caramel-colored young woman taller than Keegan, closer to six feet. She sported an explosion of thick curly black hair.

AJ gave a little wave. "Maryann's not-quite-adopted daughter," she said, and grinned. "My parents regularly threaten to ship my clothes to the Keegan house and pay for a meal plan."

"It is a pleasure to meet you, AJ. And Maryann. And Keegan."

"Judging by your reaction, you must have known my mother," Keegan said, forcing the visitor to make an awkward about-face. She thought *Oil me, the Tin Man creaked.*

"*Oui.* At the University of Maine at Orono. UMO. I learned that she had died but I had no details. Just now when you walked out of that room, though, Zelda sprang to life again right in front of my eyes. The resemblance is amazing. You also look like Maryann here, but you look exactly like Zelda as I remember her."

"I'm sorry," Maryann interrupted. "But you know our names and we don't know yours."

"Luna," the voice with no face said. "After Zelda left college, we talked by telephone a few times. Then when the calls stopped, I found out she had died. It was a shock. Zelda was amazing."

"You mean an amazing student?" Maryann asked.

"That, too. But I mean she was an amazing person and friend. When people stared at me because of this outfit—Zelda told them I was a Muslim exchange student and a brilliant Middle Eastern scholar. She was so imaginative, so resourceful. She just made that story up on the spot one day. That was before 9-11, when nobody knew enough about Muslim women to recognize this is not a burqa."

The four of them laughed.

"That'd be my sister," Maryann said. "I wish you could've been at her memorial service, Luna, to tell that story."

"Me too. And though I'm 17 years late, let me say how sorry I am for your loss."

"Thank you," Maryann replied. "And for your loss, as well."

Three customers came in. Maryann greeted them and excused herself. AJ returned to her dusting. Keegan moved behind the counter to work with Luna.

"I'd love to talk more, Luna, but on Friday mornings we get busy, as you can see. For now let me get your books ordered." She pecked at the computer and brought up a screen. "Two cemetery books and a reprint. Working on a family genealogy?"

"Something like that."

Keegan glanced down at the veil. With Luna's head tilted up a bit, the fabric was tented out a little where it rested against her nose.

That nose must be broad and flat like a gorilla's. Keegan turned the monitor 90 degrees so they could both see the screen.

"Are these the correct titles?" Keegan asked.

› *The Dirt on Maine's Burial Grounds,* Richard Laymon (SK Books, 2017).

› *Ancient Maine Cemeteries, Public and Private: Volume 27 York County,* compiled by Austin Call (Co-publishers: York County Historical Society and State of Maine, 1968).

› *General Joshua Chamberlain's Night Hawks: LeClair and Champaigne, the Scouts from Wells* (Wm. Coburn, privately printed Limited Edition 25 copies, Brewer, Maine, 1919; reprinted by Maine Civil War Press, Portland, Maine, 2017).

"Yes, those are the three."

"As I explained on the phone yesterday, *Chamberlain's Night Hawks* is the reprint that just came out, not the 1919 original. There were only 25 copies of that, which makes it a very rare book."

"The reprint is fine."

"Okay, today's Friday. My best guess is, we'll have all three here for you on Tuesday afternoon. Slight chance of Monday for the two cemetery books. We switch to summer hours in July, which is next week, so we'll be open 10 to 4 o'clock."

"How much money do you need from me?" Luna asked.

"How about $20 and the balance when you pick them up? Then we can talk more."

"Very well," Luna replied, working a gloved hand through a hip-high slit in the robe.

It'd be easier to grip a purse without that glove, Luna.

Luna's hand emerged with a clump of bills. She handed the wad over like a first-grader at a candy counter. Five twenties.

"Take one, please," she said, the veil puffing at her words. "It's hard for me to separate them."

Arthritis? "Looks painful," Keegan said. "You're still so young."

"Not as young as you think."

"Weren't you in college with my mother?"

"I was an older student."

Keegan let the subject drop and scooped the twenties off Luna's palm. She picked off the top bill and slipped it into the cash drawer. She rolled up the remaining twenties like a rug, picked a rubber band out of a woven bowl on the counter, and snapped it around the roll.

"That'll make it easier to pull your money out."

"Thank you, Keegan. Now I just need to find gloves with fingernails." She watched Keegan's mouth open and her eyes widen. "I'm joking, Keegan. I can do it myself once the gloves are off."

Keegan caught the playfulness in Luna's voice and, even though she couldn't see her mother's friend's face, she imagined a broad grin. She placed the little tube of bills on Luna's palm. *For such a little person, she's got huge hands.*

The glove closed stiffly over the money and with effort she worked it through the slit in the robe, into what must have been an inside pocket or pouch. When the hand appeared again, it came through the slit, the glove snagging, the leather back peeling away from her wrist. Keegan caught a quick glance.

What is that? Not skin. Leather? Scales? Is that what sunlight does to her?

The glove snapped back to its original shape, hiding the skin again. The veil and hood moved, and Keegan sensed Luna had cocked her head upward again and slightly to the side. *Owlish,* she thought, and felt sure Luna's eyes were staring straight at her through the veil, gauging her reaction to the exposed hand and wrist. *Did she catch me looking?* Keegan smiled as if nothing had happened.

"Can you give me a last name for the order?" the girl asked.

"Just Luna."

"Phone number? Email?"

"No email. I'll give you a local phone. It's not mine. Seldom does anyone answer. You can leave a message." She recited a 7-digit number and Keegan inputted it using the keyboard.

"We're all set for now, Luna. I'll call when the books come in. It's been a pleasure meeting you."

"*Moi aussi,* Keegan."

Keegan translated the French in her head. *Moi aussi. Me too.*

Then Luna added, "You're so like your mother."

Keegan grinned. "Which one?"

They chuckled and Luna made her wobbly Charlie Chaplin turn, then leaned forward and shuffled toward the front door. She rested a glove on the knob, pausing like a farmer about to head from house to barn in a blizzard. Except Luna's blizzard wasn't blinding, freezing cold snow. It was dazzling, blistering sunlight.

Maryann looked up. "*Au revoir*, Luna," she offered in her best high-school French.

"*Au revoir*," came the reply, and the little woman in the black Grim Reaper robe opened the door and trudged out slowly like a prisoner mounting the gallows.

CHAPTER 2

Two hours later, after a busy morning with customers at Annie's, things had slowed down enough so AJ and Keegan could grab lunch in the work room. AJ glanced at the special-orders shelf and pulled the three newest tickets.

"Why would a priest want these three books?" she asked Keegan.

"What are you talking about?" Keegan said.

"The two cemetery books and the Civil War book. You took the order." She recited the three titles.

"AJ, those are for Luna, the woman in the robe. They're not for a priest. Why would you say that?"

"I know she's the one who placed the order, but a priest called an hour after she left and said she was getting them for him. Father Joseph, he said his name was."

"Where was I when that happened?" Keegan sputtered. "You didn't tell me."

"You and your mother were both with customers. I took the call, answered his questions, and then I got busy with a mother and two kids who wanted picture books. I forgot about it until just now when I saw the three tickets again. It was no big deal."

"Tell me what he said."

"He asked if one of his nuns had come in, so I asked if he meant Luna. He said yes, that was her, but she sometimes gets confused, and he wanted to make sure she'd gotten his order right."

Keegan looked thoughtful. "Luna didn't seem confused to me. She was very clear this morning when she came in, and she was clear yesterday when we talked on the phone and she first asked about the books." AJ gave an I-don't-know shrug, and Keegan continued, "And why didn't this priest call the order in himself?" AJ shrugged again, and Keegan said, "But let's back up. First of all, Luna's not a nun. She said she wears that outfit because her skin can't handle sunlight."

"But the priest asked if one of his nuns had been in to place an order," AJ said, a little defensive. "Why would the priest ask about one of his nuns if she's not a nun?"

Keegan waited for the imaginary bulb to go on over AJ's head. It did.

"Because he's not a priest," AJ said. "He was playing me."

"He got lucky," Keegan said. "Mom and I knew Luna isn't a nun, but—"

"But I missed the first part of the conversation when she came in. I was by the front window. The most I got into it was when I waved hi after your mother introduced me. Even just now, I assumed she was some sort of retired old nun in an outdated outfit."

"Okay, okay, let's put that behind us. You didn't know. The question is: Why did he do that? What else did he say?"

AJ scrunched up her face and looked thoughtful, remembering. "He had some kind of a French accent. He asked if one of his nuns had been in yet. She's easy to spot, he said: her robe fully covers her. I told him she had just left and had ordered books."

Keegan's antennae went up. "So he asked about them—the books — right?"

"He did. She was ordering for him, but she sometimes got things a little mixed up. He asked me to read him the titles so he could double-check and make sure they were the ones he needed."

"So you recited the list."

"Yep. All three. It seemed innocent enough. After all, I thought he was a priest, and although I hadn't been sure about Luna when she came in, he made it sound like she was a nun. And it wasn't like I was giving away credit card numbers or a bank password."

"I know, AJ," Keegan said, her voice trying to soothe now. "It could have happened to me or Mom just as easily. Did he say anything else?"

"Nope."

Keegan shook her head. "The guy just wanted to know the titles."

AJ still hadn't let it go. "Are you sure Luna's not a nun? Did she actually say she wasn't?"

"I don't remember, but I'm pretty sure she's not. Know why I think that? She didn't have a cross around her neck. I don't know if all nuns wear crosses, but I'll bet most of them do. Or rosary beads. Wouldn't she have a string of those? Luna had nothing overtly religious. She told Mom not to call her Sister, and she explained the outfit as a precaution against sunlight."

"Well, nun or no nun," AJ replied, "I think we should call and tell her what happened. Maybe this Father Joseph guy is a real priest, maybe he isn't. I don't know. Either way, he's shadowing her. Even if it's no big deal, she should know that he doesn't trust her enough to get a simple book order right."

"I'll call in a minute. But since we're on the topic of Luna, let me tell you something else weird."

"What?"

"When she went for her money, her glove got hung up on the edge of her pocket. It pulled back and I saw her skin. Her hand and wrist had, like, reptile skin."

"You mean dry? Like she needs moisture lotion? She said she has a problem with sunlight. It probably dries her out or burns her."

"This was more than dry skin. This was *big-time* dry skin. Like alligator or frog or lizard skin."

"Okay, so she's got weird skin. If we had it, we'd cover up, too."

"I think the outfit is about more than avoiding the sun. I think she doesn't want to be seen."

"Look, Keegan, the woman has a medical condition, so she dresses oddly. And she may have a cloak-and-dagger thing going with some stalker pretending to be Father Joseph—or maybe he really is Father Joseph. As far as you and I know, though, she's just another customer who ordered books."

"She isn't just another customer, AJ. She knew my birth mother. She couldn't have made that up. I saw her reaction when she met me. What are the odds of that?"

AJ gave her shrug again.

"Something weird is going on here," Keegan said, "and I feel like we need to do something. But I don't know what."

"Call Luna and warn her. That's all you can do for now. The other thing we can do is, when she comes by to pick up her books next week, we can get her license plate number and ask my brother to run it. We can also look through the books and see what the attraction is."

They agreed on that course of action and Keegan called the number Luna had given her and left a message.

"Hi, Luna. This is Keegan at Annie's Book Stop. After you left the bookstore this morning, a man called and identified himself as Father Joseph. He didn't talk to me, he talked to AJ. He gave her the impression he was your superior and said the books you ordered were for him. But then he asked AJ for the titles—which she told him. Something about this sounds fishy to us, and we wanted you to know. Watch your back, Luna."

☙ ☙ ☙

That night Keegan had just finished loading the supper dishes into the dishwasher when her cellphone rang.

AJ.

"What's up?" Keegan asked.

"You're not going to believe this," AJ blurted.

"Believe what?" Keegan replied.

"Aaron was home for dinner ..."

"He usually is," Keegan quipped. "He still lives at home."

"Funny, Keeg," said, clearly annoyed. "Are you going to listen or not?"

Keegan sensed AJ's seriousness. "I'm listening."

"Good. Now, remember me telling you the Toil & Trouble break-in Tuesday night?"

"Aaron and Trooper Smitty responded. Have they caught somebody?"

"No. But there's something new. Swett is missing a book."

"A book?" Keegan asked.

"A rare one," AJ replied.

"How rare?"

"Very rare. Swett expected it to bring about $50,000 in his online auction. Bids were already up to $35,000."

Keegan whistled her surprise. "So it wasn't somebody after drug money. This was somebody who knew what they wanted."

"Yep. And here's the kicker. *You and I know the book.*"

"We do? What is it? *Charlotte's Web,* copy #1? A Stephen King high school story typed on a manual typewriter with hand-written corrections?"

"Nope. We heard the title today at the store."

"Quit stringing me along," Keegan said impatiently. "What is it?"

"Here's a hint," AJ said. "A Civil War memoir. Twenty-five copies printed in 1919."

Keegan gasped. "Not the Chamberlain book, the one the nun—I mean Luna—special-ordered? *Night Hawks*?"

"You got it," AJ answered. "It's getting weirder by the hour."

CHAPTER 3

On Monday afternoon FedEx Freddy delivered two flat cardboard mailers, each containing a book. One was Richard Laymon's *The Dirt on Maine's Burial Grounds*, the other was *Ancient Maine Cemeteries, Public and Private: Volume 27 York County*, compiled by Austin Call.

Keegan riffled through both books and set them on the awaiting-pickup shelf with their tickets. She checked the tracking information for the third book on the work room computer. The reprint of *General Joshua Chamberlain's Night Hawks: LeClair and Champaigne, the Scouts from Wells*, by William Coburn, was projected for Tuesday delivery.

She pulled the *Night Hawks* ticket and called the number Luna had left. It rang a half dozen times then switched to what sounded like an answering machine, not voicemail. A male voice said simply: *Leave a message after the beep*. It beeped.

"This message is for Luna. It's Keegan calling from Annie's Book Stop in Wells. It's Monday at 3:58. Two of your three books came in—the cemetery books. The Civil War book will be here tomorrow afternoon. We open at 10 a.m. You can pick up the two books in the morning or get them all after 3:30." She left the bookstore number and clicked off.

Why would Luna—or anybody—want those three books?

The workroom door opened and Maryann stuck her head in. "Ready to go?"

"Let me collect up my stuff, Mom. Be right out."

The door swung shut again and Keegan did something she'd never done before. She pulled the two special-order books off the shelf and slid them into her backpack.

She's not coming until tomorrow. I'll have them back in the morning.

After a stop at Mike's Fish Market for haddock, they got home around 4:40. Maryann headed into the kitchen and Keegan padded upstairs to her room.

"Dinner at six," Maryann called after her. "I'll do the fish and rice, you fix the salad."

Two minutes later Keegan settled on her bed with the backpack and pulled out Luna's books. *She never said I couldn't look.* She skimmed a few chapters of *Ancient Maine Cemeteries.*

The author explained that Maine was home to more than 50,000 known burying grounds, with a hundred times more private family graveyards than public ones. Larger public cemeteries had come into existence as towns and cities grew, while many of the smaller burial grounds had developed of necessity in Maine's frontier days as a rural population dealt with geographic isolation, harsh winters, poor roads, and lack of embalming processes and persons with the expertise to use them. Such factors influenced body disposal procedures, leading to the creation of family, clan, and crossroads community graveyards close to where the deceased had lived—like a roadside meadow or a dedicated corner on the family farm.

Keegan understood why people around Wells joked that you couldn't walk a dog in town without tripping over a grave. She and AJ had walked or ridden their bikes past dozens of small boneyards—five Littlefield graveyards, a Hatch cemetery, a Littlefield-Hatch cemetery, two slave cemeteries, a tiny Civil War soldiers' burial ground, and many others—all less than three miles from home—and those were just the ones that came to mind at the moment.

What do they say in politics and mystery novels? He's been around long enough to know where all the bodies are buried.

Among the listings at the end of the book she found a three-page registry of more than 150 Wells cemeteries, numbered and keyed to a one-page map. How many had the Town and the Historical Society added since 1968 when Call's York County book came out?

"Keegan, time to fix the salad!" came Maryann's voice from downstairs. She slipped the books into her backpack and set it aside.

Luna must want to know where the cemeteries are.

CHAPTER 4

Maryann and Keegan ate on the back deck: pan-fried haddock, wild rice, and a garden salad with diced pears and glazed pecans.

Keegan's index finger was at her temple, twirling the strand of white hair around the fingertip, something she often did when she was musing about something and about to ask a question.

"Here's a piece of trivia for you, Mom," she said, sure she had a stumper. "Any idea how many cemeteries we have here in Wells?"

"Two hundred and one," Maryann answered without hesitation.

Keegan was caught flatfooted. "What? Seriously, Mom. What're you, psychic? You didn't even stop to think about it. I'd have guessed 40 or 50."

"I didn't have to guess," Keegan. "I knew the answer. I was leafing through the town history last week and saw it there. It was a project your mother worked on when she was in college."

In 2002 the town historian and a committee of volunteers had put together *The History of Wells* for the 350th anniversary celebration. The town historian, now in her middle 90s and still sharp as a tack, occasionally stopped in at Annie's Book Stop.

"That figure may have gone up since it came out 15 years ago. But in 2002 their census was 201, all plotted and numbered on a foldout map. The book's in the den—middle shelf over my computer—if you want to check it out."

"I never noticed it there. I've sold a few of them at the store, but I never really looked at it."

"Hiding in plain sight, Keeg, for years. Zelda got U Maine to approve her for a nine-credit independent study one summer, then nine more credits the next, which was when she worked on the project. She researched the sections about graveyards and quarries, plus some other stuff that made it into the book. Her notes are in a blue and yellow banana crate in the attic."

"You kept them?"

"Of course I kept them. They're ours—yours and mine. They've been up there waiting for you to look at them."

"Hey, just show me the box."

Keegan had thought she'd combed through all-things-Zelda over her 17 years: photo albums, yearbooks, report cards, sports photos and varsity letters—she had played soccer and run track, just like Keegan—and they both wrote for the school newspaper. But Keegan had never given any thought to the banana box of research notes and files.

"Let me dig it out tomorrow. That'll give me a chance to see what else in the attic might be of interest. I think you've seen just about everything else. It didn't occur to me that you might want to look at class notes."

❦ ❦ ❦

Maryann settled in for the evening news and Keegan went back up to her room and cracked the second book, *The Dirt on Maine's Burial Grounds.* She had unpacked it at the store and knew from the provocative title and campy cover that it wasn't a scholarly tome. Books like this were tourist-trap staples, designed for impulse purchases. They had titles like *True Maine Ghost Stories, Maine's Haunted Lighthouses,* and *Shipwrecks of Maine.* Bread and butter books, Maryann called them, stocked mostly by seasonal merchants who needed to capitalize on Maine's short summer selling season. Besides the paperbacks they sold saltwater taffy, silkscreened tee shirts, sea shells, and ball caps. Even before she opened *The Dirt on Maine's Burial Grounds,* Keegan knew what to expect: a couple dozen colorful stories and legends with a scattering of black-and-white photos and sketches. She was right.

There was the story of the Reverend George Burroughs who, before coming to Wells, had been an assistant minister in Salem, Massachusetts. When the 1692-93 Witch Trials commenced, Burroughs was accused of witchcraft by the hysterical girls of Salem. Reverend Cotton Mather, leader of the lunacy, had Burroughs arrested in Wells—Maine was then still part of Massachusetts—and brought back to Salem to stand trial with four other innocent people. All five were convicted and hanged.

The story of Mackworth Island's pet cemetery was included. A former Maine governor donated the island with the stipulation that his pet cemetery—containing the bones of his Irish setters, horse, and other pets—never be disturbed. Laymon ended the Mackworth entry by inviting speculation: could this have been the inspiration for Maine author Stephen King's bestseller, *Pet Sematary?*

Keegan found two other Wells-related entries, the first a one-pager about handicapped Theodore "Thed" Heard, who at his own request had been buried in the family tomb sitting up in his wheelchair without shroud or coffin.

The second described a long-lost stone house. Laymon inserted a quote to attest to its authenticity but never cited the source. "Described in an old document as *a stone cabin constructed of four walls made of stacked blocks of pink granite, capped with a granite slab roof, approximately twelve feet by twenty feet by eight feet in height.*"

Laymon didn't try to make a case for the stone cabin being a crypt or a mausoleum but let the image suggest it. He wrote that the old-timer he interviewed could not disclose its location, saying only that "it's a granite chamber that has no connection to human remains." Which led Laymon to pose a cryptic teaser: "No connection to *human* remains? Could it be a vault filled with animal bones like the Mackworth Island pet cemetery—or the skeletons of extraterrestrials who visited southern Maine but did not survive?"

What grabbed Keegan's attention was the description of the structure. Even without a cited source it felt authentic—not granite but specifically *pink* granite. And the dimensions were specific, reminding her of the directions Noah had received from his God for building the ark—so many cubits by so many cubits. As precise as the dimensions for the granite cabin were, though, there was no mention of doors or windows.

No wonder Laymon slipped in the idea that this might be a tomb. But I've lived in Wells for 17 years and never heard that story. I wonder if AJ knows it.

She called AJ and summarized the high points of the book. When she got to the story about the pink granite cabin, she read the chapter in its entirety and waited for AJ's reaction.

"Never heard that one till just now. Maybe the author mixed up his notes, switched town names. I think there's a Weld up near Farmington."

"If he interviewed an old-timer, he wouldn't forget which town the story goes with. It's got to be us."

"Maybe he needed to pad the book—you know, a certain number of pages—and made it up. You said he didn't list a source."

"I don't think he used this to pad it. He was too specific about the materials and the dimensions." She read the sentence aloud again. "I'll do an Internet search after we hang up, see if there's anything else out there about it."

CHAPTER 5

Maryann and Keegan discovered the break-in Tuesday morning when they went to work. The front door at Annie's Book Stop was ajar and a pane in the upper half of the door was clearly shattered. Maryann dialed 911 and they waited in the car.

Three minutes later Cliff Bragdon pulled up in a Wells Police Department SUV and climbed out. He knew the Keegans well. Cliff was an insatiable consumer of mysteries, thrillers, and police procedurals, and dropped by Annie's at least once a week. While many of his Wells High classmates had been gym rats, Cliff had been a bookstore rat.

Maryann and Keegan got out and the three of them approached the store. A few shards of glass lay on the floor inside the doorsill. Cliff cautioned them not to touch anything then pushed the door open the rest of the way with his foot. It wasn't dark inside, but it wasn't bright either, so he gripped his flashlight in his left hand and placed his right hand on the grip of his holstered weapon, then carefully stepped over the broken glass. He scanned the interior of the bookshop, shining the light in its darker areas.

"Can we come in now?" Maryann asked from behind the big cop.

"Let me check the back room first."

He swept the main and side rooms with his flashlight, saw nothing out of place, and walked to the work room door. Before he opened it he shone his beam into the interior room that was his home away from home, the one that housed the paperback mysteries and thrillers. No one was there and nothing appeared disturbed. He opened the door to the work room. No one inside.

"Now you can come in," he called to Maryann and Keegan. "Don't disturb the broken glass and don't touch anything."

Maryann couldn't contain her anger. "For crying out loud, Cliff," she complained. "Who breaks into a bookstore? The sign on the door clearly says: *No cash on premises after hours.*"

Keegan was angry, too, but her response came out as sarcasm. "Haven't you heard, Mom? Bookstore burglaries are in vogue this week in Wells. Toil & Trouble was number one, we're number two. Who's next—Arrington's or Doug Harding?" Arrington's dealt in rare and used military books and maps. Douglas Harding's barn-like warehouse was jammed with used and hard-to-find books.

Cliff notified dispatch that he had cleared the premises. "Need a detective to investigate. M.O. similar to Toil & Trouble last week."

A woman's voice acknowledged Cliff's request.

"Look around," he said to Maryann and Keegan. "See if anything's been disturbed. But don't touch. Start with the register."

Maryann went behind the counter while Keegan checked out the book rooms.

"Register looks fine," Maryann said.

"Stacks look the same as we left them yesterday afternoon," Keegan said, and walked to the door of the work room. "Cliff, is it okay to turn on the light in here?"

"Let me do it," he answered. "Dispatch is sending a detective over—probably Elly Stedman. He'll want to check it for prints." He used his flashlight to flick the wall switch up, and an old ceiling fixture with three long tubular fluorescent bulbs flickered on.

Under the brighter light Keegan saw what Cliff had missed when he first looked in. The special-orders shelf was empty, its dozen or so books strewn on the counter and floor below. Three special-order tickets lay on the table—all Luna's. Keegan had set them beside the special-orders shelf when she borrowed Luna's two cemetery books. Everything else seemed to be in its place.

Keegan said nothing.

"Don't touch," Cliff reminded. "Leave it for Stedman. This gives us a few minutes to look at the security cameras. One of our patrol cops drives by here every night and checks the place out. Last night it would've been Aaron who made the pass. As far as I know he didn't report anything out of the ordinary, which suggests the break-in happened after 3 a.m., probably before 5 a.m. when it started to get light out."

Maryann showed Cliff the two recorders. One was for the wall-mounted camera watching the checkout counter and cash register. It also offered a view of the front door. The second recorder worked with the front window camera that covered the parking lot and the street beyond. Both set-ups were inexpensive but were enough to meet a small business' insurance policy requirements. For cost reasons, they recorded black and white stills every 30 seconds.

Cliff checked the parking lot camera first. He started it at 2 a.m., hoping it had captured the intruder's approach. The 3:35 frame showed a figure in a black robe and hood approaching from the street.

"Holy crap," he said. "Look at the shoulders on this dude. He's like Arnold Schwartzenegger in his prime. Must be about six feet tall and pure muscle."

He switched to the counter/door camera for a different view. There was no frame of the intruder breaking the pane or reaching in to unlock, but the camera had caught a still of the burglar framed by the open door. The tip of his hood was close to the top of the doorframe.

"Definitely over six feet," Cliff said. "And look at that outfit. Thinks he's Darth Vader. Must have gotten it at a Halloween store. Oh, wait, look at his face."

The visitor's face was bright white, and he appeared to be grinning grotesquely. He had a thin mustache and a narrow goatee.

"That's not a face," Maryann said. "That's an *Anonymous* mask. It's from *V Is for Vendetta*, the movie. Activists wear them now when they protest economic summits."

"And kids wear them for Halloween," Cliff added. "They're easy to get."

The next helpful frame came several minutes later: a back view of the burglar passing the counter on his way out. Cliff shifted back to the front window cam covering the parking lot and found a frame showing the robed burglar beyond the lot, turning left up the side street called Highlands.

"Definitely a man," Cliff commented. "Got to be. Look at the Incredible Hulk shoulders and torso. It's obvious even under the loose clothing."

"Why the hood?" Keegan asked. "A ski mask would be easier. Even if he had long hair, he could just push it up under the ski mask."

"Maybe he's covering his baldness," Maryann suggested.

"A robe is kind of elaborate for a smash and grab," Cliff wondered aloud. "Like you said, Keegan, a simple ski mask would do the trick. The robe hides the body, the hood and mask hide the face and head. This person must know he'd be easy to recognize on the street."

"*If* he comes out on the street," Keegan said. "I'm betting he avoids the public."

I wonder what his walk is like, she thought. *Does he shuffle like Luna? Does he make wobbly turns? Too bad our cameras don't show him in motion.*

She considered the robe. It was black and tent-like, yet it wasn't like Luna's habit. This wasn't Luna in an evening outfit with lifts. The person in the security footage was at least a foot taller and probably a hundred pounds heavier—maybe more. Luna had worn the habit, hood, and veil for practical purposes—to avoid sunlight—the burglar had used the robe, hood, and Anonymous mask to hide his identity. Clearly two different people. Besides, why would Luna break in after hours? Not to steal a couple of books she'd be picking up in twelve hours anyway.

"Cliff, back the tape up to the two shots inside the store," Maryann said.

He replayed the footage.

"Look there," she said, pointing. "Gloves."

"So much for fingerprints," Cliff lamented.

Another similarity to Luna's dress, Keegan thought. She had wanted this second figure to be gloveless, not so much for the fingerprints, but so she could see if the skin was reptilian. This might not be Luna, but the two of them shared physical similarities.

Bet this is Father Joseph.

Cliff did the math and said, "Less than five minutes in and out—maybe three to four. Shops like a man after Christmas presents—targeted approach, knows what he's hunting for. He wasn't after cash for drugs."

A car drove up and someone big and bulky got out.

"Elly Stedman," Cliff said, and backed away from the security equipment.

Stedman came inside and everyone did the hello thing. The detective went through everything again with Maryann and Keegan, and when they were done in the work room, Keegan retrieved her backpack from the Subaru. She showed the two "borrowed" books to her mother and the two cops.

"I think he was looking for these," Keegan said. "When they weren't there, he got mad and knocked stuff over." She held up one of the three older tickets. "This is the last one in the special order. It's due in this afternoon."

Bragdon and Stedman wrote it all down. But neither cop let on that the third special-order ticket—for *General Joshua Chamberlain's Night Hawks*—bore the same title as Geoff Swett's rare first edition that had been stolen from Toil & Trouble five nights earlier.

Keegan already knew it was the same title, but didn't dare mention that fact because she'd heard it from AJ, who'd learned it from her Aaron, who had been on the Toil & Trouble call. She wasn't sure if pointing it out would get her brother in trouble.

Stedman suggested that Maryann call her insurance company. "They'll have somebody here in an hour or two to fix that broken glass so you can be up and running again in no time."

Stedman was right. Annie's Book Stop was up and running by 12:45.

Section II

The Civil War Memoir

CHAPTER 6

At 2:45, two hours after the glass pane was in place, FedEx Freddy delivered a single flat cardboard book mailer. Keegan opened it and found *Chamberlain's Night Hawks* inside. She called Luna again.

"Luna, this is Keegan at Annie's Book Stop. Your order is complete and ready for pickup. We close at 4 o'clock."

Tuesdays were always slow, so AJ had the day off. Maryann covered the selling floor and Keegan turned toward the work room.

"Give me a holler if there's a rush," she said, and disappeared. A moment later she was cracking Luna's third book. The back cover description said:

GENERAL JOSHUA CHAMBERLAIN'S NIGHT HAWKS reveals the previously unknown story of two Civil War scouts from Maine known only as Le Clair and Champaigne. They report only under cover of darkness to two men: Colonel (later to be General) Joshua Chamberlain, the hero of Gettysburg, or Reverend Clayton Lussier, Chamberlain's aide de camp. The two men, after meeting during their years at Bangor Theological Seminary, personally recruited the two scouts in 1862.

LeClair and Champaigne—operating without firearms—were responsible for conducting night raids behind Confederate lines, where they spread so much terror and inflicted so many casualties that the rebels began referring to the pair as "the banshees" or "the harpies."

Author William Coburn has skillfully woven together material from previously published books including Chamberlain's, to which he has added new material drawn from recently discovered sources: Chamberlain's divinity school diaries and the war journals of Chamberlain and his aide de camp Clayton Lussier.

The Preface gave a lot of basic background information.

Joshua Chamberlain died in 1914 at the age of 86. A graduate of Bowdoin College in Brunswick, Maine, he also attended Bangor Theological Seminary in the 1850s. He returned to Bowdoin as a professor of languages and traveled to Europe. When the Civil War broke out, he joined the 20th Maine Infantry as a Lieutenant Colonel, and by the war's end had earned the rank of General. *The Passing of the Armies*, his Civil War memoir, was published a year after his death in 1914. A prolific scholarly writer and lifelong journal keeper, his voluminous writings were handed over to the Bowdoin College Library for curation.

It was believed at the time that all his writings were included in the donated materials. Two years later, however, Chamberlain's childhood friend William Coburn acquired four previously unknown journals that Chamberlain had kept during his seminary years. Coburn also obtained several journals written by Reverend Clayton Lussier, Chamberlain's Bangor classmate who later became a pastor in Calais, Maine. When the 20th Maine Regiment formed in 1862, it was Lussier who was asked to serve as Chamberlain's *aide de camp*, which he did.

Using the two men's journals and materials from the Bowdoin collection, Coburn pieced together *Night Hawks*, a narrative about Chamberlain's fierce warrior-scouts, LeClair and Champaigne.

The Introduction to the 2017 reprint pointed out that Coburn's 1919 book, released so soon after Chamberlain's 1914 death, should have been a bestseller, but publishers' resources had shifted from Civil War books to books about the Great War in Europe or the 1917-1918 Influenza Epidemic. It was bad luck for Coburn, who was forced to privately fund and publish *Night Hawks* as a limited press run of 25 copies.

That explains the value of Geoff Swett's rare first edition. No wonder Maine Civil War Press saw the need for a reprint.

Keegan kept an eye on the clock. *Take your time, Luna.* She plowed ahead with *Chamberlain's Night Hawks.*

In 1862 when the 20th Maine Volunteer Infantry Regiment was formed up, Chamberlain was offered command of it at the rank of colonel, but declined. Adelbert Ames, a recent West Point graduate, accepted and asked Chamberlain to be his second-in-command at the rank of lieutenant colonel.

Clayton Lussier, Chamberlain's *aide de camp* and seminary classmate had worked as a surveyor before enrolling at Bangor. Accompanied by an assistant, Lussier had been charged with mapping northern Maine's Allagash Wilderness.

According to Coburn, Chamberlain wrote in one of his student journals:

> *Our classmate [Lussier, a former surveyor] described a harrowing ride with his assistant down a gorge through a series of boiling rapids, the result being the capsizing of their canoe. The unfortunate pair were drawn down into the tumult and smashed about against the river's rocks. Lussier awoke to find himself sitting up in a hardscrabble clearing, propped against a rock, knowing his arm and both legs were broken. His mind held no clear recollection of what transpired after the capsizing of their canoe. Nor did he recall how he had come to his present dry position.*

> *The clearing was lit only by the moon. He turned and gazed upon his drowned companion's pummeled body. The corpse was positioned sitting up as in life, as it was leaned against the rock, except there was no breath of life left in him. Our classmate found himself at a loss to explain how either of them arrived upon that spot. It was as if they had been placed beside one another. When he considered his own broken limbs, he was certain it had not been he who dragged his companion from the angry waters.*

Chamberlain continued:

> *What he [Lussier] told us next, I shall never forget. Twenty yards away in the shadows at the forest's edge he perceived two slump-shouldered figures silently watching. They appeared hawk-like, crouching upon their haunches. Were they preparing to attack, or could they be*

standing a watch? Lussier called to them in English, but hearing no answer he addressed them in French, his other language, asking if it had been they who saved him. One of them answered oui [yes].

[Lussier] fell to weeping then and asked if they might approach him that he should gaze upon his saviors' faces and shake their hands and thank them. They declined, claiming they were of a different race, and their countenances were sure to alarm him.

What happened next I found nearly impossible to believe. But our classmate swore it to the class then and later to me when I questioned him privately.

A pack of eight or ten wolves entered the clearing, snarling and threatening. With no ability to stand or to make himself appear for- midable, it was all poor Lussier could do to shout and wave the one unbroken arm. The pack divided, approaching within ten feet. Then they crept slowly forward, prepared to spring upon him and rend his flesh.

It was at that moment that his guardian angels—in his words— "sprang to action, drawing their weapons with lightning speed, each brandishing a sword and a dagger." They flew at the wolves—flew, he said—setting upon them from the rear, slashing, stabbing, the moon- light glinting off their flashing steel as they worked in tandem. This pair Lussier described as "the fiercest warriors I ever set eyes upon." They dispersed the pack in a minute, leaving four dead and those in retreat gashed and limping.

[Lussier] said he glimpsed his saviors close at hand then. Their countenances were indeed terrifying—sardonic, grinning faces helmet- ed in scales that bore short horns, their heads set atop powerful hunched bodies that were balanced on thick legs ending in wide clawed feet.

[Lussier's] injuries and exhaustion delivered him to sweet uncon- sciousness then. When he awoke, he found himself lying at the door- step of settlers in the frontier settlement called The Oxbow, north of Bangor. As the crow flies, that outpost lies more than fifty miles east

of the Allagash, the wilderness region where he had faced the wolves.

The couple who found him at their door tended his wounds for three days—dismissing his story as delirium—then entrusted him to the care of a passing parson who transported him by wagon to Bangor, where his broken bones were set.

When Lussier finished relating his story to the class, one of our classmates joked that it constituted either a call to ministry or a call to lunacy.

Keegan kept reading. Coburn cited a different Chamberlain journal, this one from 1862, more than half a decade after his Bangor years, penned during the forming up of the 20th Maine Volunteers that summer.

My classmate from Bangor Seminary, the Reverend Clayton Lussier, recently pastor of the Congregational Church at Calais, has accepted my invitation to join the 20th Maine as my aide de camp.

While the regiment was coming together, Chamberlain and Lussier journeyed to the Allagash Wilderness to find the spot where the "two strange sentinels" had appeared and saved Lussier more than a decade earlier. Chamberlain saw their battle potential and was determined to recruit them. If they were as fierce as Lussier claimed, they would prove invaluable against the Confederates. Both men kept diaries of their Allagash sojourn.

After 10 days traveling to northern Maine and another three trying to find Lussier's rock outcropping, they set up camp. For four nights they took turns—two-hour watches—calling out in French, inviting the two sentinels to approach the campfire and talk. Lussier's "angels" eventually made their presence known one night, remaining far back from the fire and hunkering down in the shadows. Chamberlain realized he and Lussier would have to go to them.

For the darkness we could not make them out clearly, but I am certain they are half a foot shorter than we, broader at the shoulder, with a more muscular breast than stone workers who lift heavy rocks all day. Their eyes reflect our campfire's light as bright stars glow in an ink-black sky. Those eyes convince me that these reclusive creatures are at once both ferocious and kindly.

Lussier wrote:

The two who saved me listened as my friend Joshua, a staunch abolitionist, eloquently defended the need to fight for the freedom of the slaves. He asked them if they would join us in the great battle for emancipation. He pleaded his case at a distance of ten yards, for the two would let us advance no farther toward them. Their warning was spoken not from malice but out of consideration. They deliberated between themselves less than an hour. One voiced a concern to us about his mate.

In time, they and the Colonel reached an agreement: they would not muster into nor gather with the Infantry, but would serve as civilians at Chamberlain's pleasure, as night scouts. They would travel near to, but not with, our Regiment, quartering wherever they saw fit. They would confer only with the Colonel or myself, and then only under cover of darkness. The dark, they said, quickened their blood, while the sun slowed it and afflicted them.

Colonel Chamberlain, for his part, must commission the construction of special living quarters for the mate within 50 miles of the Regiment's home. The quarters shall be, of necessity, built at a location remote from townsfolk. The dimensions of the structure were stipulated, with the insistence that the walls be of granite block, windowless, and the roof of similar material. To this humble clergyman it described a vault, a crypt, not a suitable dwelling place for a living being.

Colonel Chamberlain agreed to their terms and gave his pledge at a distance, without a handshake, for they shied from his touch. They offered no Christian names, only the surnames LeClair and Champaigne, which is how the Colonel directed me to register them.

Lussier wrote in a later entry at Portland:

At the Colonel's direction, I have secured LeClair's mate an iso-lated property 30 miles south of Portland in the Town of Wells. The Colonel has charged me to contract with a local quarry there for the construction of the stone abode.

In Chamberlain's Allagash diary he reflected:

How could I not agree to these warriors' terms, if they will fight the rebels? If these two engage the armies of the South with even half the fury unleashed on Lussier's wolves, this war will end sooner, God willing.

Chamberlain's troops must have gotten clearer views of the scouts in night battles, for with highest respect they nicknamed the pair the *Night Hawks*. The Confederates on the receiving end of the Night Hawks' night-time forays referred to them as *the cursed banshees* or *the damned harpies*.

Coburn cited a letter from rebel Private Henry Mosby, who wrote home after his unit's assault on Gettysburg's Little Round Top was rebuffed:

We tried a night charge and I seen one of the harpes swoop down on my friend Burgess. It clampt its claws into his sholders like a owl grabs up a field mouse and carryd him to a promntory and droped him off. Poor Burgess dashed his head on the rocks.

Referencing that same night charge, one of the 20th Maine's junior officers sent a note to Chamberlain:

Sir, your two hunchbacks fought like Roman gladiators, saving many lives including my own. God bless them, sir, and you for enlisting them to our aid.

Keegan set the book on the table. *Hunchbacks?* She thought back to Luna in the bookstore. They had mistaken for a hunchbacked nun, and she had thought it about the black-robed burglar in the Vendetta mask.

Luna and the burglar aren't hunchbacks, but something about their physical appearance connects them to each other and to the Night Hawks, LeClair and Champaigne. Banshees? Harpies?

The door to the work room opened.

"Keegan," her mother said. "Five minutes to four. Shall we lock up and go home?"

"Luna didn't pick up her books."

"No, she didn't. Maybe she's out of town," Maryann suggested. "Or couldn't get a ride. You saw her walk. I can't imagine her driving a car."

"But we can't leave her books here. We've already had one break-in."

"Okay, so bring the books home again. You can tell me all about them in the car."

Keegan slipped the three books into her backpack and they left.

CHAPTER 7

About the time Keegan and Maryann were closing the bookstore, Aaron was getting out of his Jeep Cherokee at the Wells Police Department. He was off-duty, but his brain hadn't gotten the memo. He met Cliff Bragdon as he walked out.

"Can't stay away, Aaron?" Cliff asked.

"Doesn't mean I'm addicted," Aaron said with a grin. "I can quit anytime."

Cliff held the station door open. "You going in?"

"Not right now. Got a minute?"

Cliff let the door go. "Minute and a half for you." The two friends walked toward the parking lot. "What's up?"

"The break-in at Annie's Book Stop this morning—you took the call, right?"

"Yep. Stedman finished it."

"And you know I got the Toil & Trouble call last week?"

"Yep."

"Two bookstores," Aaron said.

"Yep."

"Coincidence?"

"Maybe," Cliff said. "Maybe not. You see a connection?"

"I don't know. What'd you find missing at Annie's this morning?"

"Nothing."

"So, was it about cash?" Aaron asked.

"Register wasn't even touched. Not sure what it was about."

"So just what *do* you know, Cliff? I had Geoff Swett's bookstore break-in, you had the Annie's Book Stop break-in. Don't you think you and I should be comparing notes?"

"I suppose. Well, okay. You're just going to go in and read it in my report anyway, aren't you? The security footage shows somebody about six feet tall, built like The Rock and dressed in black like Darth Vader, except this guy had on a *V for Vendetta* mask and gloves. He busted the glass—Maryann's hasn't got an alarm like Swett does—then he reached in and unlocked. Walked in, strolled to the work room, knocked a few books over, and exited the premises—all in about three to four minutes. Keegan—not Maryann but her daughter—thinks he came in looking to grab one or more of these three special-order books somebody ordered. That didn't happen because she took the first two home the night before, and the third hadn't arrived by the time of the break-in. What I'm saying is, if the guy broke in for the books, he went away emptyhanded, because they weren't on premises."

"So nothing's missing?"

"Not that the Keegan or Maryann can determine."

"And Stedman's got the store security footage to follow up on?"

"Yep. A few stills. I got a quick look at it before Elly showed up."

"Any prints?"

Cliff shook his head. "The guy wore gloves. And no footprints."

"You sure it was a guy?"

"Pretty sure, considering the still shot of him in the doorway. A body-builder, would be my guess."

"How about the front window cam? Did it get a vehicle or a plate number?"

"Nope. The guy hoofed it, took a left out the door and probably walked up the Highlands road into the neighborhoods."

"And you're sure nothing was missing?"

"Looks like no. But there is one odd thing."

"What's that?"

"There were three special-order tickets on the work table. Keegan had two in her backpack in the car: a couple of cemetery books. The third special order hadn't come in yet, but was due later in the day: a Civil War memoir, a reprint."

"Don't tell me, Cliff. It was the same title as the first edition that's missing from Geoff Swett's."

"You got it. I wrote it down here in my scratch book." Cliff pulled a small notebook out of his back uniform pocket and flipped to a page. *"General Joshua Chamberlain's Night Hawks: LeClair and Champaigne, the Scouts from Wells."*

"So we've got more than two bookstore break-ins," Aaron said. "Now we've got two bookstore break-ins connected by the same book—the rare one and the reprint of it."

"Stedman figured that, too. But he pointed out that it doesn't mean the perp who broke into Annie's was after the Chamberlain book. If he's the same guy who hit Toil & Trouble, why go for the reprint if you already have a copy?"

"Right," Aaron said. "He may have wanted one of the other two books—or both. Can you tell me their titles?"

"Don't see why not. I just transcribed them from my pad to the report." Cliff read out the two titles and Aaron wrote them down.

"You say Keegan has both of those books?" Aaron asked.

"Either at the bookstore or at home," Cliff answered. "Why? You going to read them?"

Aaron stared at his friend. "Of course I'm going to read them. Last week after Swett's break-in I thought it was about the value of the rare book on the black market. Now I'm not so sure. It could be about something else."

"Like what? I mean, I agree—and Stedman probably will, too—but what could that something else be?"

"I don't know. I'm hoping it'll make more sense when I see the books or read them. I'll keep you in the loop. You do the same for me."

"I will. But Aaron, remember what they told us in class. Don't take the job home with you. Maintain a separate life. Remember that, buddy."

Aaron forced a smile. "I know, I know. But thanks for reminding me." He got back into his Cherokee, leaving Cliff standing there. If he hustled, he could make it to the Keegan house before they started dinner.

CHAPTER 8

On the ride home from the bookstore Keegan filled her mother in on Luna and some of what she had learned from reading the special-order books. She read part of the Coburn *Night Hawks* reprint aloud.

"So," Keegan asked, "do you think Luna's shaking the family tree to see what kind of nuts fall off?"

"You mean ancestors?" Maryann replied.

"Exactly. I mean, you've seen her posture, Mom. Don't you think she could be descended from Chamberlain's scouts? Obviously that York County cemeteries book is to help her find the right cemetery."

"But that's just cemeteries," Maryann pointed out. "It won't give her individual graves. Besides, it's got to be about more than genealogy. Somebody broke into Geoff Swett's and stole the same book Luna ordered. It wasn't about cemeteries. Who did that, and why?"

"I don't know who did it, Mom, but I don't think it was Luna. First of all, look how she walks. There's no way she could manage a second-story job at Swett's. Also, she's way too short to be the Grim Reaper who's on our security tapes. Plus, you've got to ask why she'd hit up Swett's for a first edition when she was about to order a reprint anyway?"

"Back up a second, Keegan. Swett's copy was stolen on Tuesday night. Luna didn't order her reprint until Friday morning. What if she couldn't find it at Swett's and had to switch to a backup plan: ordering the reprint through us?"

"Then where'd Swett's copy go?" Keegan challenged.

Maryann shrugged. "No idea. I'm just tossing the ball back and forth with you."

"Okay, for the sake of argument, let's assume the obvious: it wasn't Luna. A different person broke into Swett's."

"Why risk it when there's a reprint?" Maryann asked.

Keegan's face scrunched in thought. "Maybe there was a time crunch—the person was in a hurry and grabbed the first available."

"Or," Maryann said. "Maybe Swett's burglar *didn't know* there was a reprint. Let's say the original appeared on Swett's online auction and the burglar had to act fast. But he or she couldn't afford the big-bucks bidding."

"And didn't want to chance losing it in the final minute of the auction," Keegan finished.

"Another possibility," Maryann suggested. "This other person was *competing* with Luna."

"And why would she and this other party want the very same book?" Keegan asked.

"It's not the same book," Maryann said. "One's a first edition, one's a reprint. What's the same is *the content*. It's not about the dollar value, it's about the information."

"Which leads to two other possibilities," Keegan theorized. "One, the Toil & Trouble thief broke into our bookstore to block or delay Luna from getting the information. Two, there's a third player who broke into our place, who is also after the book's information."

Maryann pulled into their driveway. "Don't forget the other two books Luna ordered. Maybe the Swett burglar was after them. Either to get the additional information the books contained—"

"Or to stop Luna from getting it," Keegan finished.

Maryann shut off the engine. "So what's the competition about?"

Before Keegan could answer, a red Jeep Cherokee crunched up on the gravel. Aaron got out. His shorts and tee shirt made it clear he wasn't on duty. He looked more like a lifeguard or a surfer than a cop.

"What, no AJ?" Maryann asked, opening the Subaru's door.

"AJ's home," he replied, shaking his head. "Do I always have to have my sister with me when I stop by? I just wanted to ask you two about the special-order books. AJ says Keegan texted her to say the little nun's third book arrived."

Keegan rested her arms on the car roof. "She's not a little nun, Aaron. AJ knows that, but maybe you can remind her."

"You knew who she meant, though, didn't you?" He made a hand gesture, as if measuring, then made the sign of the cross. "Little. Nun."

She conceded his point. "Yes, the robed customer's third book did arrive. I've been reading it."

"The Joshua Chamberlain book, right?" Aaron asked. "AJ said you already read the others."

"Yes, the Chamberlain book. It's about his scouts. I read the other two last night. Why?"

"I'd like to borrow all three this evening, so I can see what's in them."

Maryann cut in. "Want to come in, Aaron? Looks like you're off duty. We can talk inside."

Keegan bristled. "If you want to read the books, you'll have to do it here. They belong to the customer." She patted her backpack. "I'm not letting them out of my sight." She started for the house.

Aaron opened his mouth to object, but Maryann cut him off. "This might be a good night to stay for supper, Aaron. I think Keegan's got her mind set."

"But—"

"I'm with Keegan on this one. Policeman or not, the books stay here. The best you're going to get is free dinner and some uninterrupted reading time. Take it or leave it."

He glanced at Keegan's back as she walked toward the house. Then he looked back at Maryann who raised a questioning eyebrow. He threw up his hands in surrender and they started up the driveway.

"You compared notes with Cliff, didn't you?" Maryann asked. "Two bookstores. You got the Swett call and Cliff got ours."

"I talked to him at the station a little while ago."

"And what did he tell you?"

"That Darth Vader broke in and rifled your special-orders but came away empty. He also told me one of the three books, *General Joshua Chamberlain's Night Hawks*, happens to have the same title as the Swett's missing book."

Keegan climbed the steps to the landing and unlocked the door. She looked back to make sure her mother and Aaron were behind her. When they reached the bottom step, she opened the door.

"Oh, no," she gasped.

"What?" Maryann asked, then saw it.

The back kitchen door that led out onto the deck was wide open. The bottom of the door was solid wood and the top half was made up of a half dozen glass panes. The pane nearest the door handle had been smashed in. There was glass on the tile floor by the sill.

Aaron muscled his way past them. "Don't move," he whispered. "Could still be in here. You two go back out and get in the car. Call 911. Somebody should be here in five minutes."

"What about you?" Keegan asked.

Aaron stepped to the kitchen island and drew a large carving knife out of the butcher-block sheath. "Just go call 911. Now." He tiptoed into the living room.

"Go, Mom," Keegan ordered, giving Maryann a nudge back onto the porch. "Call 911."

Keegan closed the door partway so her mother couldn't see what she was about to do. Then she went to the butcher block and grabbed a long serrated bread knife. She was halfway up the stairway when Maryann pulled out her phone and dialed 911.

Keegan made her way up the stairs like a swordsman ascending a parapet, the serrated bread knife in front of her. She stopped on the top landing, checked the hallway left and right, stepped over the creaky board, and tiptoed past the master bathroom toward her bedroom. The door was open, as usual. She pressed her back against the wall on the door side and inched closer, then peeked around the door frame. No one.

The books from her shelves were scattered on the floor. She stepped inside, knife in front of her, angry enough to use it. The room was empty.

A board squeaked. She peeked back out the door and up the hallway. Aaron was at the top of the landing, brandishing the carving knife. He spotted the serrated bread knife in her hand and shot her an are-you-kidding look.

"Keegan," he whispered impatiently. "What are you doing?"

She lowered the bread knife. He lowered the carving knife. Her hand was trembling.

"He was here. In my room. He came for the books."

He walked toward her. "You haven't checked the other rooms, have you?"

She shook her head. "No, but I think he's gone."

They stepped back into her bedroom and stared at the books strewn on the floor. Keegan's bedcovers had been pulled back, too, and the mattress was off-center on the bedspring.

"He checked under the mattress," she said. "I'll bet he came in as soon as we left for work. He didn't find them at the store, so he figured out where we live."

Aaron saw she was both angry and on the verge of tears. He'd seen that same mix of emotions in other homeowners who felt violated by break-ins.

He put an arm around her shoulder. "I'm glad you weren't sleeping here when he came in."

She rested her head against his chest for a couple of seconds, then straightened up and stepped away. She started for the scattered books.

"Don't," he ordered, grabbing her arm. "It's a crime scene. We wait for our backup."

"*Our* backup?"

He raised the carving knife and smiled. "Didn't *we* clear the house?"

She grinned back and lifted the serrated bread knife. They crossed swords.

"At least he didn't get the books," she said, and slung the backpack off her shoulder.

They heard Maryann and a male talking downstairs.

"Keegan and I are up here," Aaron called down. "Somebody ransacked

Keegan's room." Then to Keegan he said, "I really need to see those books. Somebody wants them pretty bad."

"Just a sec," she said, and pulled out her iPhone. She punched in a web address, did a search, and said, "Guess what? The two cemetery books, *Dirt on Maine's Burial Grounds* and Call's *Ancient Maine Cemeteries*—are available as e-books. Cheap, fast to download, and easier than sitting here reading these copies."

Aaron replied, "I'll download them when I get home. What about *Night Hawks*? Maybe a Kindle or a Nook?"

Keegan's fingers tapped away. A moment later, "Nope. Not yet."

"So can I borrow your copy?"

"The answer is still no. It's not leaving this house except with me. But once your buddies finish their house call, you can read it here. It doesn't leave my sight."

❧ ❧ ❧

By 6:15 the reports were done and the photos were taken. For the second time in the same day Maryann called to have broken glass replaced.

Aaron phoned AJ to tell her about the break-in at the Keegan home. She already knew about the Annie's break-in.

"So here's the deal. I'm inviting you to join us here for dinner," he said to AJ. "There's only one catch. Before you come over, you have to call Coastal Pizza and order two large pies—whatever toppings you, Keegan, and Maryann usually get. Stop and pick them up on your way and I'll pay you back when you get here." He clicked off and turned around.

Maryann's tense face relaxed a little and slowly broke into a what-a-nice-thing-to-do look.

He shrugged. "Seemed crazy to ask you to cook after this."

"Aaron Stevenson," she said. "You are such a sweetie," and shook her head.

CHAPTER 9

While they were waiting for the pizza, Aaron caught up on some of the chapters Keegan had already read in *Night Hawks*.

"This'd be a great read even if it wasn't connected to a crime," he said. "All of us in the Maine public schools know who Joshua Chamberlain was, but I'll bet nobody's ever heard of these two scouts and the Wells connection."

They were all starving by the time AJ arrived with dinner, so they set the pizzas out and gathered around the kitchen table. Before anyone finished a whole slice, the talk returned to the break-ins.

"I don't get it," AJ said. "Are these three books—or even one of them—worth three burglaries?"

"Apparently they are," Keegan said. "We have one customer who wants them, and somebody else."

"You mean Luna?" AJ said.

"AJ!" Keegan said, annoyed. "Confidentiality? I was trying not to use the customer's name."

"Oh, Aaron already knows," AJ answered. "I told him about Luna's grand entrance after work Friday."

All eyes went to Aaron.

"What else did she tell you?" Keegan demanded.

"That this Luna has a sunlight disorder," he said. "And that someone calling himself Father Joseph was checking up on her."

"Did AJ also mention," Maryann said, irritated, "that Luna took classes with my sister Zelda at Orono?"

"She did. But let's not be too hard on AJ. When she told me, it was over dinner. It was just another how-was-work story. Her telling me isn't what caused the break-ins. We're all just feeling more sensitive after two burglaries."

They quieted down and returned to eating.

Maryann said, "Keegan and I were wondering if there might be a blood connection between Luna and the scouts, an ancestral thing. Luna seems to have a bit of a curvature to her upper spine. I haven't read the *Night Hawks* book yet, but according to Keegan, that's how the two scouts are described."

"It is," Aaron said. "I just read that part."

Keegan added, "It's worth noting that they only fought at night. Luna is a night person, too."

"She called herself a moon child," AJ said. "She wears the nun outfit so she can come out in daytime."

Keegan said, "Best guess is, she wants the three books for genealogical research. The same could apply to our other person, the guy who called himself Father Joseph, who seems to be after the same books. And although he's big and muscular, he looks hunched, and he covers up, and he comes out at night. Maybe these are two apples from the same tree."

"It's possible," Aaron said. "But it's too soon to draw that tight a connection. Remember, when he crashed Annie's, it was nighttime. So the robe was about covering up for the camera, not for the sunlight. He broke into this house after you two left for work, so it was in broad daylight, but with no cameras to tell us how he was dressed. We don't know if he wore the robe or not."

"But between the books and their body shapes," Keegan argued, "we have enough to link the two of them."

"Agreed," Aaron said. "That doesn't make them twins separated at birth, or even long-lost cousins."

"But you agree they're in competition?" Keegan pressed.

"Yes," he said. "Probably."

They went back to the pizza and had taken the last slices out of the boxes when Aaron said, "By the way, I did check with the registrar's office at the University of Maine yesterday, hoping to get a last name for Luna, maybe a current address."

"What'd they say?" Maryann asked.

"It's a pretty unique name. They've never had anyone there named Luna, first or last name. Not in your sister's college years, not ever."

Keegan insisted on trying Luna's number again. She got the same recording.

"Luna, this is Keegan. You need to call me if you want your books. Please call. This is an emergency." She left her iPhone number this time as well as the store phone. Then she and Aaron excused themselves from the table and went back to reading *Night Hawks*.

***

William Coburn cited a Chamberlain journal entry written in December 1862 after the bloody battle at Fredericksburg, where the Union armies were humiliated. Maine's untested 20th Volunteers, formed barely four months earlier, had arrived in time to cover the retreat of Union's main army. The troops of the 20th were forced to spend a frigid night on the battlefield, where they employed extreme measures to stay warm.

Colonel Chamberlain wrote:

It was a cold night. Bitter, raw north winds swept the stark slopes. The men, heated by their energetic and exciting work, felt keenly the chilling change. Many of them had neither overcoat nor blanket, having left them with the discarded knapsacks. They roamed about to find some garment not needed by the dead. Mounted officers all lacked outer covering. This had gone back with the horses, strapped to the saddles.

So we joined the uncanny quest. Necessity compels strange uses. For myself it seemed best to bestow my body between two dead men among the many left there by earlier assaults, and to draw another crosswise for a pillow out of the trampled, blood-soaked sod, pulling the flap of his coat over my face to fend off the chilling winds.

Several times enemy soldiers approached the place where I had secreted myself. As it was nighttime, L and C [LeClair and Champaigne] were able to stay near me, and regularly dispatched the enemy.

At one dark hour I looked up and saw my loyal guardians' fierce and terrible countenances illuminated by the light of a burning tree trunk on the battlefield. Seeing them perched atop two stacks of corpses nearby, I was reminded of my visit to Paris, when I enjoyed viewing the Cathedral de Notre Dame with its grotesque ornamental drain spouts, gargouilles they are called, colorful but frightening creatures strategically placed to shunt rainwater off the roof and away from the structure.

My two faithful scouts, my night hawks, perceiving that I was even then still shivering with cold, placed two additional rebel corpses over me, and those barely moments after they slew them. By the time dawn approached, I could feel the last traces of warmth draining away from those unfortunate souls' bodies. Had it not been for L and C on that bleak and terrifying night, it might have been my lifeless body blanketing some other shivering soul. At which good use I would have taken no offense. One cannot help but bring to mind the Eucharistic liturgy of the Church: My body, broken for you; my blood, shed for you. I am overcome with emotion as I write these words, for they have hit close to my heart.

Keegan choked back tears and gasped, "My God, this is so different from what we learned in school. They taught us about battles. But this is about people."

"The unsanitized version," Aaron said, his own voice thick. "In school I thought Stephen Crane's *Red Badge of Courage* was powerful. This, though, is more like Ken Burns' documentary, *The Civil War*, with all those old letters and brown photographs."

"Is this harder for you than for me—the war being over slavery and all?"

"You mean, is reading this harder because I'm black?" he asked, and paused a moment. "I think you're asking a white person's question, but you don't realize it. You're attempting to be sensitive. But it's a non-question, really. You and I are reading this man's words and we're responding because it's about people—plain old human beings—fighting and dying. It's not about politics. There's only the suffering, the agony, the death, and here Chamberlain's fight for survival. You're white and I'm black, and regardless of how liberated or socially conscious we think we are today, underneath we're just human beings responding to what Joshua Chamberlain needed to share on paper."

"I guess it was a stupid question, wasn't it? I'm sorry."

"It wasn't a stupid question, Keegan. It was simply a question. And I don't think my answering it with a yes or a no would have done it justice."

She looked confused.

"For now we can leave it at that and read on, okay?" He handed her the book. "Your turn to read."

A little more than six months after Fredericksburg came the war's bloodiest battle, Gettysburg. Fought in the first few days of July, the two opposing armies suffered more than 50,000 casualties. In the aftermath, Reverend Lussier noted in his aide de camp journal:

The battle for Gettysburg is over. Lee's troops are retreating to northern Virginia. After days of fighting, with our ammunition at an end, Colonel Chamberlain led a bayonet charge against General Hood's infantry, routing them.

Shortly after that Lussier wrote:

Colonel Chamberlain has granted scouts L and C leave to return to Maine to visit L's mate in Wells. Without their wicked blades and night-fighting prowess—their night vision akin to a bat's—it is doubtful our 20th Maine would have held the high ground at Little Round Top, which strategically turned Gettysburg to the Army of the Potomac's favor.

My friend Joshua, as always, has downplayed his own heroism. He is of a mind that L and C's forays behind Hood's lines the two nights prior to the bayonet charge struck such terror into the rebels' hearts that they were ready to flee the fight when the charge came. I am inclined to agree. The battle, I am certain, would have gone far differently had it not been for these hunchbacked scouts who once saved me from wolves in the Maine wilderness. So both my friend Joshua and I owe our lives to them.

We have been reinforced and resupplied with food, medicine, and ammunition, and we have the strength of numbers now. Yet the Colonel and I will feel more confident once our night hawks return from their leave. They have promised the Colonel they will return within the month. How they can traverse that distance and back in four weeks, traveling only at night as they do, we cannot fathom.

"How far is it from here to Gettyburg?" Keegan asked.

Aaron asked his phone. "Over 500 miles. Eight hours one way by car. Probably a couple of months to do a roundtrip on foot or by horseback in those days. Railroad would have been fastest back then, but I doubt anything was direct."

"Yet Lussier writes that LeClair and Champaigne will be back within the month."

Aaron shrugged. "Maybe LeClair's mate met them halfway, someplace like Hartford. Who knows? All we've got is the journal account."

A month after Robert E. Lee surrendered to Ulysses Grant at Appomattox in 1865, Chamberlain wrote in his journal:

My scouts L and C have given everything and asked for nothing in return. As civilians they cannot receive military medals or honors, which they would undoubtedly refuse if offered. What else can I do to reward their service except guarantee life use of the pink granite house in Wells? It seems a pittance. I personally and we as a nation shall be forever indebted to these two brave warriors.

Keegan and Aaron tried to absorb the unbelievable tale Coburn had constructed out of old and new sources. Could the "lost" sources, Chamberlain's and Lussier's seminary and war journals, be authentic? Even if they were, how much of Coburn's cobbled together version was true, and how much was a skillfully woven piece of fiction?

Keegan searched Coburn's name and the book title online. Reviews and opinions were split. *Wikipedia's* brief bio presented Coburn as a respected small-college history professor who, when challenged numerous times to produce the "found" journals, refused. The journals were not found after his death in 1966. Either they never existed, or they were purposely hidden, or they had disappeared.

Many of *Night Hawks'* cited writings were verifiable, including quotes from the personal letters and reports of Confederate officers and soldiers, in which they referred to the scouts as banshees, harpies, and hunchbacks. Chamberlain's junior officers' journals and letters also mentioned them.

Keegan and Aaron talked a while more until he said, "It's getting late. You've got to work in the morning and I want to get home and download those two e-books and skim through them. I'll get back to you tomorrow."

He went downstairs, found that AJ had already left, and said goodnight to Maryann, who walked him to the door.

"Thanks again for dinner, Aaron," was all she said, and locked up after he left.

Section III

Zelda's Blue and Yellow Banana Box

CHAPTER 10

It was 9:10. Aaron had been gone fifteen minutes and Maryann was relaxing in her recliner in front of a sitcom rerun, her eyelids drooping.

"Mom," Keegan asked, rousing Maryann. "Before you fall asleep, can I ask a favor?"

"Try me," Maryann replied, without fully opening her eyes.

"That box of my mother's files and notebooks—the banana crate? You said we'd get it out of the attic today."

"Now? Keegan, aren't you worn out, too? This has been a long stressful day for both of us."

Keegan didn't relent. "Last night you said you'd find it for me."

"True. I did say that." Maryann's sounded resigned now. She was going to have to get up from the chair and go to the attic.

"And can you pull out that town history, too?"

"I told you yesterday, it's on the shelf right above my computer." She leaned forward and pressed her palms on the arms of the recliner. "You get that while I find the box."

Ten minutes later Keegan sat propped against the headboard of her bed, the town history beside her on the nightstand and a blank spiral-bound notebook on her lap. At her feet rested the blue and yellow banana box.

Her head was still spinning from the images in the *Night Hawks* book. She jotted notes and questions, marking some of the action-needed items with asterisks.

›　*"Pink granite house in Wells" (Chamberlain journal, 1865). Built for LeClair's mate. What? Where? Mentioned in other historical documents? *Check town history. *Check historical society. Mom says Zelda took notes for college internship. PINK granite?*

›　*Champaigne, LeClair and mate. Buried where? In/near Wells? Who would know? *Funeral homes, cemetery associations. Did they return to Allagash after war? May be buried there.*

She retrieved Luna's phone number from the special-order ticket in the book then texted AJ: *Here's Luna's number. Can you get Aaron to track it down? Where is she?*

Then she pulled up Amazon and downloaded the Kindle version of *The Dirt on Maine's Burial Grounds* so she'd have it at her fingertips after Luna picked up her print copy. She went back to notetaking.

› *Joshua Chamberlain's journals. Originals at Bowdoin College Library. Are they available in paperback or e-book?*
› *Clayton Lussier. Bio? Journals? *Maybe Geoff Swett knows about Chamberlain and Lussier journals. He knows rare books.*
› *William Coburn. Additional info/bio?*
› *Check Ancestry.com and other genealogy sites for Champaigne and LeClair. Maine or Canada connections? *State of Maine or Veteran's Administration may know if they're buried in a Civil War vet cemetery. (Lussier said they were civilians.)*
› *Hunchbacks. Read up on them.*
› *Sunlight allergy/disorders?*
› *Chamberlain mentioned the scouts reminded him of Cathedral de Notre Dame's rainspouts.*

She set the notebook aside, drew the banana box up between her knees, and pried the top off. It was like lifting the lid of a casket; she had no idea what might be staring up at her from inside. She closed her eyes, set the lid aside, and opened them. Her heart thumped. The manila folder on top had notes scrawled across it. The handwriting had to be Zelda's. It could easily be mistaken for her own.

She lifted the folder out. It was jammed with handwritten notes. She flipped it open and leafed through, her mind numb and not grasping content. She was aware only of her birth mother's flowing cursive script. Before this she had seen practically nothing written in Zelda's hand, and now here she was, uncovering a treasure chest full. The tears welled up and stung her eyes. She stopped turning pages, closed her eyes again, and sobbed. She had seen school pictures and photos of Zelda at different ages, but this was like meeting her. Finally.

When she regained her composure, she began sifting through things. She didn't try to open or read them all. It was late and the weariness of the day was catching up with her.

One of the files she did pause to examine was marked *Quarries*. She fanned the photocopied book pages. There were black and white photos on plain copy paper, not glossy photo paper, and a raft of notes. Pages had dates penciled at the top to indicate when the information had been acquired. Keegan set the folder on the floor. She could look at it more closely in the morning.

The next four folders were all marked *Cemeteries* and formed a sequence: 1-50, 51-100, 101-150, and 151-. She grabbed *The History of Wells* from the night table and opened it to the cemeteries section Maryann had said Zelda helped research. There were 201 cemeteries listed, all numbered and keyed to a foldout map. Zelda's files included nearly 50 more graveyards than the 150+ Austin Call had listed in his decades earlier *Ancient Maine Cemeteries, Public and Private: Volume 27 York County*.

Keegan wrote in her notebook: *Compare Call's list with Zelda's files and with final version in History of Wells*.

Another of the cemeteries folders had notes of interviews Zelda had conducted around Wells. Some of the interviewees gave her information about a particular family graveyard or a crossroads cemetery. Others detailed—in some cases *surmised*—whose bones might lie beneath the ground. Keegan placed all the cemeteries folders on the floor with the *Quarries* folder.

Three thick folders of notes related to Zelda's interviews with town elders. Further down was a shoebox containing 20 microcassette tapes and a handheld recorder, the headset looking like it had once belonged on a McDonald's drive-thru worker's head.

There were also some thinner manila folders, one tagged *Historical Societies* and another *Libraries*. Alongside them sat a small stack of historical books that included Call's *Ancient Maine Cemeteries, York County*.

In the very bottom of the box lay a yellow spiral-top notebook, something a person might keep in a breast pocket or in a handbag for grocery lists or reminder notes. Inserted in the wire spiral binding was a stubby green golf pencil with no eraser. On the front cover was the name *Zelda Keegan* with an address and phone number. Keegan's fingers felt suddenly weak and tired. The little notebook slipped from her grip onto her lap, landing with the back cover up. *Jan* was scrawled near the top--perhaps a reminder to do something in January during or after semester break—with a name below it, her name: *Dauphine*. Seeing it took her breath away.

CHAPTER 11

"Keegan?"

Keegan felt a warm hand gently shaking her wrist. She opened her eyes and saw Maryann sitting on the edge of the bed. The digital clock on the table read 12:14 a.m. She turned her head a few times to get the tightness out of her neck and realized her hips were stiff, too. She had fallen asleep with her legs wrapped around the banana box, which was still between her knees.

"I fell asleep reading."

"Me, too. Not reading, but in the recliner watching TV. Find anything interesting in the box?"

"Don't know. I haven't really looked closely. I set aside the quarry files and the cemetery files." She pointed to the folders on the floor.

"You look through the town history?"

"Just the cemetery list. I wanted to compare it to the list in Call's York County cemeteries book." She lifted the box from between her legs and handed it to Maryann who balanced it on her lap.

"Does that go in the box, too?" she asked, and pointed to the little spiral notepad on the spare pillow. She saw *Dauphine* scrawled on the face-up back cover beneath *Jan*. "Is that notebook yours? I see your name on it, but I can't recall when you last used your first name."

"It was my mother's. I found it in the bottom of the banana box." She turned it over and showed Maryann the front cover with Zelda's name, address, and phone number.

"So your name was on the back before you were born? Must have been a reminder. You know, you hear or see a baby name you like, so you jot it down. What's in it?"

"I don't know yet. I fell asleep."

"Want to look now?"

Keegan swung her legs around and let them hang over the side of the bed so she and Maryann were sitting side by side. Their hearts stood on tiptoe as they waited for Keegan to flip up the front cover.

On the first page Zelda had written:

6/20/99

General Joshua Chamberlain's Night Hawks: LeClair and Champaigne, the Scouts from Wells, William Coburn. Brewer, Maine, 1919. 25 copies pub.

› *Bowdoin College Library—no*
› *UMaine Libraries—no*
› *UNH Library—no*
› *Maine State system—no*
  Bangor Theological Seminary Library—in rare books collection

6/23/99

› *drove to Bangor Sem, read Coburn on site*
› *librarian confirmed with registrar that Lussier and Chamberlain were classmates*
› *librarian and predecessors have tried for decades to no avail to locate "lost" Lussier and Chamberlain journals around country. Librarian suspects Coburn is fiction.*
  Q: If journals exist, where did Coburn get them? Where now?
  Q: Lussier/Chamberlain, LeClair/Champaigne. Are first letters L and C a coincidence?

6/27/99

*Check Byron Littlefield interview. Said he and his pals on a dare (1948 or 49?) camped out near Stonehedge (his word) in/near High Pine section of Wells. Ask town historian about Stonehedge.

› *Is there an aerial photo of High Pine? Maybe Stonehedge shows up. * Check Town Office for photo and info on Stonehedge. Historical Society? Archived photos?*

Keegan stared at the handwritten page. *She takes notes and asks questions the same way I do.* She felt a strong connection, not only to the mother she never knew but to the college intern she'd never met. *Are you and I trying to unravel the same mystery?*

Maryann said, "I read in the *Portland Press Herald* a couple years ago that Bangor Seminary closed its doors. Some other institution—another seminary, I think—must have acquired the library collection. And before you ask, I'll tell you—in all the years I've lived here, I've never heard of anything local referred to as Stonehenge."

"Stonehedge," Keegan enunciated. "She made it clear that Byron Littlefield called it Stonehedge."

Other research notes followed, but both of them were too tired to continue. Keegan closed the notepad, turned to the back cover again, and stared at her name—Dauphine. She ran an index finger under it.

"It's like she knew one day I'd find this," she said.

"Maybe, maybe not. Your mother and I came up with plenty of baby names during her pregnancy. But she never mentioned Dauphine until the day she went into labor. She made me promise to use it if anything happened to her."

"So either she liked the name or she wanted to draw our attention to this notebook. Do you think she knew someone named Dauphine?"

Maryann shrugged and shook her head. "Not that I know of."

"Let's look it up," Keegan said. "I've got a little energy left before I fall asleep."

She went to her desktop and Googled Dauphine. Several encyclopedia entries came up.

Dauphin with no E was French, pronounced doe-fan. The eldest son of the king of France (title in use from 1349-1830), early 15c., from Middle French dauphin, literally dolphin. Originally the title attached to "the Dauphin of Viennois" whose province in the French Alps north of Provence came to be known as Dauphiné.

"The name of the province has an accent," Maryann pointed out. "That changes the pronunciation to doe-fan-ay."

"Guess she didn't name me after the province," Keegan said.

A dictionary site defined dauphine—no accent—as the wife of a dau-phin. The silent E at the end served to feminize the word.

"Maybe it could apply to a sister of the male heir, too," Maryann said. "Not just a wife."

"So my name, depending on whether there's an accent or not, could refer to a region in the French Alps or to French royalty. You think there's a connection?"

"Well, Zelda's first notes here are about Chamberlain's scouts. Didn't you say that when Lussier met them in the Allagash, he tried communi-cating with them in English? And when they didn't answer, he switched to French."

"How about this? They weren't French Canadian—even though the Allagash is near the border—they were from France."

"Possibly," Maryann said. "But we're not going to solve this tonight. It's bedtime." She put an arm around Keegan's shoulder, pulled her close, and gave her a kiss on the forehead. "You remind me so much of my sister at times." She let go, stood up, and walked toward the door.

"Mom?"

Maryann turned back. "Yes, Keegan?"

"Nothing. I just wanted you to hear me say it. Mom."

"Thank you. I like how you say it, too. See you in the morning, Dauphine."

CHAPTER 12

Keegan dreamed she and Zelda were sitting on a bench in the warm sunshine. She was seventeen and her mother eighteen or nineteen. In spite of there being only a year or two age difference, she felt the connection and knew it was a mother-daughter outing.

The bench they were sitting on was one of about twenty in the court yard and faced a shimmering pool that had a three-tiered cascading fountain at its center. She could see over the low wall that encircled the pool. Its bottom was littered with tossed coins. Water flowed from the mouth of a huge statuary fish at the top of the fountain and spilled over a catchment bowl at the top to a second and then to the lowest before reaching the rippling surface of the pool.

Keegan was reading a book and her mother was gripping a green golf pencil and taking notes in a little notebook that had pages the size of index cards. Every so often Zelda would raise her writing hand, touch the golf pencil to her lip, and look thoughtful. Then she'd go back to notetaking.

There was a sudden commotion in front of a two-story brick building on the other side of the pool. Zelda looked up, tried to see around the fish fountain, then got to her feet and moved left a few steps to see what was going on.

"Wait here," she told Keegan, and started around the fountain at a brisk pace.

Keegan, however, didn't wait. She followed her mother.

A group of about 10 students, some with books and notebooks in hand, others with backpacks, stood clustered on the sidewalk facing away from the fish fountain toward the brick building. They sounded like angry protesters, voices rising and thick with impatience, certain of their moral rightness.

Zelda marched around the wall of students and disappeared from view.

Keegan tried to catch up, but more students drifted closer to see what was going on, making it hard for her to do the end run Zelda had done. She stopped and stood with the crowd, getting the same view they had.

On a bench by herself sat Luna in her black habit, hood, veil, and gloves. The crowd was rude, throwing out demanding questions, catcalls, and insistent challenges. Keegan couldn't understand the words, but the tone and meaning were clear. They were not angry at Luna, but wanted to free Luna from whatever enslavement required her to wear such garb. Luna sat with her gloved hands folded on her lap, not trying to raise a hand or speak.

Keegan saw Zelda approach Luna's bench. She expected her mother to face the crowd and give a firebrand speech, to play the beleaguered sheriff facing down the torch-bearing lynch mob. She wanted to push through the crowd so she could back her mother up like the sheriff's faithful deputy. But the crowd was like a thicket of heavy vines she couldn't move.

Zelda stepped in front of Luna, keeping the crowd at her back, then threw up her arms, the stubby green golf pencil in her right hand and the small yellow notepad in her left, looking like a woman whose immigrant great-grandmother had just stepped off the boat onto the dock. She placed her palms together and gave a nod of the head, bowed at the waist, then widened her arms again and hugged Luna, adding a theatrical double kiss, first to the left outside of the black veil and then to the right outside the veil.

The mob fell silent. Zelda straightened up.

"Thank you for agreeing to meet with me," Keegan heard her say over the hush. She sat down beside the woman in black and said loudly enough for the crowd to hear, "We can do the interview here, if you like, or I can find us a place a little more private." She crossed a leg over her knee, golf pencil and yellow notebook poised over her lap, as if ready to start her notetaking. When the crowd of students didn't disperse, she looked up at the gawkers and said, "You can all read about it later this week."

The crowd broke up in twos and threes and drifted away until no one was left between Keegan and the bench where her mother sat next to the black-robed Luna. She caught herself thinking, *I can't wait to read Mom's newspaper interview*, then realized there was no interview, that this was an intervention. She had a little insight into the mother she had never met.

When she approached them on the bench, her dream began to dissolve—but not before she saw Luna's black-gloved hand reach out and clasp Zelda's hand.

☞ ☞ ☞

At 7:22 a.m. Maryann and Keegan were having toast and black coffee. The Channel 8 weather lady was on the kitchen TV, giving another sunny forecast for the rest of the week in southern Maine.

Keegan asked, "When my mother was in college, did she write for the campus newspaper?"

Maryann squinted thoughtfully. "Maybe. I don't recall. Why?"

Keegan told her about the dream.

"That's interesting. But remember, Aaron said he checked with the registrar at Orono. The college has never had a student named Luna."

"Maybe she wasn't registered under that name."

Maryann sipped her coffee. "Taking the dream pretty literally, aren't you? You saw the golf pencil and the yellow notebook before you went to sleep. And the dream was a lot like what Luna told you when she came into the store: Zelda leading curious students to believe Luna was a visiting Middle Eastern scholar. Could be your subconscious wove a few aspects together for the dream."

"Probably. But I love the way she came to Luna's aid in the dream. She wasn't just brave, she was clever and resourceful. She sold it."

"She was brave and resourceful." Maryann had a little catch in her voice. "It was a beautiful dream, and I'm glad you shared it with me. I needed to hear it, too."

"You still miss her."

"How could I not? I see her in you every day."

They ate quietly for a few minutes, half-listening to the end of the news but mostly lost in their own thoughts.

When the news ended, Keegan asked, "Don't you think it's strange that Luna hasn't called back? She wants those books. And I left messages with both our store number and my cell number."

"Maybe she's away. Or not feeling well. You know—the sunlight thing."

"Or maybe something's wrong," Keegan said.

"Keegan, it's a book order."

"Mom, you know there's more to this than a book order. She could be …"

"Could be what?" Maryann asked.

"Oh, I don't know."

Maryann took the last gulp of her coffee. "Okay, so call her again when we get to the store. That's about all you can do."

Keegan got up from the table. "I'd like to take the banana box to work today. When things are slow I can go to the work room and read through some of her folders."

"Okay. AJ's in today, and we can yell if we need you."

Keegan went upstairs, showered, and dressed for work. She was tying her running shoes when a text from AJ dinged in. Call now. She pressed the phone icon for AJ.

"This must be important," Keegan said when AJ picked up.

"Aaron ran the phone number and got an address."

"Seriously?"

"Yes. It's the Christian Brothers monastery in Alfred. We went for the Apple Festival a couple years ago. About 20 miles from here."

"Does she live there?" Keegan asked.

"No. Just staying there. One of the brothers said she's a visiting nun on retreat."

"You're kidding. She's actually a nun?"

"That we don't know. I'm just saying, that's what they told Aaron. They treated her as one and let her use a room there."

"And the phone?" Keegan asked.

"It's not their main line. It's a separate line for the guest room. Aaron says it has an old-fashioned answering machine."

"How does he know that?"

"How does he know what?" AJ said.

"That it's an answering machine."

"He just got back from the monastery. He saw the answering machine. He heard it."

"And?"

"Your messages are on it."

"Could he tell if she listened to them?"

"Wait a sec," AJ said. "He's right here. Let me put him on."

Keegan heard AJ passing the phone to her brother.

"Keegan? Aaron. The monks say she packed up her tent Monday night and hit the road."

"And she hasn't been back?"

"According to them, no."

"What about the messages I left?"

"They're all still on the answering machine. The new, unchecked ones were still blinking. Looks like she got your first two—when some books came in, then the one when you warned her Father Joseph was shadowing her. That was probably the one that spooked her."

"So she's not picking up the books because she didn't get my later messages. I left one a few minutes ago, before AJ texted me. But that would have been after you left the monastery."

"Doesn't matter. She won't get it."

"But Father Joseph might. I don't suppose one of the monks is named Father Joseph?"

"Nope. I asked. The brothers don't have a clue who he might be."

"So for now we have no way to get in touch with Luna."

"True. But the good news is, she heeded your warning," Aaron said, trying to sound positive.

"Yeah, there's that. But I really need to talk to her."

"You've got to hope she comes in for the books."

"Any thoughts?"

Aaron held her with hmmm, then said, "Let's assume the character posing as Father Joseph followed Luna to Wells. He knew she took the room at Christian Brothers, slipped into her room when she was out, and checked the answering machine. When you called from the store Monday to say some books were in, he wanted to beat her to them and broke in late Monday night, expecting they'd be on the special-order shelf. But you had taken them home. So he waited until you and Maryann went to work, then broke into the house. But he missed again, because you had taken them back to the store so you'd have them for Luna."

"You think it was also Father Joseph who broke into Toil & Trouble?"

"Who else? It's unlikely there's a third party after the same book."

"But why?" Keegan asked.

"Still no idea."

"Me either," she said. "Are you dropping AJ off at work, or is your mother?"

"Mom was going to."

"If you bring her, come in and I'll show you some of Zelda's notes. I'll look them over before you get there. Maybe by then I'll have something more for us to talk about."

"Sounds good. Oh, one other thing."

"What?" she asked.

"Luna didn't leave Christian Brothers by car. The brother I talked to says she left on foot. He wondered if somebody was picking her up at the end of the driveway. He couldn't remember anybody dropping her when she arrived last week, which was also after dark. He says she came and went with nothing but the black outfit she was wearing and a long flat wooden case that was three or four feet long."

CHAPTER 13

Maryann and Keegan got to the Book Stop first. Maryann set up the register and Keegan carried the banana box to the work room. She removed the lid and set some of the folders on the table.

Quarries was as good a place as any to start. She only knew of one working quarry in town, Millenium Granite, which covered a massive tract of land in the Bald Hill section of Wells' High Pine district. It included a huge water-filled pit near the high end of Quarry Road. Keegan wasn't sure who owned it, but she and AJ had ridden by it on their bikes and seen workers operating machinery. No Trespassing signs were posted near the road, and she knew the pit was off-limits for a reason—to keep teens from leaping off its high side cliffs into the deep green waters.

She skimmed Zelda's internship notes. A few were typed, but most were either printed or written in cursive script. There were also photocopies of articles, including one that gave an excellent summary of granite mining.

Runs of granite or ledges in the ground were known as motions. In the early days, quarries were mined with hand drills and gun powder. Teams of oxen dragged the gigantic slabs and blocks to nearby locations where they could be used as foundations for homes. Later, when there was a demand for granite for large buildings, the slabs were shipped by railroad or transported down to Wells Harbor for loading onto southbound coastal schooners. Wells granite was used for many structures including the Seagram Plaza and Tiffany's in New York City and the Tomb of the Unknown Soldier in Washington, DC.

Zelda had noted that locally mined granite came in various colors. North Berwick produced black granite. Pine Hill in York shipped green granite. But the pink granite from Wells was the most in demand.

In the 1800s the quarry had been mined for local consumption, mostly house foundations. In 1925 Pasquale Miniutti purchased it from William Colby, then in 1929 Miniutti passed on three-quarter interest to the John Swenson Granite Company of Concord, New Hampshire. By the early 1970s foreign competition forced its closure.

But it's not closed. It's being worked.

Below Zelda's printed notes were several blocks of script written like a journal entry.

> *When I was in middle school and Maryann was in high school, we'd ride our bikes to the Swenson Quarry with our friends. The trails through it were runs for moto-cross bikes and four-wheelers. Sadly, the area right around the pit was a dumping ground for junk cars. But for us the pit was our illegal swimming hole, and it was heaven on a hot summer day. It was deep, a catch basin for rain, snowmelt, and runoff water from the high ground all around it.*
>
> *We'd jump off the cliffs, yelling and screeching to high heaven, our voices echoing off the side walls, then we'd plunge feet-first into the cool, emerald waters, disappearing beneath them for a few seconds. We'd do it again and again until whoever was our lookout spotted a Wells cop car pulling into the driveway. Those cops knew we were there. They'd open the driver's door, stand next to the car, and use that speaker to yell a not-very-serious warning. Most of the cops, if they grew up in Wells, had jumped from those cliffs when they were in school.*
>
> *The cops usually stopped once in the morning and once in the afternoon. We could almost set our watches by them. It was a formality for them and a ritual for us. They'd drive off and five minutes later we'd sneak back in from where we were hiding in the trees. I never saw one of them walk all the way into the quarry as far as the pit or give chase. It was great fun. It was also where my sister and I first jumped and skinny-dipped with two boys.*

Keegan's eyes widened in surprise, then dampened. That revelation had caught her off-guard. One minute she was reading dry historical notes, the next she was catching a glimpse of the Keegan sisters—her two mothers—near the age she was now. At the end Zelda had penned an intimate detail that, had she lived, she might have shared in a mother-daughter talk.

How old were they when they skinny-dipped? No year noted. Did anything else happen or was it all innocent? She wrote that it was two boys, not boyfriends.

Keegan fought back a sob. She hadn't realized until this week how much she missed the mother she'd never met. And she had no chance to know her father—not only personally but even by name—because Zelda had died of an aneurysm in childbirth without divulging it. Maryann swore she had no idea who he was, either, and wondered if Zelda had planned to name him on the birth certificate. In the end, the lack of a name had forced her to put down father unknown on the form. Zelda's unexpected death had left everyone with unanswered questions. *Had the pregnancy been accidental or intentional? Had Zelda herself been certain who the father was?* Maryann and Keegan had nowhere to turn for answers. The only two things Zelda had shared with her sister was that she was excited about being a mother and—after the sonogram revealed the fetus as female—that the baby's name would be Dauphine.

There were more pages of quarry notes and a handful of pages photocopied from old books. There was also a black and white aerial photograph with wording penciled under it: *Granite Quarry at Bald Hill.* It occurred to her then that Zelda's notes had been taken in the late 1990s, when the inactive quarry was still an illegal dumping ground, dirt bike track, and unofficial swimming hole. Time to Google.

She used the work room desktop and searched: *granite quarry in Wells, Maine.* It brought back a business listing: *Millenium Granite* and *Stoneworks.*

The owner was a Wells native with a U Maine degree in civil engineering. He had foreseen a growing demand for ornamental granite for driveways, walls, and capstones, so in 2000 he bought the old Swenson quarry that had been inactive since the 1970s. With plenty of previously mined granite already stockpiled on the 100-acre property, he guessed it would be a decade or more before he'd have to reopen the water-filled pit for excavation. His bio mentioned that he himself had been one of the quarry cliff jumpers when he was in school.

Was he also a skinny-dipper? No doubt dozens, maybe hundreds of kids were over the years.

The Millenium website's *About Us* page had a stunning color photo of the swimming hole. The shot had been taken from above—too low to be an aerial image—probably from the top of a crane boom. The cliffs were clearly perpendicular and the waters were the lovely emerald green Zelda had described.

Keegan remembered stopping to sneak a peek once with AJ. For her entire childhood the quarry had been a working establishment, posted with No Trespassing signs. If they tried sneaking in to swim now, the cops wouldn't give a wave and a bullhorn warning. Nowadays any cliff divers or skinny-dippers would be arrested and charged with trespassing.

She Googled *quarry swimming in Wells, Maine* and got two search results. *Quarry Jumping You Tube* had been uploaded March 10, 2007. The man who posted it stated it was a video of himself and his friends 20 years earlier—1987—jumping from the cliffs into the old Swenson Quarry in Wells.

Keegan did the math. Maryann and Zelda had been in elementary school, not middle or high school. The video was between two and three minutes long, and she watched it four times. It was thrilling, and she could imagine the Keegan sisters taking part.

The second video was less than a minute long. Same Swenson Quarry cliff, almost the same camera location. A dozen teens ready to jump, laughing, giggling, and calling across to the camera person. The year was 1993, the upload information said. In less than a minute six kids jumped. Boy, then girl, then boy, then boy, then two girls several years apart who looked enough alike that they could be twins—except for the size difference. *High school and middle school.* Even at a distance it was clear that two of the six were Maryann and Zelda—starting far back, holding hands and running, leaping off together, letting go of each other's hands mid-air so they could windmill their arms until they hit the water and disappeared beneath the surface. They reappeared moments later among the other four kids, all six grinning and yelling up at the camera person. The film ran out.

Keegan stared at the screen, too numb to replay the video yet. She needed a minute to recover. When she did she'd call Maryann into the work room to watch it with her. Right now, though, she felt limp, the strength drained out of her.

When there were no customers in the store, Maryann came back to watch the video with Keegan. She, too, choked up to see Zelda young and alive again. Still photos could be powerful, but old movies were an emotional punch in the gut. She regained her composure and asked Keegan to play it again so she could point out the actors.

"Eddie Hartung had the video camera. Until now I'd forgotten he shot this. He showed it to us in his little viewer that day, but that's the last time I saw it. I had no idea he posted it on You Tube."

"That cliff looks pretty high," Keegan said. "I'm not sure I'd have the nerve to jump. But you two did."

"Hah! Funny thing is, that was our first time. I didn't want to jump, but Zell insisted. 'I'll go with you,' she said. She wouldn't let me back out."

"Seriously?"

"Yep. I was the fraidy-cat. That was my only jump of the day. She went back up three or four times and jumped by herself."

"And the skinny-dipping?"

"What skinny-dipping?" Maryann asked, a scowl coming to her face.

"Maybe it wasn't the same day. You two, with two boys."

Maryann blushed. "Who told you that?"

"Your sister ratted you out. In her quarry notes."

Maryann's mouth opened. "That little snitch." She tried to look stern while holding back a devilish grin. "Nothing happened, if that's what you're wondering."

"I'm not asking if anything happened, Mom. I'm just wondering whether she talked you into it or if it was the other way around." Keegan stared unblinking at her mother. It was a small detail, but she wanted to know.

Maryann's glance turned up and a little to the left as she recalled the incident. "I'm pretty sure it was the boys' idea."

Keegan's mouth curled into an impish smile. "So you let yourselves be talked into it?"

Her mother's face flushed even more. "I repeat: nothing happened."

Keegan turned the thumbscrews. "So that's the story you're sticking with?"

"It is." A long pause. Then she laughed. "Unless you come across another note from Zelda."

They laughed together then and would have giggled longer if the front door bell hadn't tinkled.

"Customer," Maryann said.

"One of us ought to take it."

"Odds or evens?" Maryann asked.

Keegan mistook it for a serious question and her face showed it.

Maryann smiled. "You can owe me one. Go back to your files. I'll call you if I need you." She turned to the door then looked back. "Anything else juicy in there, you call me. I can explain away anything." She grinned and left.

The *Cemeteries* files were next.

Keegan laid out her three sources next to each other on the work table. Laymon's 1968 Dirt listed 151 cemeteries. Zelda's files from 1998-1999 showed 48 new discoveries. The 2002 first edition of *The History of Wells* added two more, bringing the total up to 201.

Zelda's files were comprehensive. They included photocopied pages of the same sources Laymon had used for his cemeteries list and map. There were also 5x7 color photos of various burial grounds, along with dated notes showing Zelda had physically traveled to each place.

Many of the 201 were small graveyards, tagged with family names like *Littlefield, Stevens,* or *Hilton.* Numbers 166, 171, 173, 176, 177, and 200 simply read *field stones.* Number 190 was labeled *ancient burial ground,* and 201, the last reported one, was marked *Campbell.*

Below Zelda's final list in her file was a note in longhand: *Byron Littlefield said Stonehedge. Like Stonehenge Circle? Where?*

Keegan thought, *There's Byron Littlefield's name again and his mention of Stonehedge. Last night I saw them in the little yellow notebook. She wanted to recheck the interview. That note-to-self was under her visit to the seminary library where she read the Night Hawks book. But now Littlefield and Stonehedge are mentioned in a cemetery file. What's the connection? Is Stonehedge a graveyard?*

She closed her tired eyes and rubbed them. When she opened them, she still didn't have the answer. But her mind made a different connection.

The Wells quarry had stockpiles of pink granite. Zelda's files said the quarry had been mining it since the 1800s. And according to Coburn's *Night Hawks* book, Joshua Chamberlain had ordered a house or a cabin or a structure of some kind be built for the mate of one of the scouts.

Somewhere in Wells. Out of pink granite.

CHAPTER 14

"Did you just see that pig fly by?" AJ asked when she walked into the bookstore.

Aaron was two steps behind her, carrying a white paper pastry bag.

"What pig?" Keegan asked. She had just stepped out of the work room.

AJ replied, "You know the saying: When pigs fly?" She made a surprise face. "Well, feast your eyes on this." She pointed at Aaron's pastry bag. "My brother actually broke down and bought us blueberry muffins from Borealis Bread."

Aaron held up the bag and put on a dopey smile. "Maine's best," he said. In his blue sweatpants and jogging jacket he looked like a Sesame Street actor pitching a message to kids.

"And the priciest," Maryann added with a disapproving frown.

"But so worth it," AJ countered.

"They really are," Aaron said. "But you two have to ante up the coffee."

"Fair enough," Maryann said. "Just brewed a pot."

They moved to the work room and sat on four stools. AJ broke out the muffins and Maryann poured four mugs of coffee.

"Did you look through the Kindles last night?" Keegan asked Aaron.

"I cherry-picked the Wells cemeteries book. I've driven by a lot of the bigger cemeteries and some of the smaller graveyards on patrol. There are some on the list I'm not familiar with. But cops don't spend a lot of time checking out cemeteries. If we see somebody standing up in one during the day, we figure they're just visiting. And at night there's not much to see. The days when medical students needed to dig up cadavers for classroom research are over."

"However, vandals still sneak in and tip over gravestones," Maryann noted.

"That's usually a mix of local kids and alcohol. Most times they'll brag to friends who then pass us a tip. It's less about malice and more about showing off for friends."

"And how about the other book," Keegan asked. "*The Dirt on Maine's Burial Grounds?*"

"A quick read and kind of fun," Aaron answered. "Reminded me of the Edwin Rowe Snow books I read as a kid: shipwrecks, ghosts, and haunted places."

"What'd you think about that 1800s guy, Aaron," AJ asked, "the one they buried sitting up in his wheelchair?"

"I know where that tomb is," Aaron answered. "So do you. It's next to Gregoire's Campground, on Sanford Road right after you come off I-95. I just didn't know the story."

Keegan spun around on her stool and cross-checked it using a Google search.

"Here's more on it. This is from Roxie Zwicker's book, *Haunted York County.* We have a copy out front. Daniel Heard, the father, was a Wells sea captain turned farmer. He had eight children between 1767 and 1788. Theodore, nicknamed Thed with an H—pronounced Ted—was one of those eight. A daughter died in 1815, which may be when the family tomb was started. Then the old man died and was buried in it in 1822. Thed, who was confined to a wheelchair all his life, asked to be buried sitting up in that chair. It doesn't say what year he died. The book says the tomb is set behind an arch of three granite slabs. Dirt and native plants conceal the mounded tomb."

"We've driven by it plenty of times," AJ said. "I never knew it was a real grave."

"We can check it in this," Keegan said, and grabbed the town history next to the banana box. "Here's the foldout. The numbered cemeteries list is on one side, the map with corresponding numbers on the flip side. Just like pirate treasure, they're each marked with an X."

A few seconds later they were all staring down at the map. The

Heard Tomb, #128, was on Route 109 near the I-95 toll booths and ramps.

AJ said, "I'll bet there are a few *Dead Thed* tales around the campground. You know, you've got some old lady walking her dog after dark. She hears something creaking behind her, turns and sees this dirt-covered old man in his mud-caked wheelchair rolling out of the pines after her."

They all laughed.

"Speaking of dirt," Keegan said, "here's one I want to know about." She pulled Richard Laymon's *The Dirt on Maine's Burial Grounds* from the counter and thumbed it open. "Someplace in Wells there's a box-shaped structure made from pink granite blocks for the sides—like bread sticks—and pink granite slabs like lasagna for the roof. Laymon doesn't say it's a tomb, but it sure sounds like one."

"Could it be the Heard Family Tomb by Gregoire's?" Maryann asked. "That's granite."

"I don't think so, because Laymon gives us both stories, the Heard Tomb and this other one. He wouldn't duplicate. And he says the old-timers won't disclose the location of this other one except to say it's not close to any human remains. Which takes the Heard Tomb out of it."

AJ said, "Maybe it was built as a tomb, but it never got used as one, which would explain why it's not near any human remains."

"What do you think, Keegan?" Aaron asked.

She scrunched up her face. "Not exactly sure. But I find it odd. Zelda left some old interview notes from her college internship with the historical society. One of the old-timers she interviewed, Byron Littlefield, mentioned an outing he and his friends went on, in the woods out at High Pine. Mr. Littlefield called the place Stonehedge. He said it was made of stacked pink granite."

"Which connects to what you and I read last night in the *Night Hawks* book," Aaron said. "Joshua Chamberlain had somebody build a pink granite cabin for the scouts."

"I'm guessing," AJ said, "that Mr. Littlefield called it Stonehedge because this was made of big stones like the Stonehenge circle in England."

"So we're saying Stonehedge is a place here in Wells," Aaron said. "And it's a home, though it may resemble a tomb."

"Which may make it the ancestral ruins Luna is trying to find," Keegan said. "Like looking for the family cabin."

The four of them sat thoughtfully sipping the last of their coffee until Maryann said, "It looks like maybe my sister Zelda, as far back as 17 or 18 years ago, was trying to help Luna locate it."

CHAPTER 15

Aaron said he was going home to get some sleep before his shift, which started late in the evening. Maryann and AJ worked the front so Keegan could keep going with Zelda's files and run a few Google searches. She ran a few using key words.

> › LeClair, Le Clair, LeClaire, Le Claire
> › Champaigne, Champagne
> › LeClair and Champaigne, Civil War
> › LeClair and Champaigne, 20th Maine Infantry
> › Civil War scouts Maine
> › Night Hawks (which brought up the William Coburn book)
> › Clayton Lussier, Reverend Lussier, Pastor Lussier

She checked out sun-related diseases and disorders, finding both popular articles and medical sites like WebMD and Mayo Clinic. *Porphyria,* she learned, was sometimes known as "the vampire disease." It was a rare incurable condition linked to sun sensitivity, affecting the nervous system and skin. Even very brief sun exposure produced burning blisters and swelling of the skin, along with severe cramping, paralysis, and sometimes psychosis.

Is that what Luna's dealing with? How awful.

She searched *hunchbacks* and *humpbacks*, which returned popular pieces, medical articles, books like Victor Hugo's *The Hunchback of Notre Dame*, and material on whales. There were images of actors who played hunchbacks, including Marty Feldman in Mel Brooks' *Young Frankenstein.* The condition was called *kyphosis*, an extreme curvature of the upper spine. For some it was physically painful, for others it wasn't at all. All hunchbacks seemed to suffer the emotional effects of social stigmatization and societal rejection.

A double whammy. A hunchback with vampire disease. Talk about rejection. Whispers. Taunts. I'd wear the habit and veil, too. I might consider suicide.

She recalled the vivid section of Chamberlain's journal that described 20th Maine covering the Union Army's Fredericksburg retreat. It was bitter cold, the 20th was pinned down all night, and Chamberlain had drawn corpses around him, to which LeClair and Champaigne added fresher, warmer ones. The scouts had stayed close and watched over him. *How did* they *keep warm?* Chamberlain glimpsed them by the light of a burning treetop and said they reminded him of Notre Dame Cathedral's rainspouts.

She searched for *Notre Dame, rainspouts* and saw sculpted and carved figures, some fanciful, some frightening, called *grotesques.* The grotesques were adapted to conceal drainpipes and rain gutters that shunted rainwater away from the cathedral. Other structures employed them, too.

The French word for the *grotesque* rainspouts was *gargouilles, gargoyles* in English. From their lofty vantage points the grinning, sardonic sentries squatted on their haunches, their nearly neckless heads set on muscular hunched shoulders, channeling rainwater away from the stone buildings while—according to legend—they also stood watch over the city.

One legend had it that *les gargouilles* came alive at night and patrolled the skies, returning to their perches before the sun rose, surviving the withering sun by cocooning themselves in a thin protective shell of stone.

Hunchbacks that can't stand sunlight. Moon children. Gargoyles.

CHAPTER 16

Aaron had said he was going home to catch some sleep before his shift. He didn't. He had an idea and drove to the station to use his work computer and phone.

Three break-ins, probably the same person. The burglar—presumably the Father Joseph who was shadowing Luna—had hit Toil & Trouble at night and taken the first edition of *Night Hawks*. Five days later he broke into Annie's before dawn, seeking one or more of the special-order books. When he came up empty, he visited the Keegan house and forced the deck door in broad daylight, hoping to find the books there. He already had *Night Hawks*, which meant he still needed the other two titles. Apparently, he wasn't a local because he didn't have a library card. Nor did he seem aware of e-books. Or maybe he didn't know how to order them or didn't have a device to read them on.

Which means he thinks he has to check local outlets for the books.

Aaron found a list of York County bookstores. He excluded Toil & Trouble and Annie's, then called the closest ones first.

Douglas Harding Books was a 14-room barnlike structure with an inventory of over 100,000 books, a place Aaron knew well. He asked Harding about the two titles. He didn't have them in stock, but said he could get them fast.

"I don't need them," Aaron said. "I'm wondering if anybody else has called for them."

"You're the first, Aaron. Is this connected to Geoff Swett's break-in?"

"Not sure. Maybe. Would you let me know if anybody calls or comes looking for either title?"

Next Aaron called Mainely Murders, five miles north in Kennebunk. It was a bookstore in a two-car garage, owned by two retired women living the dream. Tucked a block off Main Street, Mainely Murders, as its name implied, specialized in mystery, suspense, thriller, horror, and police procedurals. Aaron knew his chances of the ladies carrying Laymon's *Dirt* book were slim to none, even slimmer for Call's *York County Cemeteries*. But Father Joseph might not know that.

He identified himself and said, "Got my police hat on this time, not my reader hat. Just called to see if, on the outside chance, someone called about these two titles." He told the bookseller the names of the books.

"Some days you get lucky, Aaron," she said. "A man phoned right after we opened this morning."

"Seriously?"

"Yep. French accent. When I said we didn't carry anything like that, he asked if I could suggest a bookstore that might stock both."

"And?"

"I told him to try something other than a bookstore, try a gift shop that also handles historical books. You know how it is when you go to a place like the Mystic Seaport Museum down in Connecticut? Their store has books for the genealogy customer and inexpensive souvenir books for the kids on class trips."

"So you suggested Mystic Seaport?"

She chuckled. "Funny. No, I did not. I suggested a historical society or museum with a gift shop. First one I thought of was Old York Historical Society, so I mentioned that. I told him I had no idea if they stocked both books, but it would only cost him a phone call."

He thanked her, clicked off, and called the Old York Museum. A volunteer answered and transferred him to a man in the gift shop. Aaron identified himself as a Wells P.D. officer and explained the situation.

"Matter of fact, a fellow called right after we opened. Since we were the ones who published the York County Cemeteries book, we have plenty: three or four on display and a few more cases in the back room. That other book—well, tourist kids can't resist the title: *The Dirt on Maine's Burial Grounds*—we'll run through five or six cases a season. We always have a couple dozen."

"Did he ask you to hold one of each?"

"Nope. Why would he, with that many on hand? He can get them anytime he comes in. He said no rush, he'd be in tomorrow or Friday."

"Tomorrow or Friday—that's what he said?"

"Word for word."

Aaron thought for a few seconds. "Was that the last thing he said?"

"Nope. He asked what time we were closing."

Why would he ask that if he said he'd stop by in a day or two?

"Did he change his mind, say he'd try to get in before you closed?"

"Nope. He said *merci* and hung up."

"*Merci?*"

"Yep. French for thank-you. Probably a French-Canadian staying up at Old Orchard Beach. You know how we joke about Old Orchard: the Riviera of the Quebecois."

Aaron thanked the man and hung up. He had a hunch, but he couldn't take a Lone Ranger approach, so he phoned Elly Stedman, who had processed all three crime scenes. Stedman, even more than Aaron, had the most investment in the three open cases. And Elly had way more clout with the York P.D. than Aaron had.

They were on the phone for 10 minutes. Aaron talked and Stedman listened, asking a few questions for clarification. Then Elly was all in.

"Mousetrap," the detective said. "I like it. Let me make some calls, Aaron. Good work."

CHAPTER 17

The house phone in the kitchen rang shortly after the sun went down.

"Got it," Keegan yelled, and picked it up. "Hello?"

"Is this Keegan?"

She recognized the voice. "Luna? Are you alright? I've been leaving you messages for days. Where are you?"

"I was not able to call you back."

"You went on the run, didn't you, because Father Joseph is following you?"

"He is not a priest and his name is not Joseph. His name is Faucon."

Luna accented the second syllable, making it sound like *faw-cone*. She spelled it for Keegan. "In English it is falcon."

"And this Faucon is after you?"

"No, not me."

"Then he's after the books?"

"Yes, for what they may tell him."

"So you and Faucon are after the same thing?"

"Not exactly, but for practical purposes, yes."

"He's the one who stole that rare copy of *Night Hawks* from Toil and Trouble and broke into our bookstore and our house, right?"

"*Oui.*"

There was silence on the line.

"Luna? If I'm going to help you in this, I need an explanation. Did this start with my mother in college? And by the way, the registrar at Orono says you were never a student there."

Still silence. Then Luna started talking.

"Your mother and I were in a course together. She was enrolled, I was not. I was just sitting in, not even auditing. The professor never challenged us, probably because of the way I was dressed."

"And why were you there?"

"I went to the university because I needed to do some—*qu'est-ce que c'est*, um, what is it called—some genealogical research. But being neither a student nor an auditor, I lacked access to the resources Zelda had—such as a library card. She agreed to help me. Remember, this was in the days before search engines like Google. Somehow, working the old-fashioned way, your mother discovered a book title, *General Joshua Chamberlain's Night Hawks*. The subtitle included a name I knew."

"LeClair or Champaigne?" Keegan asked.

Luna didn't sound surprised. "Both, actually. But my interest was more in LeClair."

"Because he's your ancestor."

"No. His connection was to my sister."

"Is your sister back home?"

"No. *Elle est morte.*"

Keegan didn't need much high school French to translate that. "Your sister is dead?"

"*Oui.*"

"I'm sorry," Keegan said automatically.

"*Merci.* It is a long time now." Luna went on. "Unfortunately, this *Night Hawks* book Zelda told me about was rare—only 25 copies—and she could not locate one back then. She told me to keep looking in case one ever became available."

"And shortly after she said that, she died—having me."

"*Oui.* But several years ago, when your Internet search engines became more sophisticated, I set up something called a Google alert using the title, author, and key words. About ten days ago I got a— *qu'est-ce que c'est?*"

"A hit. Your alert got a hit. Let me guess. The hit was Geoff Swett's Toil & Trouble online book auction. He somehow got his hands on one of the 25 copies, probably from somebody's estate."

"*Oui.* I traveled to Wells, hoping to see Mr. Swett and examine the book. I did not need to buy it. I only needed to read it, to see what it could tell me."

"But Faucon beat you to it. He broke into Swett's office and stole the rare copy before you could get to it."

"*Oui.*"

"But how did Faucon know about it? Did he have a Google alert set up, too?"

"That would have been unlikely. Apparently, I made the mistake of telling someone I trusted back home that I had finally located the book. That friend must have mentioned it to Faucon."

"Which allowed him to follow you here and beat you to the punch."

"*Oui.* But there was a lucky accident. When I arrived, my plan changed. Before I could call Mr. Swett and ask to meet with him, I checked to see how the bidding for *Night Hawks* was going. Because it was already online, I used a simple Google search. Not only did Swett's auction come up, but so did a link to the newly published reprint. So I abandoned my plan to see Mr. Swett and I called Annie's Book Stop."

"And talked to me, asking about the reprint?"

"*Oui.*"

"But you also asked me about two other titles. I said we could order all three. Why the other two?"

"They sounded like they might be helpful. I had not mentioned them to my friend back home, the one I suspect told Faucon about *Night Hawks*."

"And when you called us, you had no idea it was Zelda's sister Maryann who owned the bookstore?"

"None. Pure coincidence. Even on the phone when you said your name was Keegan, it didn't occur to me that it was your last name. I was quite surprised when you walked out on Friday morning. I thought I was seeing my friend Zelda again."

"So, if Faucon already had a copy of *Night Hawks* that he stole from Toil & Trouble, and he didn't know about the other two paperbacks, why did he break into our bookstore?"

"I think he was watching me and followed me to Annie's. When I left with no books, he called and spoke with your friend AJ, pretending to be Father Joseph."

"Which is when AJ told him you had ordered a reprint of *Night Hawks* along with two other books. He got her to supply the titles."

"*Exactement*," Luna said. "They may be of little value, but Faucon does not know that. He assumes they are important, which is why he decided to steal them as soon as they arrived."

"So he must have listened to my message on your machine Monday afternoon," Keegan said, "when I said your first two books were in. The *Night Hawks* reprint wouldn't arrive until later, but he didn't care because he already had the original. If he didn't need your reprint, he could break in before dawn Tuesday. What he didn't know was that I had taken them home in my backpack. When he didn't find them at Annie's, he took a chance, broke into our house, and ransacked my room. But by then they were back at the store."

A short silence from Luna, then, "And where are they now?"

"They're here with me at home." Another silence. "Luna, do you think he'll try again? Here? Tonight?"

"I doubt Faucon would risk contact. For all he knows, your friend AJ has them, or that tall policeman who must be her brother. Faucon will find another way to obtain copies."

"So Mom and I are safe here tonight?"

"I believe so."

Another silence. Keegan broke it. "You still need the books, don't you?"

"*Oui*. Faucon has *Night Hawks*. I do not."

Keegan said almost apologetically, "We open at 10 o'clock tomorrow. I can go in early and meet you."

Again the silence, then Luna said firmly, "I need them, Keegan. Please. Tonight."

"But how?"

"You have that large back porch."

"You mean our deck," Keegan corrected. "How did you know?"

Luna ignored the question. "Does it have a motion light?"

"No. It has a light, but the switch is inside."

"Good. And do you have something you can put the books in?"

"Yes. How about a cloth book bag?"

"*C'est parfait.* Can we meet in half an hour on the deck? Leave that light off."

"I thought your problem was sunlight," Keegan said. "Will you need your habit for a spotlight?"

"I will come without my robe. I do not want you to see me."

Hesitation, this time on Keegan's end of the line. Then, "Okay, half an hour. But I have a condition. You showed yourself to Zelda, didn't you?"

"*Oui.*"

"Then we'll meet on the deck in the dark and I'll hand you the books. But I'll have my flashlight. If we're going to be friends, I want to see you."

Section IV

Luna Unveiled

CHAPTER 18

When local lawyer Bill Keegan died unexpectedly of a heart attack in 1996, he left everything to his daughters, Maryann and Zelda Keegan. The estate included savings and investments, life insurance, a college fund, and the house in the woods.

As Maryann and Zelda worked through their grief, they made one major decision and one minor decision together.

The first was to buy Annie's Book Stop, with Maryann the working partner and Zelda the silent partner. Maryann had recently gotten her master's in library science and was starting her second year as a librarian outside Boston. Zelda was a high school senior planning to attend the University of Maine at Orono, three hours north of Wells. It was clear they could either rent out their newly inherited Wells house, leave it empty, or occupy it themselves. Buying the bookstore not only fulfilled Maryann's childhood dream but allowed her to move back into the house while drawing a basic salary from the store. Zelda would have the childhood home to return to on vacations, semester breaks, and summers.

The minor decision was to add a deck onto the back of the house, something they had always wanted but their father had balked at.

The deck stretched half the length of the house and, after a dozen tall pines and oaks were taken down, extended fifteen feet out. Because the land behind the house sloped downward at a fairly steep angle, the outer support beams sat atop tall six-by-six timbers that rested on dug-in concrete piers. A waist-high safety fence enclosed the deck's three sides, and a gate accessed a long stairway to the ground. The sole change to the house was a new door between the kitchen and the deck, the same door that Faucon had used for the previous day's forced entry.

Keegan stood inside the door with the kitchen lights out. In her left hand she held a tan cloth UMO bookstore bag containing Luna's three books. In her right was a penlight the size of a fat Magic Marker. She stared out the glass pane above the newly replaced one, ready to thumb the flashlight switch. She kept her eyes on the gate at the top of the stairs, waiting for Luna to waddle up the long stairway.

Nothing moved.

She pressed the little button to light her watch.

Two minutes late. Luna, where are you? Did Faucon grab you?

The moon was out, its light filtering through the tree canopy overhead. She could make out the square clear-top table at the center of the deck, four chairs around it, and the center-post umbrella folded above it. Beyond it was the picnic table she used when her friends came over. All the familiar shapes appeared ghostly in the moonlight.

She watched, willing Luna to appear. Although she had said she wouldn't be in her black robe and veil, Keegan found herself expecting Luna to appear the same way she had when she visited the bookstore. But no dark figure materialized by the gate at the top of the stairs.

Keegan pressed her watch button again. Five minutes overdue. *Trust the force.* She placed her hand on the doorknob and whispered the same mantra aloud, "Trust the force." She turned the knob, pulled the door in, and pushed the screen door open. She stepped out, quietly pressing the screen door shut behind her, and glanced around the entire deck. Nothing. Nobody.

She walked to the gate, switched on the penlight, and aimed it down the steps. No sign of life. She tried shining it at the sloping ground below, but the distance was too great, and the light was weak and diffused.

"Keegan." Somewhere behind her.

She froze, the sound of her name startling her. She turned slowly to face the house and aimed the light at the back door, expecting to see Maryann framed in it. But Maryann was upstairs in bed, and the voice hadn't been hers. She knew now—she was certain—it had been Luna. Or had she imagined it?

Again. "Keegan."

It wasn't imaginary. She was facing the right direction. The voice had come from somewhere near the back wall of the house. Her eyes strained to make out a figure, but none was there. The penlight was pointing in front of her feet now. She raised it and flashed it across the entire shake-shingled back wall. Nobody.

"Turn out the light, please." Somewhere above the eaves.

Keegan snapped off the penlight and scanned the roofline. Nothing except the huge stone chimney that vented the living room fireplace.

"Luna," she called in a loud whisper. "Where are you?"

"Behind the chimney," came the response. "Go to the gate again and look away. I'll come down."

"Do you have a ladder?"

"Just do as I ask."

Keegan went to the gate and turned toward the back woods. She was about to say something, but before she could open her mouth she heard a *whoosh* sound above and behind her. A second *whoosh* brought a rush of air on her back. She felt the slight vibration of the deck under her feet, accompanied by a clicking sound on the planking, then a rustling like a crinoline petticoat.

"Not yet." Right behind her now.

Keegan waited. "Now?"

"*Un moment.*"

"Oh, come on, Luna," she said impatiently. "This is like waiting for AJ to come out of the dressing room at Macy's. What're you doing—combing your hair or putting on lipstick?"

"I don't have to worry about either of those. I have no hair and very thin lips."

That stopped Keegan's joking fast. "Seriously?"

"*Oui.* I want to prepare you. I don't look like you or Maryann or AJ."

Keegan said nothing.

"You do not have to look, Keegan. I can simply take the book bag from your hand and leave. It would be much easier."

Keegan closed her eyes and, without turning, said, "Let me guess, Luna.

No hair, almost no lips. You can't handle sunlight. Your English is good but your first language is French. You got down from our roof without a ladder, which means you either glide or fly. How am I doing?"

"*Tres bon*. You are as funny and as perceptive as your mother Zelda was."

"Okay then, please excuse me if I mispronounce the word, Luna—my French is only second year—but are you actually a *gargouille*?"

A pause, then, "*Oui, mademoiselle. Je suis une gargouille.* I am indeed."

"Then may I turn around?"

"If you dare. Humans seldom find us beautiful."

"That's because we judge from a human perspective. May I turn around now?"

"As I said, if you dare."

"I dare," Keegan said, and turned slowly, eyes cast slightly downward.

The first thing she saw was *la gargouille's* clawed feet. *Toes and talons. That was the click I heard when she landed on the deck.*

Luna squatted on her haunches—at most four feet tall in her folded-down position—muscular, leathery arms resting on her knees as if she were intentionally mocking one of the Notre Dame grotesques that Keegan had seen online. But those were masonry depictions of the creatures of legend. This creature before her—this creature she had met and spoken with, who knew and had been friends with her birth mother—was not inanimate stone. She was flesh and blood, muscle and bone.

Keegan could see that what had appeared to be a hunched back under the loose black robe was not a deformity at all. The leaning-forward crouch contributed to such a misconception, because her folded wings, when tucked together, rose slightly above her shoulders like an angel's.

At first glance *la gargouille* appeared to be wearing a helmet, but when Keegan leaned in closer she saw that her head was ringed and capped with tough skin similar to the brownish, leathery hide on her legs and arms, except the head skin was thicker.

"You have no horns," Keegan gasped.

"Some *gargouilles* do," Luna said calmly. "My clan does not."

And you have no breasts, Keegan thought.

Luna sat, unmoving, eyes and mouth closed, while Keegan looked her over. Her face was like nothing Keegan had ever seen before. *In its own way, it's exquisite. She's lovely. I'll bet the males in your race find you stunning.*

"May I?" Keegan asked tentatively, and when Luna nodded slightly, she placed her open right palm on *la gargouille's* left cheek and caressed the skin. It was softer than she had thought it would be, like an iguana's. Her nose, as Keegan had guessed when she saw the black veil rest on it in the bookstore, was broad and flat like an ape's. Two canine teeth—longer than Keegan's canine's but too short to be called fangs—protruded slightly between an extremely thin pair of lips.

"I wouldn't rule out a little lipstick," Keegan said, running her finger across Luna's lower lip, grazing the two canines.

Luna smiled slightly—was it at the touch or the comment—and her mouth opened a little wider to reveal upper and lower rows of teeth surprisingly like a human's.

"Open wide," Keegan said, and when Luna started to, she said, "Kidding, Luna. My grandmother was a dentist. That's what dentists say."

"Funny," Luna said, deadpan. "Are you finished with your examination?"

"For now," Keegan answered, and stepped back.

Luna came up out of her resting crouch into a walking posture that put her at almost five feet. When she opened her eyes, they were a stunning emerald green, staring directly into Keegan's. They held each other's gaze for a full twenty seconds.

"Thank you for trusting me," Keegan said, and handed Luna the book bag.

La gargouille took it and stepped back. "There is still much to talk about. Allow me to read these and I will call you."

Keegan watched Luna's wings unfold. "You still owe me the balance on the order," she said, and flashed a grin.

"I believe the English word," Luna said, "is *smart-ass*—like your mother." Then she added, "I left my money in the habit."

Keegan chuckled.

Luna flexed her knees, took an eight-foot run across the deck, then used her powerful legs to launch herself upward, flapping her wings like an eagle, catching the air under them.

Whoosh, whoosh, whoosh.

Keegan watched open-mouthed as *la gargouille* rose to the roof and continued beyond the chimney, skyward, the light of the moon glinting off the white tips of her black wings.

CHAPTER 19

About the time Luna was clearing the Keegans' chimney, Detective Sergeant Elly Stedman was pressing the button on his watch to illuminate its dial. It was 10:55. He flexed his shoulders without standing, trying to shake out some of the stiffness. He'd been sitting in a corner of the York Museum gift shop since it closed, and for six hours had stayed relatively motionless. His numb butt wasn't happy with the straight-backed wooden chair the gift shop manager had let him borrow. To be fair, though, the manager had offered a swivel-and-tilt office chair, but it squeaked and might give away his position. So, because he agreed with Aaron that the bookstore burglar would likely hit the York Museum next, Elly had spent four hours on the chair in the fading daylight, and now two hours in the dark. But if Aaron was right, their bookstore burglar would show up soon, and he'd make the collar.

Elly Stedman hadn't done a stakeout in years. The last one had been on a drug bust near the Rachel Carson Preserve in Wells when he'd been in his own vehicle in a comfortable bucket seat. He remembered that seat's contour now, the feel of the leather and the back support and the head rest, and wished he was in it instead of the hard chair.

Stakeouts were boring. Hours of waiting and no guarantee of a takedown. But if something did happen, you got to move, plus you got a rush of adrenalin that jazzed you afterward. And there was the satisfaction of the arrest.

Stedman had been a high school football star 25-years earlier. He'd been 6'2" and rock solid, a fullback who set rushing records for his high school and for the league. In the service he had boxed as a middleweight, ending up with a respectable record. Now, even though he weighed in at 50 pounds over his fighting weight, he wasn't obese. He could still handle himself.

The gift shop's lights could be snapped on from three different wall switches around the room. One was next to his right shoulder. His silenced cellphone sat on the lamp table beside him. His detective badge was clipped to the breast pocket of his shirt. His service piece was holstered on his hip. Handcuffs hung off his belt along with a telescoping baton—he still called it a nightstick. Standing up on the floor was his flashlight. He had on a communications pack with a shoulder-mike so he could call in the York patrol cops helping him on up the stakeout. He was as ready as he'd ever be, the mousetrap baited and set. All he needed now was the mouse. *Let it be sooner rather than later*, his sore butt cheeks groaned.

The front door was solid wood, with no glass panes like at Annie's Book stop and Maryann Keegan's home. The back door was also solid and had no windows on either side of it. The third door in the building was up at the second level, a solid fire door with a panic bar on the inside. It opened off the hallway opposite the storage rooms where the gift shop kept its backup stock. To either side of the fire door were six-over-six windows like those at Toil & Trouble, but these weren't close enough to the fire door that a burglar could smash a pane and reach in to press the panic bar and gain access.

With none of the three doors easily accessible, whoever showed up—*if* he showed up—would have to crawl through a window, either down or up. Stedman's guessed it'd be down. The perp would sneak up to a lower window at the building's rear away from York Street, the main drag, and let the shadows hide him. He'd climb into the gift shop, use a pen to locate the two books on one of the shelves or on the spinner rack, and would then leave by either the back door or the entry window.

Stedman guessed wrong.

The sound of glass breaking came at 11:10. Upstairs. At Stedman's request, the manager had left the door at the top of the stairs open. Elly fought the adrenaline surge and the jumpy tummy, remaining as still as he could, listening, eyes locked on the staircase.

The initial smash—probably created by a protected elbow or a cloth-wrapped fist striking the pane—was followed by the sound of more glass: the knocking out or pulling out of the remaining shards and wood strips. Stedman was sure the burglar was outside the window, dropping or placing the pieces on the floor just inside it, as had been done at Toil & Trouble. He remembered the bear claw-like scratches he had photographed on Geoff Swett's outer sill.

Is there a ladder this time?

He heard someone climb through, the sound of feet—weight—on the floor upstairs. Then creeping across the creaky wide-pine floor. He drew his service piece with his right hand and switched it to his left. He was comfortable with it in either hand. He gripped the nightstick in his right and waited. Once the intruder came down the stairs, he could hit the lights and temporarily blind the perp while yelling the old standby, "Police. Freeze." And he'd have his man. Or boy. Or woman. Whoever.

But nobody came down the stairs. He heard a clicking on the floor, followed by the distinct sound of a door latch and the rub of a tight door against its frame as it was pushed open.

He's checking the storeroom, making sure nobody's in there.

A sliver of light glinted off the polished staircase bannister. Not a flashlight beam but light seeping down from the open storeroom. The intruder had switched on the light.

He's not coming down here, he's checking the inventory. Aaron said the manager had told him there was plenty of backup for both titles. Whoever answered the phone probably told the bad guy that, too.

The intruder was looking for what he needed upstairs. He'd leave the way he broke in—through the broken window or by the fire door—without ever coming down.

Stedman knew that if he wanted the collar, he had no choice but to cross his own minefield—to cross the squeaky floor and run up the squeaky stairs. He'd have to move fast, which meant snapping on the light switch, getting his stiff body off the chair, and sprinting across and up in hope of surprising the burglar and trapping him in the storeroom. Elly clipped the nightstick onto his belt again, replacing it with the heavy flashlight, a suitable substitute in close quarters.

Upstairs he heard boxes being moved around. Soon the intruder would find the right cases of books and open them. Stedman took a couple of deep breaths, counted silently to three, and tried to ease himself to his feet without scraping the chair legs on the floor. He got his boxer's balance then touched the shoulder mike and whispered, "He's upstairs. Need backup." He flicked the light switch and broke for the staircase, taking the stairs two at a time, yelling near the top, "Police. Freeze."

He made it to the top landing and a step beyond at the same moment the intruder exited the closest stockroom. In his gridiron days Elly Stedman had been cross-body blocked by players who had hit him like a truckload of granite. In hockey he'd been cross-checked so hard he was once carried away unconscious on a stretcher. In boxing he'd been knocked out six times, the last time by a first-round haymaker he never saw coming, the one that concussed him and ended his career.

None of those matched the sheer impact of the freight train that plowed through him in the hallway.

CHAPTER 20

Keegan couldn't fall asleep. Her mind was racing. She had not only seen but *touched*—*examined*, really—someone who could fly. Until now the only flying humans she knew were literary creations: Greek mythology's wax-winged tower escapees, Daedelaus and Icarus; James M. Barrie's Peter Pan; and James Patterson's flock of flying lab experiments—98% human and 2% bird: Max, Fang, Iggy, Nudge, the Gasman, and Angel.

Is that what Luna is—a mix of human and bird? She walks like I do and she stands upright like I do. She speaks like me—even better, because she's bilingual: French and English. But unlike me or anybody I know, she has wings—and her wings aren't vestigial like my tailbone and appendix. Hers actually work, and from what I saw they work very well. But her skin . . . I saw and felt her skin, and it speaks to me of reptiles. Or amphibians. Alligator, iguana, frog, snake.

But she's not a reptile or an amphibian. She and my birth mother were friends. And now she and I are friends.

Keegan couldn't wait for their next meeting. She had a million questions. But tonight they'd barely had time for a hello and here-are-your-books. In her mind she could hear Ricky Ricardo's Cuban accent on *I Love Lucy Show* saying, "Luna, you got some splainin' to do."

❧ ❧ ❧

Aaron was on patrol near the Maine Diner when he heard that the York P.D. had an Officer Down call. He had a bad feeling and called Wells dispatch.

"It was Stedman," Marcy Stonestreet told him. "He's not dead, but somebody really rang his bell. York P.D. was standing by the whole time. They were only a minute away when he radioed that somebody was inside the museum."

"So he's okay?"

"First responders found him unconscious in the upstairs hallway and transported him to York Hospital."

"Anything else you can tell me?"

"The chief's on her way down there. She'll let me know when she gets to the hospital."

Silence on the line.

"Aaron, you okay?" Marcy asked.

He cleared his throat and swallowed hard. "I'm the one who got Stedman into this."

"Elly got himself into it. He knew there were risks and he made his choice. It was his plan, wasn't it?"

Aaron didn't answer.

"Look, Aaron, Elly Stedman's one tough old bird. He's been knocked out before. He'll get back up."

After a long silence, "If you hear anything new, let me know, okay?"

"I will, Aaron. Promise. Everybody's calling and asking. Right now, all you can do is finish your shift."

CHAPTER 21

When Aaron's shift ended at 6 a.m., the first thing he did was call home.

"Hi, Mom. Just off shift. Can't make it home for breakfast."

"Everything okay?" she asked.

"Everything's fine, Mom. I'm going to grab a McMuffin on the way to York Hospital. I have to visit a friend there."

"York Hospital?" The hint of alarm was there. "Or the Wells clinic?" York Hospital's Wells branch was on Route 9 in Wells near the schools.

"No, the main hospital in York. One of our guys got the wind knocked out of him during a burglary last night."

"It's not a shooting or a stabbing then. You said he got the wind knocked out of him."

"Correct."

"Who is it?"

He knew she'd ask. She knew everybody on the force.

"Stedman. He got knocked down, that's all."

"Elly?" Disbelief in her voice. She knew the guy was built like a tank and had a head as hard as a gravestone. "Knocked down? Or hit over the head?"

"I don't know, Mom. Could have hit his head in the fall. All I know is, he was knocked out cold."

"You said it was last night? How's he doing now?"

"He came to a few hours ago. Word is, he's got a concussion and some broken ribs."

"Thank God."

"And a broken collarbone," Aaron added.

"What?"

"And a dislocated shoulder."

"Land sakes, it sounds like he fell out of an airplane."

"He'll be fine, Mom. He's just going to need time to heal."

"You tell him . . ."

"I know. You're thinking about him and will pray for him. Look, Mom, I'm turning into McDonald's—"

"Wait. Is it alright to tell AJ? I don't want to break some kind of confidentiality."

"I didn't share any specifics on the case. Just tell her Elly got hurt on a stakeout."

"And you know she's going to call Keegan first thing."

"And Keegan will tell her mother. I know, Mom. By the time Maryann and Keegan get to work, half the town will have heard it through the grapevine anyway." He said goodbye and clicked off.

Need to stop and see Keegan later. Stedman could have gotten killed. This is bigger than a couple of stolen books.

***

Four police cars were already in the lot when Aaron turned into York Hospital: a State Police cruiser and vehicles from the York, Wells, and Kittery police departments. The Wells car he recognized as Chief Sandra Warren's. He parked his Cherokee away from the cop cars, near a well-worn Ford F-250 pickup. A magnetic sign on the driver's door read: Cliff Bragdon, Firewood Cut, Split, Delivered, with a phone number. He walked to the hospital entrance and through the electric-eye door. Cliff was sitting on a couch in the reception area by an artificial fern.

"Cliff," Aaron said with a nod. "Aren't you off duty?"

"Yuh," he replied glumly.

"What's the deal—nobody needs campfire wood today? I see your truck's out there."

Cliff ignored the question. "Don't tap dance around it, Aaron. Elephant in the room and all that. You're off duty, too. We're here for Elly."

Aaron sat beside his friend on the couch. He leaned forward, forearms on thighs.

"Okay. How's Elly doing? Other than the broken bones, I mean. I heard he's conscious? Is he remembering things?"

Cliff breathed like a man forcing himself to count to ten. "It was the guy in the V mask, wasn't it?" His voice was thick with anger. "That *Vendetta* guy from Annie's security video."

"Probably. Pretty sure it's the same guy who hit Geoff Swett's and the Keegan house, too. Difference with this break-in was, we figured out the pattern and we had Stedman waiting for him."

"So what went wrong?" Cliff asked.

"We expected him to hit the downstairs gift shop, grab what he wanted from the display books. But he came in on the second floor where the inventory is. Stedman went up to get him."

They sat together quietly for a minute.

Aaron asked, "You been up to see him?"

"An hour ago. A quick look. He was asleep, which is better than unconscious."

"Has he said anything about who hit him?"

"Doesn't sound like it," Cliff replied.

"Maybe in time," Aaron said, and changed the subject. "I saw Sandy Warren's car outside, and three others. She upstairs with Stedman now?"

"Chief came over last night as soon as it went down. I think she went home for a few hours and caught some sleep, then came back about the same time I got here. The York chief's been in and out, too, on about the same schedule as Chief Warren. The Kittery chief got here a half hour ago. The stakeout was joint Wells and York, not Kittery, but since they're right next door I guess their chief wants to keep abreast of it and show his support."

"And the Trooper car?" Aaron asked.

"Dawson. CID. He and Stedman were pretty good friends, worked a lot of cases together over the years. You know him: older guy close to retirement, about 6'5", lanky. A runner, I think."

"So the four of them are putting their heads together?"

"It would seem that way," Cliff answered. "When I went upstairs a few minutes ago, the nurse was giving them the boot from the ICU waiting room. She moved them to a small conference room on the same floor."

"Okay. So Stedman's banged up but stable and the brain trust is up there strategizing. If the situation's under control, why are you still here?"

"You haven't asked the obvious question." Cliff looked sideways at his friend.

"Which is?"

Cliff's eyes narrowed. The cat-and-canary look. "When the Grim Reaper broke in last night, did he get the books?"

Aaron's mouth made a little O. "He did, didn't he?"

"Apparently. Not guaranteed, but almost. Chief Warren knew the two books he was after. When Elly went down last night, she was here in a heartbeat. Before the EMTs got Stedman to the hospital, the Chief had the gift store manager taking inventory."

"So the guy has all three books now," Aaron said.

"Which is why I was waiting here for you. I haven't been in the loop. There's more to this than Stedman knows and more than the Chief and the others know." Cliff stared right at Aaron. "But you have an idea, don't you? You're the one putting the pieces together. Maybe it's time you told me what the hell's going on."

Aaron didn't answer right away. Then he stood up and said, "Let me run up to ICU and look in on Elly. Maybe he'll wake up and have something to say, maybe not. On my way back down, I'll poke my head in and see if Chief Warren or the others have anything new."

"See if *they* have anything new to share with *you?*" Cliff said mockingly and shook his head. "You have it backward, old buddy. *We* share with *them*. You and I, we're just patrol cops, we're not detectives."

"Our lead detective is out of action at the moment," Aaron countered. "You and I may not have his title, but somebody's got to work this case."

Cliff looked like he was considering the challenge. He got up and faced Aaron eye to eye.

"Look, someday you'll make detective, Aaron. You want it, and you think like a detective. It's in you. Me, I'll never be a detective. I can read all the police procedural books and mysteries in the world—and I love them—but that stuff's not in my makeup, it's not me. I'm a patrol cop, and I like that. I think I'll like it until retirement, if I get that far." He held out his left hand. "Don't forget, I'm the doofus who accidentally cut off his own pinkie with a chainsaw."

"Your hand still works fine," Aaron replied. "Having nine fingers won't disqualify you from making detective, if you want it."

Cliff licked his lips, tried to remember where he was going with the thought, and swallowed. "Look, Aaron, if you want to be play detective, fine, but you're going to have to include the rest of us. You're not the only one who picks up clues, you know. We peons have something to contribute. Know what I mean? I think you and Stedman—now you *without* Stedman—have a piece of some big puzzle that we can't see yet. But if you let us in on it, maybe, just maybe we can help."

Aaron considered what his friend had just said. "Cliff, I really don't know anything at this point except to say that I think it's a single perpetrator who really, really wants these three books."

"I know that, Aaron. That's kind of obvious, I'd say. What I want to know is, what's in the books that's so important?"

"Good question."

"Have you read them?"

"Yes."

Cliff didn't respond.

Aaron tried to figure out what was going on. Then he had it. "You've read one or two of them, too, haven't you?"

Cliff gave a sly smile. "Two. I downloaded the e-books."

"I thought you had no desire to be a detective."

Cliff shrugged. "Maybe there's a little detective in all cops." He added, "I'm driving up to Augusta this morning. The Maine Civil War Press is holding a copy of *Chamberlain's Night Hawks* for me. I didn't want to order through a bookstore and have to wait days."

Aaron smiled and shook his head. "After you read it, we can compare notes."

"Deal," Cliff said, and headed for the electric-eye doors.

""Cliff, wait."

"What?"

"Would you do me a favor? Swett's copy is gone, and the copy I was reading belongs to Keegan's customer. There's no e-book version of *Night Hawks* yet."

"I know. I checked," Cliff said. "Are you asking me to pick up an extra *Night Hawks* for you in Augusta?"

"A couple, if you don't mind."

Cliff seemed to consider it. "Okay," he said with a shake of his head. "I suppose I could. This is why you detectives-in-training need us patrol grunts."

"Thanks, Cliff. I'll let you know if anything changes here."

Cliff raised the four-fingered left hand and gave the OK sign, which came out looking like the *Playboy* logo.

CHAPTER 22

Aaron went upstairs to check on Stedman. The upper half of the hospital bed was tilted up at a 30 degree angle to allow him to sit up without stressing the broken ribs too much. A soft pillow was tucked behind his neck. His right arm was in a shoulder sling. The plastic tubing of a nasal cannula rested under his nose and pumped oxygen into his nostrils.

A nurse appeared at the entrance to the cubicle and walked past Aaron. She adjusted the neck pillow, asked Stedman something Aaron couldn't hear, and checked the sippy cup and straw on the bedside table.

"Why is he on oxygen?" Aaron asked the nurse.

"It's easier to breathe with the broken ribs. The less he has to strain, the more comfortable he'll be."

"Any idea how long he'll be in here?"

"We're waiting for a room to open up," she explained. "Maybe by noon."

"So he isn't critical?"

"No. He'll be in for a day or two. But he doesn't require round-the-clock attention, if that's what you're asking."

Stedman stirred and his eyes opened, fixing on Aaron. He groaned something.

"I think he said you can come in," the nurse said. "Keep it under five minutes." She disappeared out the door.

Aaron stepped in next to Stedman's left hand, the one not in the sling. The hand opened and Aaron gripped it.

"Heard you got run over by a bull."

"Mmm. That's what the Chief told me earlier. I don't remember."

"I'm glad you're okay," Aaron said solemnly, then added, "Sorry I wasn't there with you."

"Not sure you'd have helped. A hit like this was would've probably taken us both out."

Aaron gave Stedman's hand a little squeeze. "So what do you know? What happened?"

Stedman closed his eyes, tried to adjust his torso but grimaced at the rib pain. He gave up on changing positions.

"I was downstairs in the dark. I heard glass break upstairs, then realized the guy was in. Waited for him to come down to the gift shop." Stedman took a deep breath from the cannula, made a face of pain as he expanded the lungs, stressing the broken ribs. "I heard him go into one of the upstairs rooms and figured out he wasn't coming down, not with inventory up there. So I called for backup and charged up the stairs, hoping to trap him in the room. Next thing I know, I'm waking up here."

Aaron sat on the edge of the bed. "So he used an upstairs window?"

"Yep, just like at Swett's. Didn't climb the fire escape, because the fire door was solid and secure and there wasn't a window within reach of it. So the same question remains: if he didn't use a ladder, how'd he get up to the window to bust it in?"

Aaron put a finger to his lip and looked thoughtful. "Maybe he didn't go up. Maybe he came down—like a window washer."

"What—like some acrobat swinging on a rope in a Vegas heist movie?" Stedman scoffed, agitated, which made him cough. His ribs hurt and he winced at the pain.

Aaron waited for him to recover. "You got a better theory?"

Stedman shook his head, too pained to speak.

Aaron said, "I'm sure York CID will check for scratches outside the window, and I wouldn't be surprised if they found some like the ones we saw at Swett's. Would you mind asking them to look at the roof, too, in case a rope was tied around the chimney?"

"May as well have them check it," Stedman managed. "We didn't check it at Swett's, but we can still send somebody back to see. I never considered access from above."

"You want me to do it discreetly?"

"No. Let the Chief know you talked to me. Tell her I asked you to do it. I'm the one who failed to check it out earlier."

"Okay. Consider it done. I'll get back to you."

They sat silent for a moment. Stedman's eyes fluttered. Probably a painkiller for the ribs. He was fighting to stay awake while Aaron was there.

"Cliff stopped in. You knew that, right?" Aaron asked. "He'd been downstairs for an hour when I came in."

"No, I didn't know that. I didn't see him. I was probably still conked out."

"He was worried. So are the rest of us."

"Nice to know I'm so revered," Stedman wisecracked.

"Hey, don't downplay it. We all really do care. And this is serious. The guy could have had a knife or a gun—or could have taken your weapon and turned it on you. You could be history."

Stedman didn't answer. When Aaron glanced down at his face, he saw that the detective had drifted off to sleep again.

☞☞☞

On the way out, Aaron stopped at the small conference room where Chief Warren was meeting with the York and Kittery chiefs and Detective Dawson of the State Police CID. He said he'd spoken with Stedman, and Stedman had suggested checking out the Museum's roof and chimney as well as Toil & Trouble's.

"He said that if there's no ladder and no tracks on the ground, it's possible the perp came down a rope."

The four senior cops stared at Aaron, considering this.

The Kittery chief asked, "How would the perp get on the roof?"

Aaron shrugged. He wanted to give a smart-ass answer like *helicopter drop*, but he simply shook his head and shrugged. "I'm just the messenger, Chief. All I know is, Sergeant Stedman told me to ask you if we can check it out."

The York and Wells chiefs nodded and said okay. When Aaron didn't move, Sandy Warren asked, "Something else, Officer Stevenson?"

Aaron fidgeted. "Did the guy get the books?"

"Looks that way," she answered. "I'd like to know what's so important about a couple of paperbacks that you can walk in and buy during the day." When Aaron still didn't move, she asked, "Officer Stevenson?"

"Chief, I was the responding officer last week at Toil & Trouble. Sergeant Stedman and a K9 team worked the scene and discovered scratches outside the window on the sill. I remember Sergeant Stedman saying they reminded him of bear claw marks. Which makes me wonder now if they were left by some kind of a climbing tool the perp used to hang on with while he broke the window. Sergeant Stedman wondered if York CID would be sure to check the museum's outside sill for marks. Maybe his idea about roof access has merit."

"I'll have our CID check it out," the York chief said. When Aaron still didn't leave, he said, "Something else?"

Aaron put on his most respectful face. "Yes, sir. Since I was partially responsible for placing Sergeant Stedman in harm's way by suggesting the break-in could be here at the museum—with your permission and Chief Warren's permission—would you allow me to take a quick look at the scene?"

CHAPTER 23

When Aaron pulled in at the York Museum, an SUV with the York P.D. was waiting there. Patrolman Bruce Grey got out and greeted him. They knew each other from their jobs and from having taken a few training courses together. Like Aaron, Grey had finished his shift a couple of hours earlier. Grey had been the first officer to respond to Stedman's call for backup.

"Have we got somebody to open up for us?" Aaron asked.

"Gift shop manager just went in. Come on." Grey led the way to the front door. "Harry Barnes, one of our CIDs, processed the scene last night. He's at the office working it now. Said you can stop by the station or call if you have questions or input."

Inside the gift shop the lights were on. A small, trim 75-ish man in a bowtie and gray tweed jacket stood by the counter. He wore tortoise-shell glasses and had thick, wavy hair and a silver mustache.

"Aaron Stevenson, Dr. Jim Alley," Grey said, and the two shook hands.

"I only manage the gift shop," Alley clarified, "not the Historical Society. Second career, sort of. I'm a retired pediatrician, which is why everybody still calls me Dr. Jim. But basically, I'm just another volunteer whose wife said he needed to find something to do outside the house." He chuckled and the two cops responded in kind.

"I just want to poke around," Aaron said. "Won't keep you long."

"Happy to give you the nickel tour, if you like," Dr. Jim said, and without waiting for an answer, he pointed across the room at a chair. "That's where Sergeant Stedman set up yesterday." He made a hand gesture in a different direction and said, "Austin Call's *York County Cemeteries* book is right there on that shelf." He placed a hand on a three-tier carousel and said, "This spinner is for the popular books kids like. Here's *The Dirt on Maine's Burial Grounds*. A fun read—I can see how kids would like it—but hardly worth stealing."

"It *was* a fun read, actually," Aaron commented.

"You read it?" Dr. Jim asked.

"I did. Skimmed the York County book, too, which is a little dry. I agree they're not worth stealing. Takes a lot less effort to buy."

Dr. Jim talked as he led Aaron and Grey up the staircase. "I guess Sergeant Stedman heard noise upstairs and ran up the steps. As you can see, there's the hallway with rooms to the right, fire door and windows to the left."

"The rooms are for storage?" Aaron asked.

"Yes. Officer Grey knows more than I do about what happened last night, but it looks like the burglar came flying out of this first room at the same moment Sergeant Stedman reached the door."

"Stedman got T-boned," Grey said. "I found him slumped over here against the fire door. See the wood trim around the frame, how it's cracked? The impact must have smashed Stedman into it before he slipped down. If he'd been a few inches to the left, closer to the center of the door, his butt or hip might have hit the panic bar and opened it."

"So he was sitting up when you found him?"

"Sort of."

"Show me. Act it out."

Grey squatted down and sat on the floor. He leaned back against the fire door's frame. Then he closed his eyes, recalled it, and shifted his position so he was tilted more toward the center of the door.

"Like that? You sure?" Aaron asked.

"Positive," Grey replied.

"And the fire door wasn't open when you found him?"

"Nope."

"So if the perp had escaped out the fire door, Stedman's upper body would have spilled out onto the fire escape landing. You'd have found the door open."

"Yep," Grey said, and stood back up. "And he didn't use either of the downstairs doors, because they were still locked when we checked them."

"So how'd the guy get out?" Dr. Jim asked.

"The way he came in," Aaron said, and walked a few steps farther to the window with its raised lower sash and it broken pane. Unlike the window frame at Toil & Trouble, this one hadn't been totally knocked out.

Aaron dropped to his knees, pulled out a handkerchief and laid it across the bottom sill. He placed his hands on it, stuck his head out the window, and checked the wooden sill. There were two sets of wide scratches. He had Grey look at them, too.

"They look like the marks we found outside a second-floor window at a burglary last week in Wells," Aaron said.

"So what does it mean?" Dr. Jim wanted to know.

"Honestly, I don't know. Is there a way we can get up on the roof?"

"The roof?"

"Yeah, I want to see if somebody swung down or shinnied down to the window."

"Let me call somebody in buildings and grounds," Dr. Jim offered. "They'll have ladders over there. Anything else?"

"Yes. While we're waiting for the ladder, can you sell me two copies each of those books—one set for me and a set for Sergeant Stedman? He'll be looking for something to read in the next day or two."

"I'll take a set, too," Grey said, fishing for his wallet. "If this guy broke in to get them, I need to get a better handle, too."

☙ ☙ ☙

The roof revealed nothing. No rope left hanging from it. And no marks on the eaves above the broken window. A burglar's weight on a rope surely would have left an impression on the lowermost shingle. The chimney idea didn't pan out, either, because it didn't line up over the window that had been the point of entry. If it had, there'd have been a chance of finding rope fibers on the corner bricks' sharper edges.

Grey listened as Aaron shared his theory that the sill's deep scratches could be from a climber's tool, something that freed one of the burglar's hands to break the pane and unlock and raise the window.

"Interesting theory," Grey said. "But it doesn't explain how our guy reached the sill with no ladder."

"Stilts?" Dr. Jim ventured, half joking.

They discussed it, but like a ladder, there would have been marks.

CHAPTER 24

Keegan was getting ready for work when Aaron called.

"Stedman's in the hospital," he said. "AJ tell you?"

"Uh-huh. She said you were driving to York to check on him. He got knocked out during a break-in. Concussion, broken collarbone and ribs, busted shoulder. And the bad guy got away. AJ get it right?"

"Yep."

"Luna's books again?"

"Yep. The York Historical Society's gift shop had both cemeteries books in stock. I figured it out yesterday and brought Stedman in on it. He worked out a stakeout with York P.D. and was waiting in the gift shop when the guy broke in. Got blindsided. Guy must've been as big as a buffalo."

"But Stedman's okay, considering his injuries?"

"That's what they tell me. I talked with him a while, but he drifted off."

"How about the books? Did Father Joseph get what he wanted?"

"Looks that way."

"What else? You didn't call just to tell me about Stedman. AJ already did that."

"I called because you and I need to sit down together and think this through. Soon. I just bought copies of both books at the gift shop. I've been looking them over again. This whole thing can't be about them. They're reference books, that's all, and they may or may not connect to *The Night Hawks*. I guess your customer Luna and this Father Joseph seem to think so. Coburn's book has to be the key to unlocking this thing. We'll go through it again."

"I gave it to Luna."

"You what?"

"I gave it to Luna. Last night. She finally returned my call, and she came by the house and picked it up. It was her book, remember?"

"I remember. And it's okay. We'll have another copy later today."

"How?"

"Cliff Bragdon's on his way to Augusta. The Maine Civil War Press printed it in Portland, but their headquarters and warehouse are in Augusta, not far from the capital. They're holding a few copies for him."

"Did you send him there?" she asked.

"No. I ran into him at the hospital. He said he was driving up to get himself a copy, so I asked him to get me some extras. Should have them this afternoon."

"So how do we proceed?"

"I'm going home to sleep," Aaron replied. "You're going to work. How about if I stop at the house later?"

"Around 5 o'clock? I know your shift doesn't start until 10 or 11 o'clock."

"Five works. See you then." He clicked off.

Keegan had no idea what to do about Luna. She hadn't left a phone number. The way Luna had left it, she'd contact Keegan, but not the other way around.

How long before she gets back to me? Does she even need me now that she has all three books? I can't ask Commissioner Gordon to flash a gargoyle signal up in the sky. How much can I tell Aaron? He'll laugh if I tell him we're dealing with gargoyles.

CHAPTER 25

That morning Keegan hung out in the work room logging in books. When she wasn't doing that, she was running computer searches for *gargoyle, gargouille,* and *grotesque,* which turned up thousands of hits. Dictionary, encyclopedia, and Wikipedia entries. Legends. Book and author fan pages. References to short stories, poems, comic books, graphic novels, historical novels, and a slew of reference books about the supernatural and occult. There were video games. There was an extensive website on the history, background, and biology of gargoyles that claimed its information was true and authoritative. There were thousands of photographs, paintings, drawings, sketches, book covers, and garden statuaries. She printed out several pages of reading lists, but the sheer volume of online gargoyle material—like that on witches, vampires, and werewolves—was overwhelming. She wasn't sure what to think, because until now she had been sure witches, vampires, werewolves, and gargoyles were all pure fiction, the products of the imaginations of superstitious peoples and creative writers.

But Luna was a *gargouille,* and if she and Faucon existed then other *gargouilles* existed. Somewhere.

It's just that they're not walking around in plain view among us humans. At least not in broad daylight.

Variations of the *Gargouille* legend appeared on many links. Centered in a weather disaster, the tale bore similarities to Noah's Ark and ancient Babylon's Gilgamesh Epic—both deluge and flood stories with innumerable human casualties.

La Gargouille (also referred to as *Garguiem*) was a serpent-like dragon that spouted not fire but water from its mouth. According to the legend, which had been coopted and retold by the Early Church for its own purposes, the dragon had appeared in 1394 in France's Seine River, terrorizing boats and flooding the land. Saint Romain, the archbishop of Rouen, lured the dragon to shore, then tamed it by making the sign of the cross with his fingers. He led it to town and had it slaughtered. A few accounts said it was burned, but the head and neck refused to burn. At Saint Romain's urging, the townsfolk mounted the head and neck high up on the town's cathedral to remind the masses of God's power and the power of the cross.

That was the essential legend. Some accounts explained that *les gar-gouilles*, variations on the dragon *Garguiem*, were carved or sculpted and used not only on the cathedral but on other buildings as ornamental water conduits—drainpipes that shunted rainwater away from a building's stone-work. When it rained, *les gargouilles* (from the root word meaning *throat*) replicated the Seine dragon's water-spewing behavior. The functional and decorative improvements to buildings were also called, in English, *gargoyles*. Several articles noted the connection to the word *gargle*.

This is what Joshua Chamberlain recalled when he saw his Night Hawks by the light of a burning tree on the battlefield that night they covered him with dead bodies to keep him warm and hide him—the Notre Dame gro-tesques that hid the cathedral's rain gutters. LeClair and Champaigne were gargouilles—like Luna and Faucon.

Two sites, www.gargoyles-fan.org and www.gargwiki.net, had to do with a discontinued animated Disney TV series, *Gargoyles*. Both sites gave extensive fictional histories and information about gargoyles in general and the show's characters in particular. Even though this was made-up stuff, Keegan found it interesting.

A banner on the first site's landing page proclaimed in Hollywood fashion that *in the age of gargoyles a thousand years ago, superstition and sword ruled.* Of course swords ruled. They were the weapons of the day. Gunpowder and guns were in the future. The banner also declared one of the show's basic premises: gargoyles were *stone by day and warriors by night.*

The day/night dichotomy fit Luna. She wasn't exactly stone by day, but she did lack the vitality she possessed at night. That had been obvious from her clothing and her gait on her visit to Annie's when she had referred to herself as a moon child.

Warriors by night didn't apply to her—she seemed gentler, more sensitive—but it fit LeClair and Champaigne, whose nighttime raids on the Confederates earned them the labels *banshees* or *harpies*. These "warriors by night" saved Lussier's life by decimating a wolf pack in the Allagash.

They were gargouilles, *and LeClair had a mate. What happened to those three? Is that why Luna is here now—to find out? And what about Faucon? Why is he here? He started out shadowing Luna, but now he seems to be off on his own.*

The second fan site, www.gargwiki.net/gargoyle, was far more extensive than the first. There was a fabricated history, biology and physiognomy, and numerous "facts" about gargoyles that fans wanted to know.

What's a gargoyle's skin/hide like? Keegan knew. She had seen Luna's face up close and touched it. It was reptilian, yet it had a softness.

How long is a gargoyle's life span? That she didn't know, but she made a mental note to ask Luna.

What about their courtship rituals? How does a pair reproduce? Who raises the offspring? More questions she was sure Luna could answer more accurately than the fan page.

What about skin/hide, legs and arms and wings, head and ears and mouths and noses, horns and fangs? She had seen and touched Luna on the moonlit deck, but it had all happened fast. At their next meeting, maybe there'd be more time.

Even though the second site wasn't accurate, it was fascinating to read. The *Gargoyles* writers and illustrators, with the help of adoring fans, had developed an amazing back story: an entire alternative gargoyle universe that existed alongside and within the present-day universe populated by unsuspecting humans.

As Keegan was about to close the site, one of the reproductive "facts" jumped off the screen at her. *Gargoyles lay eggs. Female gargoyles nurse their young with breastmilk, however.*

"I beg to differ," she whispered aloud to whoever had written the back story. "Real *gargouilles* may lay eggs, but I doubt they breastfeed. Luna doesn't have breasts. I think you made that up to humanize your gargoyles for an audience." She avoided the temptation to email the webmaster her correction. Instead she noted both web addresses in her journal and closed the sites.

CHAPTER 26

I t was 3:35 when Aaron got to the bookstore. He had on black jeans and a black tee shirt.

"Special ops night mission?" Maryann joked from behind the counter.

"Funny," he said, and gave his usual nervous fidget that tipped her off he was about to ask for Keegan. "Keegan in?"

The work room door opened and Keegan appeared, with AJ a step behind.

"Did you put a peephole in that door?" Maryann asked.

"What?" Keegan asked.

Maryann let it go.

Aaron held up a fistful of books and fanned them out like a poker hand.

"*Night Hawks?*" Keegan asked.

"Yep, thanks to Cliff. I've also got the Call and Laymon books I bought at the York Museum this morning." He held them up in his other hand. "E-books are nice, but it's good to have paper available." He stood there as if awaiting instructions.

"You three have about a half hour before we close," Maryann said. "I'll yell if we get a rush."

Aaron followed Keegan and AJ into the work room.

"I think I've found a connection," Keegan said. "Aaron, go to the *Night Hawks* passage about the pink granite house. AJ, look in the *Dirt* book for that story I read you on the phone, about the Wells crypt that may have alien bones in it. I'll change the batteries in Zelda's cassette player so we can check it against the note she left."

They set to work. Keegan pried the corroded 20-year-old batteries out of the recorder and fished some fresh ones out of a drawer then pressed them in. She lifted the shoebox of cassettes out of the banana box and found the Byron Littlefield interview tape then slipped it into the player. She tried it. It worked.

AJ read aloud the Wells story from Laymon's *Dirt*.

"… a stone cabin constructed of four walls made of stacked blocks of pink granite, capped with a granite slab roof, approximately twelve feet by twenty feet by eight feet in height."

"Remember, he said it wasn't near any cemetery," Aaron reminded. "Or any place or thing containing human remains. Which let him invent that teaser about aliens' bones."

He read from *Night Hawks*:

"My scouts L and C have given everything and asked for nothing in return. As civilians they cannot receive military medals or honors, which they would undoubtedly refuse if offered. What else can I do to reward their service except guarantee life use of the pink granite cabin in Wells? It seems a pittance. I personally and we as a nation shall be forever indebted to these two brave warriors."

"He calls it a cabin," Keegan said. "Not a crypt. We know he had it built for LeClair's mate to live in while the scouts were away. So it was a dwelling place, which is why it's not near a cemetery. It just sounds—and must look, because of the granite walls and roof—like a tomb."

"A pink granite cabin?" Aaron said. "They used pink granite for foundations in the old days, but I'll bet this is the only time it got used for the whole thing."

"The two books have to be referring to the same place," AJ said.

"I agree," Keegan said. "Now let's check Zelda's interview with Byron Littlefield, which was around 1997. Her note about *pink granite* wasn't in her *quarries* file, it was in her *cemeteries* notes, even though you'd expect *pink granite* would refer to a quarry. Why cemeteries?"

She pressed the Start button.

"I'm Zelda Keegan, and I'm interviewing Byron Littlefield at his house in Wells, Maine. May I call you Byron?"

A male voice, clearly older, said, "You always have, Zelda. I've known you since you were a baby. Why stop now?" Then a mix of their laughs, the flirty back-and-forth between an avuncular neighbor in the twilight of his life and the pretty young girl from up the road who was in college and just starting her adult life.

Keegan had to press Stop. The voice and the laugh had dried her mouth and left a lump in her throat. She had expected a flat interview—had mentally depersonalized the interviewer before turning on the cassette—but this was her birth mother, and right from the start it was so human, so personal. It felt like seeing the scratch pad with her name Dauphine written on it—etched there before she was born and named, the exact opposite of a tombstone. This was again the skipping heartbeat she felt when she saw the You Tube video shot at the quarry swimming hole—Zelda, before she was a mother, before she was a teenager—running and jumping from the cliff hand-in-hand with Maryann, Keegan's other mother. She tried to blink away the salty tears, then wiped them away with the back of her hand.

Aaron and AJ exchanged a glance, but didn't know what to say, so they kept silent.

After a couple of deep breaths Keegan restarted the cassette.

Background on Byron, then his family and upbringing on the farm. The tone was conversational, not like a lawyer's deposition. Keegan could imagine Byron and Zelda sitting in porch rockers, sipping iced tea, and enjoying each other's company on a warm summer day, her facilitating the conversation by asking probing but not intrusive questions. And there was always her gentle inviting laugh.

Byron recalled the Great Depression and the war years when families had received "the visit" from a pair in uniform bearing sad news. He spoke of the changes he'd observed in his hometown, his state, and his country. In time he returned to his early twenties and the year before he got married.

"We were at a barn dance in 1948 or '49—me, Ed Whitcomb, and Hiram Brooks—when we took a dare to impress some girls. The three of us hiked out to the High Pine district. The Swenson Quarry was still open back then—it closed in the sixties or seventies—and there were blocks and chunks and slabs of granite piled everywhere. Pink granite was the rage then, and it outsold the black and the green granite the other quarries produced around us. Swenson's, though, had enough of the pink already out of the pit that they could have supplied everybody's needs for a hundred years to come.

"Now back to that dare from the girls. It required us to camp out on top of one of this stack of granite, except this one was way back in the woods away from the quarry pit. But this wasn't some haphazard stockpile, this was granite that had been *arranged*—it was a structure put together like a log cabin, built into the side of a hill. We wondered if it might have once been a sort of mausoleum for the undertakers to put bodies in during the winter—you know, cold storage until the ground softened up enough for burials—what we called spring planting. It was also rumored to be a sacred shrine dedicated to some Civil War soldier from Wells who died at Gettysburg, but nobody ever came up with a name. And there was another Civil War story about the place being where a soldier's wife stayed while he was away in the war. Truth be told, it was a granite blockhouse, and nobody really knew what it was out there for.

"But the challenge was before us—the girls had thrown down the gauntlet—and we had a scratch map somebody drew us. Whoever sketched it put an X on the spot and wrote *Stonehedge* next to it. I guess the stones reminded them of that Stonehenge Circle in England, which some folks speculated was arranged that way by spacemen.

"We followed the map and got there before dark. It was this huge stone box. It reminded me of the Nazi bunkers at Normandy—pillboxes, they called them—only those were concrete and this place was granite and smaller. Hiram and Ed and I agreed it would've made a perfect root cellar if there'd been a door in one of the walls or a trapdoor in the roof. It was hemmed in tight by pine trees—and I mean tight—that had grown right up against the block walls like a stockade fence.

"Since it was built into the hill, we went around to the high side and climbed up onto the roof—which was granite, too, not blocks but slabs laid side by side—and we tried to look down inside through the spaces between them. But it was too dark down there. It smelled like loam that's accumulated from years of rotting plants. Ed dug graves for extra money when he was younger, and when he smelled it, he called it graveyard dirt.

"We sat up on top like kids sneaking cigarettes in a treehouse. We ate our apples and bread and cheese, and we drank our warm beers. Then we set out our three candle stubs in jelly jars—we didn't want them to blow out—and we laid out our bedrolls.

"It was our intention to spend the entire night on Stonehedge regardless of what might be entombed below us. So we stayed up joking and talking, then bedded down for the night, which was the dare. If you kept your head under the covers, the dirt smell wasn't so bad.

"I woke sometime in the middle of the night. The moon was about half full and almost directly overhead, and from where I lay—I'll never forget it—it looked like it'd been skewered by one of those tall pines that had us hemmed in.

"Something moved out in the bushes. You know how a rabbit or a raccoon can rustle the leaves, and in the dark the sound is amplified? I tried to convince myself that even if it was a deer or a fox, we were safe up on the roof. The downhill wall was about eight or nine feet high, as I recall, and the uphill side where we'd climbed on was maybe six.

"Ed woke up and we heard the rustling again, so we shook Hiram awake and relit the candles. Seeing each other's faces was cold comfort then, because holding those candles in front of us only made us look like jack-o-lanterns. Even with three of us there together, we wanted to bolt.

"We heard more rustling, and it felt like the woods were closing in on us. My heart turned to skim ice. Even now, 50 years later, I can smell that burning candle wax mixed with the dank and the decay that wafted up through those cracks between the roof slabs.

"Which is when the tension got to Ed. He hollered, 'Who's out there?' Which spooked it, I guess, whatever it was, because no sooner had he yelled it than something flew straight up out of the bushes—the way a startled pheasant or a wild turkey will make your heart stop.

"Pheasant, turkey, it didn't matter to us at that point. We grabbed our candles, left our bedding right there, and jumped off the roof where we'd climbed on. Ed took the lead and we lit out together in a line. We lost the path in the dark, and Ed said it didn't matter because he was going straight until he hit a road. Which is what we did—the Quarry Road—which we followed back to the truck. I drove home—it was my pickup—and all the way back we talked about it, trying to calm our nerves. By the time we got back to town, the tension was gone and we laughed and joked about what fraidy cats we'd been."

There was a moment's pause on the tape, after which Zelda said, "That doesn't sound like a funny story at all, Byron. Sounds pretty scary to me."

Byron Littlefield replied solemnly, "Stonehedge was only funny after we put the distance between us and that crypt or whatever it was. You're right, though. I never had such a fright in my life as that night. To that I can attest, and I think Hiram and Ed will, too."

The interview ended. Keegan snapped off the cassette player.

"So now we have three mentions of the pink granite cabin," she said, "two in print and one in the Byron Littlefield interview. Think they're all the same place?"

"I do," Aaron answered. "Chamberlain had it built for his scouts in the 1860s using pink granite from the quarry that's now Millenium Granite. We know the dimensions and the shape, and Byron just told us it's set back from Quarry Road in the woods. If it was overgrown when they hiked up there in the late forties—I mean, nobody's mentioned it since—it's probably even more hidden now."

"So we should be able to find it?" Keegan asked.

"Sounds like it," Aaron said.

AJ chimed in, "There are plenty of old cellar holes with foundations out in the woods. What makes this one so different?"

"Joshua Chamberlain makes it different," Aaron said. "It's about history."

"Luna makes it different," Keegan said. "It's about family."

CHAPTER 27

After they locked up the Book Stop, Maryann and Keegan stopped for groceries on Route 1. The parking lot was the usual July pre-dinnertime zoo.

"I shouldn't be too long," Maryann said, and headed for the cart corral.

Keegan pulled out her cellphone and called the town historian at home. She said hello and they did a quick catch-up before Keegan said why she was calling.

"I need your help. I'm trying to locate a long forgotten structure that's supposedly in Wells. It's probably overgrown or sunken or damaged by roots and the elements."

"I hope you're going to give me more than that to go on."

"I am. My source says Joshua Chamberlain had it built for the mate of one of his scouts. He referred to it as a *pink granite cabin*. When Zelda did her internship with you, she taped an interview with Byron Littlefield. He called the place Stonehedge and said it reminded him of a German bunker—a pillbox at Normandy—only smaller."

The historian didn't hesitate. "I've been in Wells 90-odd years and never heard of a place called Stonehedge or Stonehenge. And that description doesn't fit anyplace I know of around here."

"Okay, Byron Littlefield said he and two friends went there in the late 1940s on a dare. They were supposed to camp overnight on its roof. Somebody handed them a map with an X on it, and next to the X was penciled the name Stonehedge."

"Sounds like a name created for the dare. Maybe the mapmaker knew the place from hunting there and, after the dare, never used the name again. Who were the two friends?"

Keegan checked her notebook. "Hiram Brooks and Ed Whitcomb."

"I should have guessed. Those three were always thick as thieves. Well,

Byron and Hiram are long gone, but Ed's still kicking. He lives in South Berwick with one of his daughters."

"So he'd have to be—what—ninety?"

"Careful, young lady. He's a couple years younger than I am. Would you like me to call him and see what he remembers?"

"Would you? That'd be great."

"I'll call him after dinner and get back to you this evening. Ed will talk for an hour, if I let him."

Keegan was at her desktop when her cellphone chirped at 8:15. She scooped it up on the first ring.

"Ed's still pretty sharp," the historian said. "He told me the story, says he remembers the night vividly, especially the smell of grave dirt coming up through the spaces between the roof pieces."

"Did he tell you where it is?"

"He did. I wrote the directions down. You ready?"

"Ready. Go ahead."

"Start at the Elks Lodge off Bald Hill Road. Follow the stream that's behind it until you run into two other streams, West Brook and Bragdon Brook. They'll cross your stream at the same spot. Ed says it used to look like a six-road intersection. Take the first stream to the right and follow it for about a hundred yards. Then look uphill to the right and—if it's still there—you'll see what looks like a picket fence of high pines surrounding the granite building like a fort. Ed says the roof will be hard to spot because it'll likely have years of pine needles and branches on it, maybe even deadfall trees. But it's bound to be somewhere under all the debris. He said to look for that crowded row of pines."

An hour later Keegan sat at the kitchen table, hoping the phone would ring as it had the night before.

At 9:40 it did. She picked it up.

"I'll be there in twenty minutes," Luna said, and hung up.

Keegan looked at the number. It was area code 207, but this time it wasn't the prefix for Alfred and the Christian Brothers monastery guest phone Aaron had tracked down from Luna's special-order ticket. This number was for Kennebunk or Kennebunkport. She jotted it in her notebook and added it to her cellphone contacts. Then she went in to tell Maryann that Luna would meet them on the deck at 10 o'clock, and filled her mother in on what she'd learned and what she suspected.

CHAPTER 28

Keegan and Maryann waited in a pair of deck chairs with the outside light off. The air was warm and still, and like the night before, the moon was still around half full.

They heard the *whoosh-whoosh* in the distance beyond the roof and glanced up. A moment later Luna glided in and alit gently on the ridgeline beside the chimney. In silhouette she looked like a round-shouldered stone gargoyle on a cathedral parapet.

"Come on down," Keegan called up. "I wanted Mom to sit in this time. She's up to speed on things." When Luna didn't move, Keegan assured her, "Nobody else here, I promise."

Luna spread her wings wide and pushed off, practically fluttering to a soft landing near them, her talon nails clicking on the decking.

Keegan gestured to a chair. "Want to sit?"

"I prefer this," Luna said, and tucked in her wings like a hen preparing to nest. Then she moved closer to Maryann. "Keegan needed to look and touch last night. Zelda was the same way. I won't be offended, Maryann." She opened her arms and her wings away from her body a little.

Maryann looked without touching, saying, "Thank you, Luna, but right now we need to talk. Twenty years ago my sister said she was helping a gargoyle. I didn't believe her."

"And now?"

"And now you're here. But I'm not exactly sure why. Keegan thinks it's a genealogy thing. Are these your ancestors—Champaigne, LeClair, and the wife?"

"I am here for LeClair's mate. We *gargouilles* do not use the terms husband or wife. I need to find where she lived."

"Where she lived—and how about where she died?" Maryann asked. "Was it here? Is she buried in Wells?"

"She lived here, but I am not sure exactly where. And yes, she probably died here and is buried here."

"How about Champaigne and LeClair?" Keegan asked. "Are they buried here, too?"

"No."

The three of them sat in silence, Maryann and Keegan puzzled, Luna waiting quietly for the next question.

"I feel like I should offer you a drink," Maryann said.

"I would not take it, *merci*."

They chuckled, and some of the unease fell away.

"By now you've read the books?" Keegan asked, and Luna nodded. "Obviously, the important one was *Night Hawks*, which confirmed the Wells connection and gave the building materials and dimensions of the cabin Chamberlain built for them."

"I have read the books. What is not there is the location."

"If the structure is even still there," Maryann said.

"That little book, Laymon's, is a recent publication, and that gives me hope it is still standing."

"How about the York County cemeteries book?" Keegan said. "Why did you order that?"

"I thought that if the granite cabin had been mistaken for a tomb, it might have appeared on the list of burial grounds."

"So, is LeClair's mate buried near it?" Maryann asked.

A slight hesitation from Luna, then, "Not near it. *In it*." That brought an awkward silence.

Keegan said, "So you're trying to find it because it's an ancestral grave."

"I am trying to find it because it is important to me."

"And now that you've read the books," Maryann said, "do you have a general idea where it could be?"

"No," Luna replied.

"So you need our help?" Maryann asked.

"Yes, if you know where it is."

"We don't know exactly," Keegan said. "But I've been working on it. As Mom said, if it's still there, it's overgrown, and everybody around Wells has forgotten it. I now have a rough idea, but I'd have to show you."

"No. You should not get more involved than you already are. Simply tell me."

They sat in silence a few seconds until Keegan said, "I've read the same three books you have, and I've seen Zelda's files and records, and a bunch of historical documents on Wells. I haven't seen it, but I think I can hike to it."

"Just draw me a map. You do not need—"

"Look, Luna, if this is only some old abandoned granite cabin that's become a tomb, what's the big deal?" Maryann asked.

Luna clammed up, with body language to match, wings and arms now pulled in tight. She looked like a large stone garden gargoyle.

"Luna, this is about more than an ancestor's cabin or grave," Maryann continued. "If that's all it was, Faucon wouldn't be here."

"*C'est vrai,*" Luna replied, then translated, "That is true."

"So he wants to find the either the cabin or the grave," Keegan said, "but for a different reason than your reason. Obviously you two can't work together on it."

No answer. Then Luna hemmed, "Faucon . . ."

"Faucon *what?*" Keegan asked impatiently.

"Faucon is not really one of us."

"Not really one of you? Meaning what?" Keegan blurted. "He's not a gargoyle?" It was the first time she had used the word *gargoyle* rather than *gargouille* in speaking to Luna, and she wasn't sure if it was offensive.

Luna didn't seem bothered.

"Faucon is *un gargouille,* but not one born into our Allagash clan, which you would think of as French Canadian. He is from the French Alps, where there are several *gargouille* clans. But Faucon has lived with us for a while. He was brought into the Allagash clan after the Great War, what you call World War 1."

Now it was Keegan and Maryann's turn to be still.

"Faucon is an interloper," Luna said. "And a pretender to the throne."

"The throne?" Keegan asked. "What throne?"

"The throne of *Les Gargouilles*. He wants to rule of what is left of our race."

Maryann shook her head. Here she was, meeting her first real live gargoyle, and not only was she learning that Luna, Faucon, LeClair, Champaigne, and LeClair's mate weren't the only ones, but there were many. She responded with nervous humor.

"Are you sure I can't get us something to drink? This sounds like it's going to take a while to tell."

CHAPTER 29

A t Keegan's suggestion they moved inside to the living room, keeping it dim, not because of Luna's skin—artificial light didn't affect her the way sunlight did—but because it was easier on her eyes. She had excellent vision at night but poor vision in daylight or under other intense light. They huddled close around the coffee table, keeping their voices low.

"In case Faucon is sitting out on a tree branch," Keegan said. "This should make it harder for him to hear us. I'm assuming *gargouilles* possess exceptional hearing, too, right?"

"*Oui*," Luna answered. "That is no doubt how Faucon knew the first two books had come in. He could not have listened to my messages inside the monastery guest room. He must have overheard me checking them."

Maryann cut to the chase. "So are you here to take LeClair's mate's bones home?"

Luna steepled her fingers and took a deep breath. Then she meshed them and pressed her palms away from her, blowing out the breath to relieve the tension.

"Zelda is the only human I've ever told my story to. That was 20 years ago. Since then it has become far more complicated."

"We have all night," Maryann encouraged.

"Thank you," Luna said. "We *gargouilles* are an ancient race, as old as humans. We live in clans—some small, some quite large. You might think of them as small kingdoms, each with its own leader. All of these clans are part of the *gargouille* race, which has a single ruler, the king. The king has always been the leader of the Allagash or French-Canadian clan."

"You said Champaigne, LeClair, and his mate were from your clan, but Faucon is not," Keegan said.

"*C'est vrai.* But first I must tell you about us as a race."

"We're listening," Maryann said.

"How old do you think I am?" Luna asked.

Keegan said, "You and Zelda took college classes together, but you said you were an older student. How about fifty?"

"I am 200."

Keegan gasped.

Maryann croaked, "What?"

Luna gave them a minute to come to grips with their disbelief.

"We *gargouilles* live about 400 years. That would be considered old age, like 90 or 100 for humans. Of course, like you, some of us die earlier of diseases, accidents, and injuries."

"You're 200?" Keegan said, still not quite believing it.

"Yes. Also, we are not mammals and we do not carry our young inside us or bear them alive. We are egg layers."

"So you're reptiles?" Maryann asked.

"Your science would place us somewhere between reptiles and birds. Look at my skin. Consider my wings. Yet we are similar to humans as well. We possess intelligence, the power of reason, and the capacity for language. We also have emotions."

Maryann and Keegan stared open-mouthed.

"Let me show you something else." Luna lifted one of her muscular legs, stretched out her foot, and flexed her toes. The talon tips that had clicked on the decking when she landed now came fully out like a cat's claws. She retracted them so that only the very tips showed again. Luna set her foot back on the floor.

"We have the grip of a raptor—the eagle, the hawk, the owl. We can perch on branches, grasp fish, and pick up prey as big as a coyote or a small deer."

"Which is what Champaigne and LeClair did in the Allagash Wilderness when they saved Clayton Lussier from the wolves, right?" Keegan asked.

"Yes. The two of them would have seized the wolves then used their swords and their *poignards*—thrusting daggers. They are the weapons of a two-handed fighting style that allows for both slashing and stabbing."

"Which was why Chamberlain sent them behind the Confederate lines after dark," Maryann said.

"Yes. LeClair and Champaigne were trained to fight alone or in tandem. They were deadly in close quarters. Their inner wings allowed them to fight side-by-side, back-to-back, or one above the other."

"Inner wings?" Keegan asked.

"Yes, also known as the short wings. Let me show you."

Luna unfurled her broad upper wings the way an eagle or a hawk might, but she didn't take off. She held them wide so Maryann and Keegan could view the wingspan—more than eight feet tip to tip.

"Look beneath them. Lower down."

They leaned closer as Luna held her muscular arms straight out in front of her. Below her armpits they saw a second set of smaller wings that Luna unfolded about two feet to the side. She tucked the large upper wings back onto her shoulders the way a convertible's top collapses back and into itself above the car's trunk. The lower wings were still exposed.

"Watch," Luna said.

The short wings began to beat at a fantastic speed, humming. She rose above the floor, hovered a moment before making two sharp, quick flits to one side then the other. As she flew she moved her hands as if swinging a sword and stabbing with a dagger.

"LeClair and Champaigne could rise, dive, lunge, and reverse—all while fighting."

"Amazing," Keegan said.

"Float like a butterfly, sting like a bee," Maryann mumbled.

"What?" Keegan asked blankly.

"Muhammed Ali, the boxer, the heavyweight champion of the world—the Greatest—he used to say it: *I float like a butterfly and sting like a bee.*"

Luna alit, the tips of her talons clicking on the hardwood floor, and retracted her small wings.

"I can see why Joshua Chamberlain went to the Allagash to recruit them," Keegan said. "They were Commandos, Special Forces, Seal Team Six. No wonder the rebels called them banshees and harpies."

Keegan's cellphone chirped. She glanced at the caller ID.

"It's AJ. Should I answer?"

"If she's calling this late, it could be important," Maryann said.

"Be right back," Keegan said, and disappeared into the kitchen.

"Luna, I can understand *you* coming here to find the granite cabin," Maryann said. "But why is Faucon looking for it?"

"He is here because I am here. But for a different reason, his own reason."

Rather than ask for clarification, Maryann switched her line of questioning.

"What was her name, LeClair's mate?"

"Diana."

"Like the Roman goddess of the moon. And your name—Luna—that's also a moon goddess."

Luna gave a snuffling laugh. "Yes. But Diana and I are not goddesses."

"Was she young?"

"She was about 50 when LeClair came back from the War Between the States."

Maryann did the math. "So she'd be your age now—200—if she had survived?"

"*Oui.*"

They heard Keegan's voice grow louder in the kitchen.

"What? You're kidding?" It was in response to AJ.

Luna said, "AJ just told her about something Faucon has done."

"But how do you--?"

Luna pointed to her ear. "*Gargouille* hearing, Keegan is off now. Let her tell us."

Keegan reappeared and said, "You're not going to believe what happened."

"Something about a graveyard?" Luna said.

"How'd you know?"

"Just tell us what happened," Maryann said.

Keegan took a breath and began.

Section V

Disturbance at Bear's Den Graveyard

CHAPTER 30

"Aaron's on duty," Keegan said.

"Aaron is AJ's brother," Maryann explained to Luna. "He's a policeman."

"Aaron got a call from dispatch about some guy freaking out up at Bear's Den RV park. Not in the park itself—in the little graveyard across the road by their dumpster."

"Freaking out *how*?" Maryann asked.

"Stabbing graves."

"Stabbing graves?" Maryann echoed.

"Yes."

Luna stood like a sentry, listening.

"Did somebody actually see this?" Maryann asked.

"Yes. A couple who live at Bear's Den. They were walking their dogs near the swimming pool. The dogs started straining at their leashes and barking at the graveyard. The husband told Aaron he thought somebody had left the dumpster lid open and raccoons might be scavenging there, which would have upset the dogs. So the couple and the dogs started across the road to scare off any raccoons and close the dumpster lid.

"But the dogs pulled toward the graveyard, and when they looked, the husband and wife saw some guy inside the graveyard wall with a big stake—they said it looked like a Samurai sword—moving from spot to spot, raising it over his head and jamming it into the ground in different places very quickly, over and over. They dragged the dogs back across the road and called 911. The guy was still poking and stabbing when Aaron came around the curve with his lights flashing, but by the time he pulled up next to the graveyard the guy was gone."

"Luna says it was Faucon," Maryann said to Keegan.

Luna said, "You said the graveyard is small. How small?"

"I don't know," Keegan replied. "Maybe ten or fifteen feet wide, twenty or thirty feet the long way."

"You said it has walls?"

"Waist high, but you can look in over them. They're thick. Stone, I guess."

"Granite," Maryann said. "I remember them from our bike rides. Long oblong blocks stacked on each other."

"So Faucon thought it might be what was left of Chamberlain's pink granite cabin," Keegan said. "Remember, all he's got to go on is the three books, which give him a general description but no location. The *York County Cemeteries* book may have led him to think Chamberlain's granite cabin is one of the listed burial grounds. Bear's Den's graveyard is about the right dimensions and is fenced in with pink granite. Who's to say the upper half of the walls and the roof weren't removed, scavenged for some other purpose?"

"Faucon does not know you have learned the location, Keegan," Luna said.

"Which means we can get there first," Keegan said.

"We?" Maryann said, voice rising. "Keegan, this Faucon is behind four break-ins. He flattened Elly Stedman and broke a lot of bones. And Elly's built like a tank, but apparently that wasn't enough to keep him from landing in the hospital. Now this guy shows up at Bear's Den playing sword-in-the-stone—which could mean he's out there at this very moment aerating any other cemeteries that happen to be the right size and have granite walls. Faucon is dangerous, Keegan, and I don't want you or AJ or Aaron or anybody else to get in his way."

"Maryann is right," Luna said. "Faucon is desperate. And this is a *gargouille* matter. You have already helped by learning the location. All I need now is a map."

"Thank you, Luna." Maryann sighed.

"Mom, can't you see?" Keegan protested. "This isn't about getting to some long-lost ancestor's cabin first."

"The ancestor's name was Diana," Maryann clarified. "Luna told me while you were on the phone with AJ." Then she said, "Luna, you didn't say how you and Diana are related."

"Diana is my sister."

"Oh, Luna, I'm so sorry," Maryann said. "I didn't mean to be insensitive."

"An understandable mistake, Maryann. Apology accepted."

Keegan didn't want to dwell on it. "Back to Faucon. This is about more than getting to your sister Diana's cabin or grave or whatever first. Faucon was seen stabbing the ground. What's that about? Is he your jilted boyfriend or something? If he is, he's got some serious anger management issues. Why would he try stabbing your sister's bones 150 years later, Luna?"

Luna said nothing.

"We've got all night, Luna," Keegan said. "Faucon doesn't know where to look—and it's driving him crazy—but I do. Without my new information, he can't beat us to your sister. So you may as well tell us. What's this about?"

Section VI

World War I

CHAPTER 31

"More than a hundred thousand *gargouilles* live on six continents: Europe, Asia, Africa, Australia, and the Americas. Our clans range fewer than 100 to more than 5,000 and function independently. But as a race—as the larger *gargouille* kingdom—we are connected. If one clan is threatened, the other clans will respond.

"Clans have their own leaders, but the kingdom has only one king, King Cyrus, who also leads the Allagash clan. His father Leander was king before him. Cyrus fathered two sons, the twin princes LeClair and Champaigne, whom you know as Chamberlain's *Night Hawks*."

"Wait," Keegan said. "Cyrus is the present king, but his sons fought in the Civil War?"

"*Oui*. Cyrus is nearly 400 years old now. When the princes fought for Colonel Chamberlain, they were in their forties."

Maryann said, "But didn't you say 400 years is about the span of a *gargouille's* life? And Cyrus is about 400."

"*Oui*."

Maryann did the math again. "So Champaigne and LeClair, Diana and you, you're are all about the same age. With Diana dead at 50, that means you three survivors are middle age. You said you're 200. Which tells me that one of the twin princes—the elder, I presume—is next in line for the throne. Would that be right?"

"It did not work out that way," Luna replied.

"But according to Chamberlain's journal," Keegan said, "LeClair and Champaigne survived the Civil War. He wrote that he was sorry he couldn't give them anything more than the pink granite cabin."

"*C'est vrai*. Both survived," Luna said. "When the war ended, Champaigne returned to the Allagash. LeClair and Diana were not with him. He did not divulge where they settled. So we did not know about the granite cabin, only that they had been in Maine during the war. It was possible they had gone elsewhere afterward, perhaps west.

"What eventually brought LeClair back was the Great War in Europe in 1917. King Cyrus sent Champaigne out to bring his brother home so he could lead an Allagash force to help the French *gargouilles.*

"Several of the smaller *gargouille* clans in the Alps were drawn into the conflict. They conducted night attacks behind the German lines in the same way LeClair and Champaigne had raided the Confederates in the Civil War here. But the German armies were too strong, and the French clans called on King Cyrus for help. Cyrus sent the twin princes and a force of twenty to fight beside them."

"So they went off to a second war?" Keegan asked.

"*Oui*, they had no choice. But remember, LeClair and Champaigne had not been in battle in more than 50 years—and that had been a 19th Century war. They were ill-equipped for 20th Century warfare. Since their years with Colonel Chamberlain, humans had developed new ways to maim and kill. Now there were machine guns, grenades, and a horrible new weapon: mustard gas. Although the princes had no equals with sword and dagger in your Civil War, this was not that war."

"What happened?" Maryann asked.

Luna went on. "We *gargouilles* sleep during the daytime in caves and cellars and barn lofts—anywhere out of the sunlight. When we awaken, we are sluggish and vulnerable. LeClair, Champaigne, and their comrades were totally unprepared for a mustard gas attack.

"LeClair had heard of the gas, but he had never experienced it. When the alarm sounded, the gas was already seeping in on them. None of them had gas masks. As soon as he felt the burning in his lungs, he covered his face and eyes with a cloth and used his body to shield his brother."

"How terrible," Maryann cried. "Did they survive?"

"One of the Alps clans had been kept in reserve, but the others that were there—including the Allagash contingent—were decimated. The gas killed many, and those who did not die immediately were rendered helpless. The German infantry entered the caves in gas masks with their bayonets fixed. With so many *gargouilles* coughing up their scorched lungs, the Germans had little need for bullets."

"What about LeClair and Champaigne?" Keegan pressed.

"The clan kept in reserve reached the caves minutes ahead of the German infantry. They were able to evacuate the twin princes, but only them. They did this because LeClair was our race's *dauphin* and Champaigne was next-in-line to the throne after him."

Keegan heard the French word *dauphin—doe-fan* with Luna's accent. Hearing it aloud reminded her of her birth certificate, *Dauphine Keegan—Doe-feen*—and the writing on the back cover of Zelda's little yellow notebook. How many times when Keegan was a child had Maryann said, 'my sister must have named you Dauphine so she could call you *princess*'?"

Luna went on. "The reserve clan was led by a gigantic *gargouille* named Drago. He was double the size of an average *gargouille* and far stronger than any male. His wingspan was four feet wider than anyone else's. He was very loyal to King Cyrus.

"As they retreated, armed only with swords and daggers, they came under withering ground fire. Drago made two flights over the glacier. First he carried LeClair—no other *gargouille* was strong enough to do that—then he returned for Champaigne.

"The German artillery saw the promontory on which Drago landed with LeClair, then watched him return for Champaigne. Rather than try to hit him in the air they zeroed in on the promontory, waiting for his second landing. As soon as he touched down they unleashed a barrage. A shell exploded behind Drago, wounding him badly. But his massive body absorbed the blast, saving Champaigne.

"With the glacier between them and the Germans, the clan carried the princes and Drago up into the mountains. Drago died there."

"But LeClair and Champaigne survived?" Maryann asked.

"*Oui.* But LeClair's lungs were badly burned, and he could no longer fight or fly. He could barely walk. When they told him Drago had died, he was concerned about Drago's son, who had accompanied his father, even though he was barely old enough to fight. The child should have been the responsibility of Drago's clan, but LeClair, feeling himself to be in Drago's debt, pledged to care for his son.

"The next year LeClair, Champaigne, and Drago's son were on a ship bound for America. It was the peak of the Great Influenza Epidemic and many of the passengers were sick. LeClair's lung capacity had already been impaired by the mustard gas. He contracted the flu and died at sea."

"How sad," Maryann said. "What about Champaigne?"

"Champaigne made it home, bringing with him Drago's son. He felt obliged to honor his brother's pledge and introduced him to our clan as his *ward*.

"The boy was unpredictable and at times difficult to control. He could be considerate and respectful one minute—even charming—then in the next he was cruel and indifferent. He grew nearly as large as his father Drago had been, but unlike his father he could be a bully with a sadistic streak. Someone reported to Champaigne that he dropped a terrified fawn off a gorge—not to kill it for food but to see if it would land on its feet."

"Let me guess," Maryann said. "This is Faucon."

Luna nodded sadly.

Keegan said, "Why doesn't Champaigne just send him back to the Alps? His clan there would have to take him back, wouldn't they?"

"*Champaigne est morte.*"

"What?" Maryann gasped. "Champaigne is dead, too?"

"*C'est vrai.* Before I started at the University. He was barely 180 years. He died a year after he adopted Faucon as his son."

"*Adopted him as his son?*" Maryann sputtered. "Why would he do that? And what exactly does that mean in the *gargouille* world? Does Faucon inherit his adoptive father's cave and belongings? The bigger question— unless I'm missing something—is: what about the throne? I mean, LeClair was the first *dauphin* but he died at sea, leaving Champaigne the *dauphin* by default, right? Don't tell me Faucon is next in line!"

"It is unclear," Luna answered flatly. "We do not have the legal systems you humans do. We have never had to face this before. The Council of *Gargouilles* has taken up the question, but now 20 years after Champaigne's death and with Cyrus still alive—though who can say for how long—they are still debating it. To answer your question, Maryann, Faucon was given what you would call Champaigne's *estate,* but the *dauphin* question is unresolved. Can an orphan *gargouille* from a clan other than the Allagash, adopted by the crown prince—succeed Cyrus?"

"So for now," Keegan said, "you have neither a *dauphin* nor—assuming a daughter or granddaughter could qualify—a *dauphine.*"

"*C'est vrai.* Nothing forbids a *dauphine,* but we have neither a *dauphin* nor a *dauphine* at the moment."

Maryann heard an inflection in Luna's answer. "*At the moment?* At. The. Moment. Just what does that mean, Luna?"

Keegan had caught it, too. "Okay, Luna, we've danced around this long enough. What's the real reason you're here?"

Luna paused, then said, "The eggs."

Section VII

The Real Treasure

CHAPTER 32

"The eggs?" Keegan asked.

"*Oui,*" Luna answered. "Remember how I said we *gargouilles* are neither reptile, bird, nor mammal—but we have something in common with each? My skin is like a reptile's, my wings and talons are like a bird's, and I walk on two legs like you humans. I have opposable thumbs, the gifts of speech, thought, and emotion.

"But we are different in our reproduction. Reptiles and birds lay eggs, though differently. A turtle digs a hole in sand or soil, deposits her eggs and covers them, then leaves, appearing to abandon her offspring. A bird—whether it's a chicken or a robin—builds a nest and lays her eggs then sits on them to warm them until they hatch. She and her mate will then care for them until they can survive on their own.

"With mammals—including your *homo sapiens*—the male fertilizes the female's egg internally, leaving her to carry that fertilized egg—what you call the developing fetus—for almost a year. The fetus draws nutrients from the mother's body through an umbilical cord until it is birthed out of the body and the cord is cut. After that, the offspring requires years of care and nurture."

"Your English is better than I thought," Maryann said. "You might want to consider teaching college."

"*Merci,*" Luna said, and went on. "*Gargouille* reproduction is a unique mix of all of those. Like a human, the female ovulates in accordance with the moon, expelling five to ten rubbery eggs that would remind you of your Gummy Bears, each the size of a duck egg. If a couple has no interest in procreation that month, they ignore the eggs and the eggs break down naturally. If the couple is ready to reproduce—and this is a one-time event in a *gargouille* couple's life—the male will build a nest so that when the female is ready she can lay her eggs in it. She will climb out of the nest afterward and the male will then climb in and fertilize the eggs one at a time using a needlelike stinger below his abdomen."

Both Keegan and Maryann stifled giggles. Luna ignored them.

"Now here is the part that makes *gargouilles* different. I said this is a one-time event for the couple. *This is when the mother sacrifices herself for the good of the race.*

Keegan and Maryann stopped giggling and paid close attention.

"An ovulating female is typically 40 to 100 years old, less than a quarter of the way through a *gargouille's* full lifespan. She—or you could say she and her mate—must make a conscious decision to give up 300 to 350 years of her life so the race can continue."

"What do you mean?" Maryann asked.

Luna continued. "The couple take turns sitting on the fertilized eggs. While the male is on the nest, the female will gorge, eating enough to double her size. Then while she is on the nest, the male is digging her a hole—consider it a shallow grave."

Keegan and Maryann were aghast, their mouths open in disbelief.

"When it is time, they say their goodbyes and she crawls into the hole to lie down on her back. Her mate places their eggs close to her sides, from her armpits to her hips, depending how many eggs there are, and hugs them close. He covers her body with dirt—not her face, for she must continue breathing for more than a year while the eggs attach themselves to her like barnacles. Their rubbery shells harden. They draw nourishment from the mother while she is alive in her hibernating state, then after that for several more years. Eventually the flesh and organs of her body will disappear. Even her bone marrow will be absorbed by the growing fetuses in the attached shells. By the time she is physically used up by them, they will have entered a holding pattern—not suspended animation but something like it—and their growth will be barely perceptible. By then they will be drawing their long-term sustenance and moisture from the roots of the trees nearby, which were planted as saplings by the couple. So, as you can see, the female sacrifices—giving not only her body but three-quarters of her life to extend her clan and her race."

"Then the mother never sees her children," Maryann said, her voice thick with sadness.

"And the children never know their mother," Keegan said, her own voice raspy..

"We have never known anything different," Luna answered.

For a long moment the living room was hushed as a shrine.

Then Keegan, steadying her voice, asked, "So how are they born?"

"The mate returns to dig them up and crack the shells."

"When does that happen?" Maryann asked.

"A batch of eggs will fully gestate over a period of about 100 years. If no one comes for them—let's say the male is killed in war or dies of a disease—they will lose viability and be absorbed back into the earth in the same way as unfertilized eggs."

"Except these aren't unfertilized eggs," Maryann said. "These are unhatched baby *gargouilles*."

"*C'est vrai*," Luna answered. "Such things happen. Another factor has been human encroachment, as with the paper industry in the Maine woods. Loggers may cut down the trees that are feeding the fetuses buried in the nesting chamber. The chamber may be bulldozed or dismantled because the loggers have no idea what they are disturbing."

"Wow," Keegan said. "A hundred years. But if Diana got pregnant at the end of the Civil War, say around 1865, wouldn't her eggs have passed their expiration date by 1965?"

"*Oui*, if she laid them in 1865. But remember, LeClair did not return to the Allagash then. He came home at King Cyrus' request when the Great War broke out in Europe so that he and his brother could might lead the Allagash force."

"So what are you thinking?" Maryann asked. "Or hoping—that Diana laid her eggs 50 years later, before LeClair went home to fight in France?"

"*C'est tres possible*. In 1916 Diana would have been 99 and still ovulating. LeClair could have fertilized her eggs before they said their goodbyes. LeClair would have covered Diana and the eggs and left."

"Which would make them," Maryann calculated, "roughly 100 to 101 years old. Meaning they're either aged out or are about to—if the father doesn't get back to crack them. There's a high probability they're already disintegrating."

"But that is not certain," Luna argued. "The eggs have rubbery shells when they are buried. Imagine them arranged along both sides of the mother like pearls on strings. Most of the pearls—eggs—have four points of contact: the mother's arm, the mother's side close to her ribs and organs, and the other eggs. The shells harden in the years the mother's body is being used up."

"But the pearls on either end of the string only make three contacts," Maryann pointed out. "The ones not on the end each have four points of contact."

"*Oui,*" Luna agreed. "So let us assume the best: three to six eggs along each side of Diana, two strings of six pearls each.

"There have been cases of two dominant eggs in a nest—one dominant egg on each string, perhaps those with four points of contact—surviving beyond 100 years. It is thought that through those shell connections the weaker ones pass along their essence—their life force—to the next in the string."

"Or maybe," Maryann said, "the strong suck it out of the weak—cannibalize them. Survival of the fittest. We really can't be sure if it's about giving or taking, can we?"

"No," Luna said. "We cannot. Either way, it is about the survival of the race."

"And that really has happened?" Maryann asked. "Ten or twelve saving two? Or by the bitter end, maybe just one survives. Can that string of pearls idea really buy the dominant egg a little more time? Or are these just *gargouille* myths, stories of hope?"

"I do not know," Luna replied. "But consider Drago, Faucon's father who was hatched with no siblings. Perhaps his size had to do with an extended gestation period."

"You mean he was big because he ate his siblings," Keegan said.

"I am simply saying," Luna said, "that Drago was the only hatchling from a nest of who knows how many."

"You said Faucon is large like his father," Maryann said. "Is that genetic—from his father—or because he too ate his siblings?"

"It must be genetic. Faucon is Drago's third son, and his two brothers are also large."

"So even if this isn't a wild goose chase," Maryann said, "finding the granite cabin, I mean—chances are we'll find two strings of crumbling pearls. Expired baby *gargouilles*."

"Or, Mom," Keegan countered, "we could find the place and dig up one really big egg that's itching to be cracked."

"Luna," Maryann said. "You said the father digs the eggs up and cracks the shells. Can someone else birth them?"

"I can."

"Okay. And if that works—let's say one survived—would he be Cyrus' *grand-dauphin*?"

"Or Cyrus' *grande-dauphine*," Keegan said, emphasizing *dauphine*.

"This is why I am here," Luna said. "For my sister's eggs."

"Faucon, too," Keegan said.

"Except that Faucon is stabbing cemeteries," Maryann said. "He has something else in mind for them. He wants to eliminate the competition."

Section VIII

Seeking Stonehedge

CHAPTER 33

"Diana's cabin—or burial chamber or birthing room or whatever it is," Keegan said, "let's call it Stonehedge."

"Stonehedge?" Luna said.

"Yes. During Zelda's summer internship here, she interviewed a man who may have camped out on its roof with two friends. This was after the Second World War. The map they used had it marked Stonehedge. One of the two friends told a friend of mine how to get there."

"So you can help me find it?" Luna said.

"Yes, but not tonight," Maryann said. "It's past midnight and Keegan and I have to work in the morning. Friday's our second busiest day of the week. We need some sleep."

Luna's shoulders seemed to droop in disappointment.

"It's not just that," Keegan said. "I'll need daylight to find it. But you need darkness, Luna. I'll go tomorrow after work, a few hours before sundown. I'll hike in and, assuming I find it, I'll set up a beacon to mark the spot for you. That way you can fly in whenever it's dark enough, probably after 8 o'clock or 8:30."

"Excuse *me*," Maryann said sharply. "You mean *we'll* hike in—not *you*. You and I will go together. We'll find the place, set up the beacon, and hike back while there's still light enough to see."

"But Mom—"

"Don't *but Mom* me! We don't want to be in those woods after dark with a six-foot gargoyle lurking in the shadows! Excuse my French, Luna, or my lack of it, I meant six-foot *gargouille*. If Faucon gets wind of this he'll show up with his sword. Even without it the two of us are no match for him. You saw him on the security tape, Keegan. He's like a sumo wrestler and a samurai rolled into one."

Before Keegan could protest, Luna said, "Your mother's right. You two go together in the daylight when Faucon cannot risk the exposure.

If you can find Stonehedge and mark it and return before dark you will be fine."

"And what about you?" Keegan asked. "What if you find our beacon after dark and Faucon appears? Will you be fine, too?"

Luna dodged the question. "Faucon does not know where or when to go. He has no idea where I am now, or where I am staying. How can he follow me? And he does not know our plan, because we just made it."

Luna saw that Keegan hadn't forgotten the question—*will you be fine, too*. She also sensed Maryann's worry.

"Perhaps it would be best if we returned to my original idea," she said. "If you draw me a good map I will find this Stonehedge. There is no sense putting you two in harm's way."

CHAPTER 34

Maryann and Keegan left for Annie's a half hour early on Friday morning. They packed jackets and flashlights for the hike, along with jeans and running shoes they could change into after work. On the way to the bookstore they stopped at a hardware store for a couple of small lanterns and a bottle of lamp oil.

When 4 o'clock arrived, they jumped into the Subaru and headed for Bald Hill Crossing. By 4:20 Maryann was parking in the gravel lot at the Elks Lodge. The two of them wriggled into their jeans and running shoes and tied their jackets around their waists. With flashlights and lanterns in hand they set out to find the stream Ed Whitcomb had told the town historian about. They followed it a half mile into the woods until they reached the confluence of several brooks, and turned according to Ed's directions. They walked uphill until a copse of tall straight pines stood in a line before them like a firing squad.

"This is it, Mom," Keegan said. "It has to be. Stonehedge should be right behind those trees."

They walked uphill. Scraggly bushes and small saplings filled the space between the big pines and oaks like caulking, rendering Stonehedge invisible from the brook trail. When they got up close they could see that behind the natural camouflage was a high wall of oblong granite blocks.

"There's no paint on it, no graffiti," Maryann said, and placed the flat of her palm against the wall. "Amazing. It's like uncovering the tip of a pyramid that's been buried under the desert sands for centuries, waiting to be discovered."

"You go that way and I'll go this way," Keegan said. "See if there's a window or a door to get in. Remember, it's supposed to be eight or nine feet high on this low side, but it's only about six feet high on the uphill side. I'll meet you around back."

They worked their way around the granite cabin, inspecting as they went, until they met exactly opposite from where they had split up.

"Solid granite," Keegan said.

"My side, too," Maryann said. "Which means there's no way in or out. The spaces between blocks are barely the width of a mail slot. You'd have trouble sliding an L.L. Bean catalog through."

"It's more like a monument than a cabin," Keegan said. "Even a mausoleum would have a door. There's no way LeClair and Diana could have lived here. How could she have gotten inside to lay her eggs, and how could he get out after he covered her up?"

Maryann shook her head. "I'm thinking Stonehedge may be an interesting find, but I'm not sure it's the place Luna's after." "It's got to be, Mom. The dimensions check out. Let's try the roof."

Maryann stretched and placed a hand on one of the roof slabs. "Your rock-climbing skills may be good, Keegan, but mine aren't. I'll need a ladder or a crane."

"Oh, come on, Mom. We do the Alley-Oop upsy-daisy."

Keegan squatted with her back against the granite wall and laced the fingers of both hands together. "Put your foot here and your hand on my shoulder. After you straighten up, I'll give you a boost. Grab the top edge of the roof and step on my shoulder. Then swing your leg up and on top."

A minute later Maryann was on her tummy on the roof. Keegan followed her by using the spaces between blocks as finger and toeholds. The roof was covered with a carpet of pine needles and blow-down branches.

"Byron Littlefield was right," Keegan said. "The walls are long building blocks—like extra-long sticks of butter—but the roof is made of thinner slabs. They remind me of our deck planks, except these are extra wide. I wonder if the spaces between were chinked or tarred in LeClair's day, to keep the rain out."

"I'm still not sure about this place, Keegan. Would Chamberlain really have this custom built for LeClair and Diana with no way to get in? It really does seem more like a forgotten mausoleum."

"It looks like what Coburn and Laymon described. The dimensions are right."

Maryann said, "Without Ed's directions we'd never have seen it from the trail. And with this canopy of trees overhead and the deadfall on the roof you'd never spot it from the air."

"Which is what the lanterns are for, Mom. So Luna can locate it from above. Let's get them going." They divided the oil between the two lamps, lit them, and set them on opposite ends of the roof.

Maryann said, "What's Luna going to do after she finds this place—rip the roof off with her bare hands?"

Keegan gave her mother a funny look, then reached over the edge and felt a slab's thickness. "Eight to ten inches, maybe a foot." She pulled out her cellphone and searched Google to find the weight of granite. She used her phone's calculator.

"It's 159 pounds per cubic foot. If my guess is about right on the length, width, and thickness of a roof slab, that's roughly 3500 pounds –almost two tons. How much do you think a female *gargouille* can bench press?"

"Not that much," Maryann said. "Luna's got some heavy lifting to do."

Keegan inspected the spaces between slabs.

"The slabs are old-school, not like the smooth polished surfaces on modern gravestones. The Millenium website says theirs are now milled with special machines they didn't have in the 1860s. So these edges resemble chipped stone tools or arrowheads. That accounts for the uneven spaces between slabs."

"Still not wide enough for Luna to squeeze through. She won't even get her hand in one of those cracks."

"Even tighter squeeze for Faucon," Keegan commented. She bent down close to one of the gaps and sniffed the air.

"What is it?" Maryann asked.

"Nothing. That's just it. Both Byron Littlefield and Ed Smith commented on the odor. Graveyard dirt, they said. But all I smell is soil."

"Suggesting what?"

"I don't know, exactly. Maybe a slower rate of decomposition. Or maybe the eggs have already rotted and returned to the earth. But it doesn't stink. Luna's chances of finding anything viable may not be so great."

"Can you see inside?"

Keegan shone her flashlight through the crack. "Pretty black. I assume there's a lot of silt and loam on the floor down there. It could be tarpaper or a pool of oil, it's that dark. And there's nothing to give perspective."

"So we're sure this is Byron Littlefield's Stonehedge, but is it the same as the granite cabin Luna is after? Or is her sister's body someplace else?"

"Don't know," Keegan answered. "What we do know, though, is that Luna's going to need a crane or some dynamite to bust in here. Otherwise she's not getting the eggs—if they're even down there."

"So can we go home now?"

"We can. We've done our part."

CHAPTER 35

By the time they got home it was 7:15, not full dark, but because the house was in the woods, there wasn't much light around it. Maryann snapped on the kitchen and living room lights first thing.

"So now we just wait?" Keegan asked, plopping down on the couch.

"Luna will get back to us, maybe late tonight. I think chances are slim that—even if she gets inside—she'll find anything."

"If she does find some eggs—or even *one* egg," Keegan moped, "we won't know about it, because she'll take it and fly like a bat out of hell for the Allagash to stay ahead of Faucon."

"Let me rephrase my earlier response," Maryann said. "If she *can't* reach the eggs, she'll get back to us tonight or tomorrow to ask for help. If she does get to them, we won't hear from her for a long time. So can we agree that no news is good news?"

"Unless something happens to her. Then no news is bad news."

Maryann shook her head as if to say, "Teenagers," then walked to the kitchen to work on an omelet. But when she opened the refrigerator and saw the two rows of eggs in door's side tray, she couldn't do it. She pulled a package of frozen enchiladas out of the freezer instead and turned on the toaster oven, then went to work on two salads.

Keegan migrated to her bedroom where the banana crate was sitting on the bed. She pulled off the lid and looked inside.

The internship files were on top. She set them aside. The little yellow grocery pad was there, and the recorder with the shoebox of interviews. She thumbed through the tapes, but nothing grabbed her interest.

There were other things in the box she hadn't looked at the day before: a stack of class notebooks. English Literature. Journalism. French History. Media in the 20th Century. Anthropology. Psychology. Creative Writing. She picked up the Creative Writing notebook, propped a couple of pillows against the headboard, and got comfortable.

Some of the pages had lecture notes Zelda had taken in class. There were also jotted-down titles of short stories and the literary magazines they had been published in, beneath which were her mother's capsule reviews in a few sentences. Zelda had copied several bullet-point lists from *Writer's Digest,* including 8 points from an article titled "Putting Flesh on Your Characters' Bones," next to which was penciled a five-pointed star and the word *Excellent!*

Keegan found short stories her mother had started—in-class "story seed" assignments—but hadn't finished, probably because time had run out. These didn't even qualify as rough drafts; they were stream-of-consciousness starts under time pressure.

Halfway through the notebook Keegan came across a piece in longhand. At the top of the page Zelda had printed the assignment: *In <750 words describe an emotional experience: funny, scary, enlightening, uplifting, etc. (*not sexual).*

Keegan chuckled at the notation *not sexual* and wondered if it had been the professor's instructions or something Zelda herself had added. Probably the professor's. She could imagine students reading X-rated essays aloud.

Twelve hours after the happiest moment of my life came the most terrifying. Early in the morning I tested positive with a home pregnancy kit, which thrilled me. I saw the color of the stick and sat on the toilet seat for ten minutes, gulping breaths of air and sobbing for joy. I had been trying for months, and I was excited at the idea of being a mother. My older sister was fine with it, too, even though I would be a single mother, and said she looked forward to being an aunt.

That evening I had to drive a classmate to Bangor so we could use the Public Library for her genealogy project. When she got in the car, I blurted out my test results. She was thrilled, partly for me and partly, I suspect, because she wasn't able to get pregnant herself. We talked about it all the way from campus to Bangor.

The library lot was full and every street spot was taken, so I left my friend, who has trouble walking, as close as I could get to the library door. I drove to the parking garage up the block and walked back.

We did our research, and when the library closed, she waited in the little lobby while I ran to get the car. I told her five minutes max.

I had left my car on the first level. There had been a dozen cars there when I parked, but now there were only two, mine and another next to it. When I got close, someone stepped out from behind a concrete support. I started to back away, but a second man grabbed me from behind and put a knife to my throat. He said if I screamed, he'd cut my throat. I was terrified and had no voice.

The first man used a key to open the trunk of the other car. He pulled a roll of duct tape out of his pocket and taped my mouth and wrists. He was about to tape my ankles when my friend suddenly appeared near the entrance to the garage and walked toward us. The men stared at her. She marched forward, not shuffling as awkwardly as she did during the daytime.

The men sat me on the edge of the trunk. The man who had held the knife at my throat turned to face my friend. He extended the knife threateningly in front of him, swishing it back and forth.

The first man pulled a pistol out of his coat and aimed it at my friend. "Pretend you didn't see anything," he said to her.

My friend kept coming, finally stopping four feet away from them. "I warned you, sister," the man with the gun said.

Her left hand suddenly came out from behind her hip with some- thing like a machete, but longer. There was a flash in the air—the light from the overhead bulb reflecting off steel, maybe—and suddenly the hand holding the knife and the hand holding the pistol were on the concrete. Two right hands! Both men screamed and clutched their wrist stumps which, after a moment, began to gush blood through their left hands' clenched fingers.

"Get out while you're alive," my friend growled. As they reached for the severed hands, she said, "Leave them. The police will want your fingerprints." When they looked up in shock, she said, "Go!"

They fled the garage on foot.

She peeled off my tape and asked if I could drive. I told her I could,
so she put me behind the wheel.

"Don't report it. The police will find the hands and the car and
tie them to other crimes. Just go."

Was Zelda's story fact or fiction? Keegan didn't know. Maybe a combination. She headed downstairs with the notebook, calling out "Mom. Mom. Come on. We've got to go back."

CHAPTER 36

While Maryann read her sister's creative writing assignment, Keegan ran out to the deck and down the outside stairs. Under the deck were two cords of firewood covered by a tarp. Next to them sat a plywood box with a hinged lid in which they stored their kindling wood and a few tools. Keegan opened it and pulled out an ax and an iron splitting wedge. She carried them around the Subaru and placed them in back with the flashlights.

In the garage on a wall spike she found the tow chain they kept in the Subaru in winter in case they needed to help someone out of a ditch. She took it down and picked up the brand new Come-Along that had been sitting in the corner since the hurricane. She had talked her mother into buying the hand winch after watching Cliff Bragdon—not in his cop hat but in his firewood business cap—use his own Come-Along to drop a hurricane-damaged tree in their back yard. Heavy rains had softened the ground around the tree and the wind had tipped it precariously in the direction of the deck and roof. Keegan couldn't imagine how Cliff was going to prevent the leaning tree from falling on the deck and roof. If he chain-sawed the base of its trunk, where else could it possibly fall but directly on the house? It was a simple matter of gravity.

But Cliff had retrieved his hand-crank Come-Along from his truck and run its cable around the damaged tree. He attached the other end of the Come-Along line to a stable tree farther out in the woods, levered the handle, and winched the tree back to the upright position and a little more. He chain-sawed a notch in the tree's base and gradually increased the tension on the cable. When the tree finally fell, it landed 180 degrees away from the house.

Wow, she'd said.

Simple physics, Cliff had answered. *And tools.*

Two days later she convinced Maryann they needed their own Come-Along.

She placed the tow chain and the Come-Along in the car and went inside for supper.

☞ ☞ ☞

The enchiladas and salad had barely had time to settle in her stomach when Maryann fired up the Subaru.

"Let's go, Keegan," she yelled. "I invited Aaron along. He'll meet us at the Elks."

"I'm hurrying," Keegan called from the garage, where she grabbed a pair of yellow reflective vests from the handlebars of their bikes. She unclipped two thumb-size flashers from their bike helmets and pocketed them and walked out to the car.

Ten minutes later they reached Bald Hill Crossing and a minute after that were driving down the long dirt road to the remote Elks Club. Aaron was standing in front of his Jeep in uniform, service piece in his hip holster.

"I've got to be on duty in a couple hours," he said when they were parked and out of their car. "I'm not expecting this to take long, but I figured if it did I wouldn't have time to drive home and change. This way I can go right to the station."

"So you can only stay two hours?" Keegan asked.

He gave a what-can-I-say shrug.

The Jeep's passenger door opened and AJ stepped out, grinning. "Hi. I didn't want to miss the party, if there is one. Plus, I was bored."

Keegan and Maryann shook their heads.

A minute later Cliff Bragdon pulled up and buzzed down the window of his Wells Police Department SUV. "Somebody call in about a gang of rowdies drinking behind the Elks Club? Which one of you specifically asked for me?"

Aaron raised a hand.

"And why would you do that?" Cliff asked.

"Before I answer, let me ask: Did you catch up on your reading this afternoon—as in Chamberlain's *Night Hawks*?"

"Cover to cover. Practically memorized it. You want to tell me what in hell *night hawks* are? They sound suspiciously like something from a *Harry Potter* movie or members of Robert Pattinson's vampire family in *Twilight*. And what does that have to do with a disturbance behind the Elks Club?"

Keegan and Maryann brought the other three up to speed fast. They didn't mention Zelda's story about the parking garage in Bangor.

"And you're spinning out this story with straight faces?" Cliff asked. "Gargoyles?"

"*Gargouilles*," Maryann said, her face dead serious, repeating the French pronunciation for Cliff. "Luna and Faucon are gar-*gwees*. Not gargoyles."

"Okay, okay," Cliff replied, and exaggerated both syllables. "*Gar-gwee*. And now you and Keegan are here to help this Luna open the tomb and gather her sister's eggs?"

"Exactly," Maryann said.

Cliff shook his head. "And you want Aaron and me to ride shotgun—to be the police presence in case Faucon the evil garglee flies in and makes trouble?"

"Gar-*gwee*, not garg-*lee*," Keegan corrected, and when Cliff didn't blink, she went on. "Essentially, yes, that's why we asked you to join us. While it's unlikely Faucon will show—considering he doesn't know where Stonehedge is—if he should happen to swoop down we'd appreciate a little protection. Keep in mind how he looked in our store security video: large and scary—as in *The Incredible Hulk*. Plus he perforated the Bear's Den graveyard and knocked Elly Stedman out cold."

Maryann added, "Luna says he's really invested in stopping her from getting to the eggs."

Cliff shook his head in disbelief and gave a little laugh. "I can almost guarantee there's not another police department in New England—maybe not in this whole wide world—that's talking about flying garglees right now. But silly as it sounds, Aaron and I have to take this seriously. Since we may encounter the guy who ran over Stedman like a snowplow taking out a road sign, I'll set my Taser to full power. Aaron's going to do the same. We've got your backs."

"I doubt you'll need the Tasers," Keegan said. "But thank you." She smiled. "Right now we need to get a move on. The sun's behind the trees. It'll be dark in the woods any minute. Let's put on the reflector vests."

Maryann and Keegan put their bike vests on, and Aaron got his traffic vest from the Cherokee. Cliff pulled two more out of the SUV, put one on and handed the other to AJ.

Keegan handed the tow rope to her mother, the Come-Along to AJ, and strapped the fanny pack around her own waist. She slipped the splitting wedge into the pouch and grabbed her ax and flashlight.

"Everybody got a flashlight?" she asked. When they all showed them, she said, "Let's go."

"We're off to see the lizard," Cliff mumbled.

Nobody laughed.

CHAPTER 37

They walked single file down the dark woods path, slowly and quietly picking their way along, trying not to slip or trip. The darkness made it different from Keegan and Maryann's hike to Stonehedge four hours earlier.

When Keegan reached the place where the two other brooks cut across the stream path, she turned and shone her flashlight up one of them, trying to locate the path she and Maryann had been on, but nothing looked familiar now. She had been counting on the two lanterns they had set out on the roof for Luna.

But there was only blackness. She aimed the beam down at the crossing brook and the lightly worn path along its bank. *This has to be the right one. Uphill. Not that far.* She tried to look confident and waved for the others to follow.

A hundred yards up the slope she turned her light toward the spot where she thought Stonehedge was, sweeping the beam back and forth across the hill. There were trees and bushes but not the picket row of pines concealing Stonehedge.

She pushed up the path another 25 yards and peered into the gloom again. No sign of the beacons that should have appeared like twin lighthouses. Without them everything seemed disproportionate, distorted, and dark. She felt disoriented, her distances off. But she was certain she had made the correct turn at the crossing brook. They had to be right on top of Stonehedge.

Another 30 yards and she turned her light up a different piece of the sloping ground. There they were—the trees aligned like a stockade wall around a fort. But no beacons. Had the oil burned that fast? In both lamps? She and Maryann had dumped in plenty of oil, and they'd barely been gone four hours.

"This is it," she whispered loudly. "You can't see the stone walls in the dark, but they're there, behind those trees."

"The lamps have gone out," Maryann said.

"Luna must have shut them off," Keegan suggested.

"Or Faucon did," AJ countered.

Aaron tried to take charge. "Okay, first thing is for me and Cliff to check it out, make sure it's safe. Wait here. Cliff, you go left, I'll go right."

"Wait," Keegan said. "You need me with you. If Luna is there in the dark, she won't know you. And you should know that the easiest place to get on the roof is on the other side where the hill gives you a few feet."

"Point taken," Aaron said. "But stay behind me."

"Aaron, Cliff, no guns," Maryann warned. "Tasers only. It's dark and I don't want Keegan, or one of you, or Luna getting shot."

They agreed and began the climb, the three of them carrying flashlights, Aaron and Cliff holding their Tasers. Keegan gripped her ax handle below the steel ax head.

Byron Littlefield had been right—it did feel like they were creeping up on a German bunker, except that when they got up close to the lower wall, they saw no firing ports or other openings. Aaron and Keegan felt their way around it to the right. Cliff went left. They met at high ground along the back.

"Not sure I could pass basic training again," Cliff said, breathing heavily.

Aaron said, "I can't believe we never knew about this place when we were growing up."

"It's like an ancient Incan temple the jungle swallowed up," Cliff said. "Keep your eyes peeled for a giant boulder rolling out of a tunnel at us."

"Funny, Indy," Keegan said. "But you're right about the jungle thing. Byron Littlefield's generation was probably the last to see Stonehedge before the trees and vegetation covered it up. It's like all those forgotten family graveyards the historical society found and cleared recently."

"They missed this one," Aaron said.

"Because it's not officially a cemetery," she reminded. "As Laymon's book points out: no human remains."

Cliff asked, "Ready to climb up onto the roof? We need to see what happened to your lanterns."

"Just a minute," Keegan said. She stretched her arm upward and set the ax on the roof, then put her lit flashlight next to it. She hooked her fingers over the edge of a roof slab, did a pullup, and peeked over the top. "Luna, this is Keegan. If you're up here on the roof or higher up on a tree limb, I want you to know that I'm down here. AJ's brother Aaron is with me, so is our friend Cliff. They're both Wells cops and are here to help us." When she got no answer she said, "Luna, if you're up here, answer me."

No answer.

She raised her voice slightly, not quite shouting. "Luna, this is Keegan. Do you need help?"

Still no answer.

Maybe she's down in the chamber. Or she could have gotten in, grabbed the eggs, and shut off the lanterns on the way out.

"Push me up the rest of the way," she said to Aaron and Cliff.

They did, and she climbed onto the roof and got to her feet, flashlight in left hand and ax in right. She swept the light over the entire roof. The lanterns were exactly where she and Maryann had left them, one on each end. Both were dark. She walked to one and checked the reservoir. Plenty of oil. She lit it and walked to the other. Also plenty of oil. She lit that one, too.

If Luna found a way to get inside, she'd have needed one of the lanterns to find the eggs. She'd have left it down there on her way out, she wouldn't have brought it back up to the roof. Which means she was here but couldn't find a way in. She's gone somewhere to make a new plan. She knows where Stonehedge is and doesn't need the beacons anymore.

"Luna," she said, giving it one last try. "This is Keegan. I'm here on the roof."

No answer. No voice. No whoosh or flap of wings.

She isn't expecting me. She had no way of knowing I was coming back. I didn't know it myself. Now I'm here again and I've brought a crowd along.

If she's watching, she can probably see Aaron and Cliff have Tasers and guns.

"Aaron, Cliff? You two need to leave. Luna may have heard us coming. She doesn't know you, and you're both armed. She may think you want to capture her."

"What is this—King Kong on Skull Island?" Cliff asked, annoyed. "We're not after her. We're after the other garglee. He's the one who's committed crimes."

"I can't leave you alone, Keegan," Aaron said.

"That's very gallant, Aaron," she replied. "I'm not asking you to go home. I just want you and Cliff to move back down where Mom and AJ are. If it's just me, Luna may show herself. Please go back down and wait quietly."

Aaron hesitated.

"I'll be fine, Aaron. I promise. You'll still be able to hear me if I shout. And the lanterns are lit."

Two minutes later Keegan was standing at the center of the roof, listening to the rustling sounds of the two cops fumbling their way downhill by flashlight. She knew what Byron and Ed had been describing when they said they heard something in the bushes that night in 1947. Cliff and Aaron sounded like grizzly bears or rhinos thrashing about in the dark.

Section IX

The Impregnable Fortress

CHAPTER 38

"Luna," she said again in her calmest everyday voice. "My friends are gone. It's just you and me, your friend Keegan."

No answer.

She pulled the splitting wedge out of her fanny pack.

If Diana and LeClair lived here from 1862 to 1916, how did they get in and out? If LeClair covered her up with their eggs, would he have sealed the chamber when he left? Since he would have planned to return, how would he get back in?

She walked over to the edge of the roof where she had climbed on. The slab ends rested on the oblong blocks, and any chinking between slabs was long gone. She inserted the beak of the wedge into the space between two slabs and tapped it with the fat head of her ax, lightly at first then harder. The nearly two ton slabs inched apart, but they could only move back so far before butting against the next slab behind them.

Luna's going to have to lose a lot of weight to squeeze through. She sat down, trying not to feel defeated, and stared at one of the slabs she had just moved an inch. Suddenly she had a vision. *A hinged door. Sure. Why not leave the slab right there but flip it up on its side—like a domino on its narrow edge?* She crossed the roof to the high side that faced the brook trail.

"AJ, can you hear me?"

"I hear you. Everything alright?"

"It's fine. But I need you to bring up my Come-Along and the tow chain. I don't need a crowd—just you and those two things."

"Be right up." A beam of light advanced up the hill and a few minutes later AJ was handing the equipment to Keegan.

"Climb up," Keegan said. "I need your help." AJ found finger and toe holds and scaled the wall.

"Your mom's getting antsy and the guys are getting bored. What's the plan?"

"See this roof piece? Imagine it's a huge deck plank, only we want to turn it 90 degrees"—Keegan used a hand gesture—"so it's balanced on its narrow edge."

"You're kidding, right?" AJ said. "That thing weighs a ton."

"Closer to two, actually. But we have physics and tools on our side." Keegan patted the ratchet lever of the Come-Along. "*We* don't lift it, the Come-Along does—same way Cliff used his to pull a leaning tree away from our house."

"You always were the tool girl. I knew it when you built our first tree-house. All I did was carry the wood."

"It's also called a portable hand winch," Keegan said, picking it up. She flicked the safety off and unwound some of the slack cable from the spool. "You stay right here and hold onto it. It's like a fishing rod: you keep playing out the line until you set the take-up on the reel and start winding it in again. Instead of catching a fish, though, I'm going to take the cable and run it around that big tree and secure it. Just hang onto the main unit." She took the cable, wrapped it around the tree, and set the hook, then walked back to AJ.

"See that other hook?" Keegan asked, pointing down at the Come-Along. "We'll attach that to our tow chain after we get the chain wrapped around the slab like a belt. Then we'll just reel it in so it tilts the slab up on its side."

"But how do we get the tow chain around the slab?"

"This is where it takes two of us," Keegan said. "Watch."

She sat down, removed both laces from her running shoes, and knotted them together to double the length. She held it between her outstretched hands so it hung down between them like a smile.

"This is exactly what you're going to do," she told AJ. "Droop it down through that narrow gap on your side of the slab." She handed AJ the line.

"What are you going to do?" AJ asked.

"Notice how the space on my side of the slab is bigger than yours? I used my splitting wedge to widen it. I can squeeze my hand through with the chain, which I'm going to get swinging. I'll see if I can catch it on your line. Once I do, you pull it up and we can connect the two ends of the chain. Got it?"

"Easy peezy," AJ said, and lowered Keegan's drooping double shoestring.

Keegan got on her tummy with the chain and inserted her arm in the gap. In less than a minute they had it, and a minute after that the tow chain was fastened around the slab with the Come-Along hook attached to it. Keegan started cranking the winch handle.

Ten minutes later the 3500 pound slab stood on its thinnest edge next to a foot-and-a-half wide opening that revealed a chamber that was open for the first time in 100 years.

"Physics and tools," a sweaty Keegan told AJ, almost gloating.

"Now all we need is Luna," AJ said.

Keegan tried the new phone number in her contacts list. A man answered.

"Franciscan Guest House. Brother Jerome speaking. How may I help you?"

Keegan hadn't expected this and had to think fast. "Brother Jerome, I'm trying to track down an old friend of my mother. I heard she's in town. A French-Canadian nun."

"Sister Therese?"

"Could be." Keegan adlibbed. "Mom would have known her by her given name—you know, before she got her nun name. All I know is, she's very short and round-shouldered and dresses in a really old-time habit with veil and gloves."

"That would be her: Sister Therese. She went out earlier. Didn't say when she'd return."

"Can I leave her a message?"

"Of course. I'll slip a note under her door."

Keegan gave the friar her message and her cell number.

"Okay," he said. "Let me repeat it back. *Zelda's daughter found your sister's can opener. Is that all?*"

"That's it. She'll know what I mean. Thank you, Brother Jerome." She hung up.

"So what do we do now?" AJ asked.

"We wait."

☙☙☙

But Keegan wasn't good at waiting. Barely a minute passed before she got onto her stomach and stuck her arm through the now wide opening into the chamber.

"Keegan," AJ hissed. "Don't do that. If this slab falls over, it'll take your arm or your head off."

"The Come-Along is still holding it in place, AJ. It can only fall the opposite way, away from the opening."

Keegan shone her flashlight into the gloom. With her vantage point limited, she had to change positions a few times. Yet no matter the angle, it looked the same: shadowy granite walls and black dirt floors. She made out several large roots along the surface.

"A couple of roots must have snaked under the walls," she commented to AJ.

"Do they connect to anything?" AJ asked. "Like something resembling a body?"

"Not that I can see."

Nothing suggested to Keegan that the room had ever been lived in— no remnants of tables or chairs or a bed, no plates or dishes, no shards of anything that might have broken.

And no outline, impression, or mound. Part of Keegan was relieved.

"It's like an empty dungeon," Keegan said. "All it needs is some shackles and chains on the walls. It'd make a great root cellar—if it only had a door. Smells like somebody just opened a bag of potting soil. But there's no obvious grave, if that's what you're asking."

Keegan's cellphone rang. She sat up and answered it. It was Maryann on the brook path.

"Cliff had to hit the road. He's going off shift and needs to get the car back and sign out. Aaron's got a couple more minutes, but then he's out, too. He's got to go on duty. Their advice is to snuff the lanterns and go home, maybe check in the morning when it's daylight again to see if Luna came back."

Mom doesn't know we have it open.

From where she was standing Maryann couldn't see Keegan shaking her head, but she sensed it. *Will she argue or will she bite her tongue and give in?*

Silence.

"Keegan, we do have to work tomorrow."

Still no answer.

"Keegan, Aaron's got to go."

A short hesitation, then, "Oh, okay. We'll be right down. Tell him he can go."

"Do you want me to come up there and help you carry anything back down?"

"No, Mom. We can leave them and get them tomorrow. Tell Aaron to go on, and you wait for us there. We'll just be a minute."

Keegan heard her mother say to Aaron, "Yes, I'll make sure the girls keep moving. Don't worry about us. We won't be far behind." Then a light started moving along the trail toward the Elks Lodge.

Keegan walked over to one lantern and AJ to the other.

"Put them out? AJ asked. "Or leave them so Luna can see the place is open?"

"Mom will wait a minute for us," Keegan answered, and carried her lantern to the opening. She sat down and once again pulled the laces out of her running shoes. "Take yours out, too," she told AJ. "I need all four."

"What are we doing?" AJ asked, and removed hers then handing them over.

"You'll see."

Keegan used all four to make a single longer hand line that she tied to the lantern handle. She lowered it into the chamber. When she ran out of string, the lamp was still two feet above the dirt floor.

"I can't drop it. It might break or go out," Keegan said. "Come over here and grab my ankles. You may have to sit on my feet to keep me from slipping in."

"What are you going to do?"

"I'm going to leave the light on for Luna."

Keegan got onto her side, still holding the end of the string, and wriggled around onto her tummy. AJ got ready to grab her ankles. A moment later the lantern touched the floor and sank a little ways into the soft soil. It lit much of the room.

"It worked!" Keegan exclaimed.

"Great, genius!" AJ said. "Now how are you going to untie it? We don't want to walk back without laces in our shoes."

"Got a good grip?" Keegan asked. "I'm coming up."

AJ put her weight on Keegan's ankles and Keegan swiveled up and out of the opening, then blinked a few times to clear away the dizziness that came from being upside-down.

"You let go of the string, didn't you, Keegan?" AJ said. "You dropped our laces inside."

"Not a problem. I'll untie it in a minute."

"What? Oh, Keegan, come on. Don't go down there. I'm serious. This isn't a good idea."

"Step back." Keegan cautioned, and released the tension on the Come-Along cable. She made sure the slab stayed balanced without the support tension, then ever so gently removed the cable hook from the tow chain. "It'll take more than a breeze to knock that thing over," she declared, and when AJ looked unconvinced, she added, "But stay out of its way just the same. A shove or an accidental bump might tip it. Keep your distance."

AJ's mouth hung open.

Keegan went to the tree and removed the other end of the cable. She connected it to a different pine at the opposite end of the roof and returned to the opening. She grabbed the winch assembly and lowered it into the hole. It hung three feet to the side of the lantern.

"Keegan! AJ!" Maryann's voice called across the quiet woods. "Let's go. Now!" They saw her flashlight waving at them from the bottom of the hill.

"Be right there, Mom!" Keegan yelled. To AJ she said, "Once I start shinnying down, you'll have to answer her."

"What? You're going down there? Great. Thanks a lot. And what will I say?"

"You'll think of something. If you have to, invite her up. Anything to buy me some time."

"Looking for the eggs is Luna's job, Keegan, not yours."

Keegan didn't answer. She removed her lace-less running shoes, stripped off her socks, then pulled the shoes back on. She slipped the socks over her hands and held them out for AJ to see.

"Gloves. Don't want my hands getting shredded on the cable."

AJ shook her head. "You idiot, Keegan. How will you get back up? The socks are fine for the way down, but they're going to slip when you come back up."

Keegan grinned. "If I have to, I can hook my belt to the Come-Along and ratchet myself up." She chuckled.

A moment later AJ watched her best friend descend into a chamber that might—or might not—hold the crumbling bones of a *gargouille* holding close her nest of 100 year-old eggs.

CHAPTER 39

Keegan went down slowly, sock-wrapped hands clutching the cable, legs scissoring it, feet and ankles braking. Going down was difficult enough, pulling herself back up the slender wire was going to be harder.

She paused with her feet a few inches above the dirt floor, not wanting to touch it, at least not right away. The space felt sacred, and violating it made her feel like a grave robber. She had no business being here; it was Luna's mission, not hers. Yet she felt compelled by some inner compass to press on.

Her arms grew shaky, though, and she needed to release her legs' scissor grip on the cable, so she untangled them and let her arms straighten above her, lowering herself until she felt her feet touch. Except it wasn't solid ground, it was a soft mulchy layer, and she sank to her ankles the way the lantern had earlier. Loose soil spilled into her lace-less running shoes. She had said it smelled like potting soil, now she knew that's what its consistency was: airy and not tamped down by anyone in decades. She took one hand off the cable and stood still, relieved to have her normal sense of balance back. She kept the other sock-gloved hand on it, not daring to take a step in any direction yet.

"You okay down there?" AJ called from above.

"I'm fine. The top layer is fluffy. I'm going to untie the lantern and walk around, check the place out more closely."

She slipped the socks from her hands and stuffed them into her pocket, then removed the line from the lantern handle and pocketed it. She picked up the lamp, noting that it left an inch-deep impression in the loose soil. She half stepped and half slid her right foot forward toward the nearest wall, then set it down, letting it sink in until it felt grounded, her weight evenly distributed over both feet. She waited.

This is like playing Twister—except I can't see where the colored circles are. And they may not be circles at all; they may be land mines or holes.

She took another step forward with the same result. Then another. She had a sense the floor was level and solid a few inches below the soft covering. A half step to the wall. She reached out and touched it. Cool, surprisingly dry, not damp. And no mold that she could see or feel. No grit, either. Unlike sandstone, pink granite apparently held up well.

"Any graffiti?" AJ asked.

"You mean like Neanderthal cave drawings?"

"I was thinking partiers."

"Well, there's something here," Keegan said.

"Seriously?"

"Let's see. Looks like one is chipped into the granite. Second is written in what looks like charcoal. Third one's in sidewalk chalk."

"Wow! Can you read what they say?"

"Let me see. Umm, first one says: *Fred and Wilma.* Second says: *Tom and Huck.* Third one says: *Puff, the Magic Dragon.*"

Silence above. Then, "Not funny, Keegan. Is there anything on them or not?"

"No, AJ, there's nothing here. No graffiti, beer cans, bottles, or Twinkie wrappers. Nobody spray-painted Wells High here, either. It's more like a windowless prison cell, a dungeon. Let me work my way around the edges and see if anything's different. If Luna's sister is buried in the center, I don't want to step on her."

"Oh, thanks a lot. Had to flash me that mental picture, didn't you?"

Keegan kept the lantern in one hand and placed the other on the wall to steady herself, then picked her way around the inside perimeter. She had gone only a few steps when she barked her shin on a thick root running along the surface. It was one of several she had glimpsed earlier from the roof. She pulled out a sock and slipped it over her hand again, then brushed the soil off the sides of the root, trying to figure out where it came from. It disappeared under the wall.

"What'd you find?" AJ called down.

"A root. Twice as thick as my wrist. Must have snaked in under the wall."

"Is it still alive?"

"Umm, wait a sec." Keegan curled her hand around it. Cool to the touch. She scratched it with her thumbnail, exposing moist tissue under the thin skin. "Yep. Still alive."

"I'm afraid to ask," AJ said, "but where does it go?"

"I don't want to know just yet. I don't want to disturb anything. That's up to Luna. For now, I'm going to keep working my way around, see what else I find." She stepped over the root and continued checking the wall perimeter. Nothing different.

AJ's phone rang up on the roof.

"Keegan," she called down. "It's your mother. Why is she calling me?"

"I probably can't get a signal on mine down here."

It rang again.

"Should I answer?" AJ asked.

"Yeah, answer it. If you have to, tell her to come up."

AJ took the call, and Keegan could hear AJ's half of the conversation.

"Of course she climbed down there. You know Keegan. I tried to talk her out of it, but—"

Impatient squawky noises from the phone's receiver.

"Keegan, your mom says to get out of there right now. She's coming up."

More impatient squawky noises.

"She climbed down that Come-Along thing," AJ said, "like it was a rope in a well. She swears she can climb up it."

More noises. Then disconnect.

"Keegan, she's on her way."

"Help her onto the roof when she gets here. And make sure she knows not to bump the slab that's on edge. I don't want you calling the fire department to extract me."

"You're coming up, right?"

"Not yet. I'm halfway around, almost directly across from that big root. Oops, there's another one on this side. It must come under the wall the same way that other one did. I'll clear away the dirt to be sure."

She started pawing back the black soil with the sock-gloved hand, working faster this time.

"Yep. Just like the first one and about the same thickness. This is the low side of the hill, so it must be from one of those big barrier trees hiding the place."

Keegan heard her mother's voice. "AJ!"

AJ responded. "Be right there, Maryann."

With the lantern in one hand Keegan sighted in on the Come-Along cable and stepped over the root. Her foot sank and kept going. She pitched forward—in her surprise releasing her grip on the lantern handle—and was suddenly blinded by white-hot pain in her leg.

CHAPTER 40

Maryann heard her daughter's cry of pain.

"Keegan!" she yelled, and without waiting for AJ to give her a hand, she found a toehold and a handhold. Powered by a surge of maternal adrenaline, she scrambled up the wall and practically vaulted herself onto the roof.

"Keegan!" she repeated, and started for the opening. "What's wrong?"

"AJ, the slab!" Keegan yelled up.

AJ hissed, "Don't touch that," just as Maryann reached for the balanced slab, expecting to lean on it so she could lower herself to her knees and peer down into the dark chamber.

The words sank into Maryann's brain in the nick of time, and she yanked her hand back as if she'd touched a white-hot woodstove.

"Come over by me," AJ said, and explained. "We need to stay away from that side of the opening. Keegan used her Come-Along to pull it up on its side like that. She had the cable holding it up, but needed to take it off so she could slide down. For now, it's just balanced there."

Maryann got on her hands and knees beside AJ and called into the opening, "Keegan, what happened?"

A moan. "I stepped in a hole and hurt my knee."

They shone their flashlights down and saw Keegan straddling a root. She looked like a runner clearing a hurdle, one leg forward and one trailing, except her torso was leaned slightly more forward.

"Can you reach the cable?" AJ asked.

"Not from here. If I can get myself out of this hole, maybe."

"Where's the lantern?" Maryann asked.

"I lost it when I fell. It must have gone out."

"How about your flashlight?" her mother asked.

"Someplace behind me. It was in my jacket pocket, but it's not there now."

"Can you feel around for it?"

She tried. "No luck."

"Use your cellphone," AJ said. "It's got a flashlight in the utilities."

Keegan fished it out of her jeans and turned the light on. First she shined it up at her mother and AJ, then at the ground around her.

"Don't see the flashlight. It must have sunk down in this soft dirt. I can see the lantern three or four feet in front of me, but it's out of reach until I get my leg out of this hole."

"Can you lean back and pull it out?" Maryann asked. "Or do I need to call 911?"

"No, Mom, don't call 911. It's not a broken leg. Just give me a minute to see what I'm dealing with here."

She held the light over her sunken leg and pawed back the soil.

"Looks like I broke through a rotten plank, like what you'd use to cover an old well. Correction, it gave way where two boards joined. I can't touch bottom when I flex my foot, so there must be some space under them."

"Want me to swing the hook your way?" AJ asked.

"First give me a chance to free my leg. If I can do that, I'll be able to crawl to it. What's a little more dirt on me at this point?"

Keegan leaned back and placed her palms on the root like she was about to rise from a recliner. She pressed down and straightened her arms, then rocked backward, one thigh leveraged against the root, the other lifting as best it could against the knee pain. She gritted her teeth and fought back tears, keeping up the pressure until her trapped calf scraped past the planks and her foot came free.

She lay back in the soft dirt behind the root, the last place she had enjoyed firm footing, and caught her breath. She was sweating from the pain, the exertion, and the chamber's warm close air. When she glanced upward, she saw a pair of faces gazing down on her from the roof.

Are those angels? Is this what Diana saw after LeClair covered her and their eggs up with soil and kissed her goodbye?

She felt the cool dirt cradling the back of her neck and clinging to her hair.

How at peace I am.

Her arms relaxed at her sides, her hands resting on the root. For a brief moment she thought she could feel the life force flowing through it. How long ago had she found that root? She didn't seem to have a grasp of time and she couldn't recall that fact.

A few grains of fine dirt trickled into the shells of her ears—*sand sifting through an hourglass*—tickling her. She had the sensation of sinking, melting into mother earth. The phrase suddenly made sense—*Mother Earth*.

"Keegan!" a voice yelled. "Wake up!"

The voice hadn't been AJ's, and it wasn't quite Maryann's, but it was close. Similar. Familiar.

A bolt of pain shot through her knee again. Had she moved it without intending to? She was suddenly violently alert, eyes wide open, jolted out of her reverie. Her fingers wrapped themselves around the root, gripping it like it was a chin-up bar. She pulled, sitting up fast, and found herself gulping air as if she'd been holding her breath underwater for three minutes.

AJ and her mother watched Keegan snap up.

"What is it?" her mother asked. "Are you okay?"

"I am now. For a minute, though, I felt like it wanted to drain my energy."

"It?" Maryann asked.

"Yes, *it*," Keegan answered. "Whatever that means." She shook her head like she was trying to dry her hair. Particles of dirt came loose. She brushed more off her neck and shoulders, then took off the sock mittens so she could use her pinkies to clean the dirt out of her ears. She pulled the socks back over her hands and slipped the cellphone into her jeans pocket.

"Can you get to the cable now?" AJ asked.

"Try and stop me," Keegan said, and dragged herself over to the Come-Along. "Got it."

"Okay, obviously you can't wrap your knees around it and come up hand-over-hand. So you've got two options. Wrap the cable under your armpits so Maryann and I can pull you up like a Coast Guard rescue. Or attach your belt to the Come-Along hook and winch yourself up."

"I'll take Door Number Two, please," Keegan said, and when AJ and Maryann didn't laugh, she added, "The theory is sound. Good idea, AJ."

She hooked herself up and started jacking the handle. A minute later she was three feet above the chamber floor, suspended by her own belt, her body spinning in a circle ever so slowly.

She heard Maryann's voice on the roof above say, "Luna?"

CHAPTER 41

Maryann's eyes had shifted heavenward at the *whoosh-whoosh* sound overhead. She and AJ first looked toward the moon then tried to focus on the airspace above the treetops. There was movement.

Something larger than a bald eagle appeared—wobbling in flight. No, it wasn't wobbling, it was tilting and circling like a turkey vulture descending on roadkill. But this was larger than a vulture, and its wingspan was broader. The spiral tightened and the shadowy outline grew larger as it got closer.

Maryann wasn't sure whether it was homing in on the remaining lantern or zeroing in on her and AJ. But she knew it had to be a *garugouille*. Which was why she had uttered *Luna*.

But when the *gargouille* was 20 feet above, she knew it wasn't her. This one, in what appeared to be a single fluid motion, retracted its large upper wings and extended it shorter, fast-beating hummingbird wings, touching down on the roof like a Life Star helicopter on a hospital helipad. The short wings disappeared under its arms, leaving the upper glide wings bunched up behind its shoulders—*the hunchback look.*

This *gargouille* was far larger than Luna, Maryann could see, and was clearly a male. A pair of red owlish eyes stared at her from above a flat rubbery gorilla nose. Unlike Luna, who was hornless, this *gargouille* had something like a rhino's horn in the center of his forehead. *Do males have a single horn and females have none?* This was definitely not Luna.

Maryann's and AJ's mouths hung open.

"Faucon," Maryann gasped, then repeated it louder. "Faucon!"

Keegan, dangling by her belt, recognized her mother's stage whisper. She had to free herself fast, but the ratchet noise would call attention to her.

Faucon doesn't know you're down here. It's up to you to get yourself off this hook.

She wrapped the socked-gloved fingers of her dominant hand around the winch assembly and pulled, straining to lift her own dead weight. As she did it, she used the fingers of her left hand to work the belt off the hook. *I only need a couple of inches.* She clenched her teeth, making sure not to grunt, and gave the one-armed pull-up all she had. But she didn't have the lift. She relaxed her lifting arm and hung suspended, limp as a wet towel.

She tried a second time, again failing to pull herself up enough to free the belt from the hook. *I don't have the strength for a third try.* Then it came to her. She placed the weaker hand on the belt buckle itself, near her navel, and grabbed the tucked-in belt tip. She counted to three in her head, gave it all she had lifting with the strong hand, and unfastened her belt. The belt loosened and her dangling body went from horizontal to vertical. Her feet touched the floor, causing pain to shoot through her knee again. But her feet were firmly planted. She let go of the cable and stood there, gritting her teeth, stifling a cry, and catching her breath.

On the roof above, Faucon said to Maryann, "You sounded as if you were expecting someone else. I see that you have heard of me."

His gargantuan torso was bursting with muscle. His head was the size of a watermelon. He would tower over Luna by more than a foot. He was broad across the eyes, with a long jawbone that culminated in a pointed chin with a few ragged goatee hairs. His head appeared to have a natural covering of thick rubbery skin resembling a 1920s football helmet. He was crouching, but even so Maryann guessed that from the crown of his head to the soles of his hairy feet Faucon would stand six-six.

Le gargouille settled on his formidable haunches, and she recalled an image Keegan had shown her online: a crouching Notre Dame gargoyle keeping watch over Paris. Was Faucon preparing to spring or was he simply getting comfortable, waiting for Luna? Maryann didn't doubt Faucon could cover the eight feet between them in a single bound, then shred her and AJ with his talons before they could blink or scream.

Where are his sword and dagger?

She squinted and saw what had to be two hilts sticking up behind his neck like arrows from a pair of quivers.

If he wants to kill us, there's no escape. Act calm. Stall. Aaron or Cliff could come back. Oh, God, please let them come back.

"Why are you here?" she asked him.

His skin is like a crocodile's, greyer than Luna's. She was more alligator, greenish. Hide, Keegan, please find a place to hide down there.

Faucon's mouth moved—a grotesque attempt at a smile. His lips were far too thick for a genuine smile, perhaps four times thicker than Luna's thin ones. And his face was sterner, stonier, and angrier—it lacked flexibility.

Fake cordiality. The good thing is, he hasn't leapt at us or drawn his sword. He won't kill us if he doesn't have to. He just wants to destroy Diana's eggs—his competition.

"One of my relatives," he said, "my uncle's wife—was buried here a long time ago. I told my grandfather I would bring her bones home."

Hide of a crocodile, warmth of a crocodile, lies like a crocodile. Come closer, little deer, I won't bite you.

"Sounds plausible," Maryann replied.

His eyes were red, unlike Luna's which were green. The red eyes dimmed for a moment—dulled—then brightened again.

He blinked. Reptile lids. Protective and also transparent, what a crocodile or an alligator does when submerging. But he wasn't going underwater. Is that blink a "tell," an unintended signal? Is he about to shift gears? Does he know I'm playing him, stalling for time? Or are those lazy lids like a schoolkid's when he's bored?

AJ had seen the blink, too, and stepped back from the cable on which hung the Come-Along assembly and Keegan. *No, the line's slack. Keegan's off the hook.* She turned slightly, keeping her left side toward Faucon, and as she turned she slowly and casually slid her right hand into her jeans pocket. She slipped out her phone, thumbed off the volume switch, and tapped Aaron's number on speed dial. She cupped the phone like she was palming a large playing card and held it behind her.

"I was here earlier," Faucon said. "But I found no entrance. I see you two have opened it. *Merci beaucoup.*" His lids dropped slowly and the bright red eyes dimmed again, then glowed once more when the lids lifted. "You two may leave and I will collect the bones and be on my way home. My grandfather will be pleased."

Liar, Maryann thought. *If your lids are drooping, you're lying. If your mouth is moving, you're lying. Not much of a poker face.*

"You say it's your uncle's wife?" Maryann asked. "Wouldn't that be your aunt?"

AJ was pretty sure Aaron had picked up and was listening by now, so she cut Maryann off, saying, "*Mister* Faucon. May I call you that? Or should I say *Monsieur* Faucon?"

I hope this is plain enough for you, Aaron. How about you and Cliff get your butts back out here?

Keegan heard the insane chatter above and found the only hiding place in the chamber—the hole she had stepped in. She pawed at it like a dog burying a bone, quietly but feverishly clawing and scratching back any loose soil that remained. When she got down to the two planks that had caved under her, she found four boards altogether, each roughly four feet long and a foot wide, making a four-by-four cover. She pried them up and found a space below that was about three feet high by three feet wide space. It didn't drop like a well, but angled away gradually at 45 degrees. She held her phone light over it and saw that the dirt was held back by wall and ceiling planks that had been braced and propped up by long stakes. Could this be a tunnel?

The supports have held up this long without it caving in.

Keegan dropped to her hands and knees then turned around and eased backwards into the hole. She didn't dare enter headfirst in case some part of it had caved in. She pulled the boards over the hole again and disappeared, as if swallowed up by the earth.

CHAPTER 42

Maryann saw Faucon cock his head slightly.

Like a hawk. He's wondering what we know and don't know, trying to figure his next move. If he can get what he wants, he won't have to kill us. But we can't give it to him with Keegan still down there.

"*Monsieur Faucon*," she said, and his head straightened up as if he'd been awakened. "You forgot to bring your shovel."

"Shovel?" He looked confused.

"*La pelle.* To dig up your uncle's wife's bones."

His mouth opened in an *ah-I-see* of recognition. "I have my hands for such a delicate job."

"And how will you carry them? Surely you will need a box or a sack to transport them back to your *grandpere*."

Faucon found himself trapped by the storyline he had begun—*I'm here to retrieve ancestral bones*—even though he knew that wasn't the reason. But he had no idea how much these two knew. It was conceivable that Luna had used the same story—*retrieve my ancestor's bones*—to convince them to open the roof for her.

"I will find them first and return with a container."

Maryann thought, *Luna told us why you're really here.*

"You won't need a container," she said, "if the bones are already in a coffin or a casket. Could they have been burned? If so, they may be in an urn? You must excuse my ignorance, for I am not familiar with the burial practices of *les gargouilles*."

Faucon stood silently brooding. He needed Maryann and AJ out of the way so he could get down inside the chamber.

"How did your uncle's wife die?" AJ asked.

"How did she die?" Faucon repeated, not sure why she was asking.

"Yes," AJ replied. "Was it old age, or an accident, or a disease, or perhaps an epidemic? I've heard that cholera germs can lie dormant for many decades and still infect the person who touches them. You wouldn't want that."

He appeared to weigh the question, then said, "*Naturellement.* She died *naturellement.*"

"So will you two take the bones back together, you and the lady *gargouille?*" AJ asked. "You must come from the same place, so it would only make sense."

Faucon wasn't sure what to say. Maybe Luna really hadn't told these two much at all, except that it was about bringing home ancestral bones. They seemed legitimately curious and eager to help.

"*Oui.* Luna and I came here in search of the bones. We will take them home to my grandfather."

"So you and Luna must be cousins?" Maryann asked. "Or are you just friends?"

"We are …"

Again he was at a loss for words. Maryann didn't know if it was because he was searching for the English or because he hadn't formulated a response before he started speaking.

He finished, "we are both eager to make *mon grandpere* happy."

Maryann glanced skyward. "So we're waiting for Luna—so you and she can do this together?"

AJ caught on and took a step forward out of the way of the slab. She pointed above the trees and said, "Is that her now?"

Faucon's raised his eyes and, as the center of his vision turned upward he caught a movement at the corner of his eye—Maryann stepping behind the slab. She shoved it. It didn't take much to shift it. By the time Faucon's attention returned to the roof, the slab fell back into its original place— *whump*—sealing the opening. The roof again looked like it had in Byron Littlefield's day—except for the silver cable leading from the tree to the crack between two slabs, where it disappeared into the dark.

Aaron and Cliff, get your asses back here, AJ thought.

Sorry, Keegan, Maryann thought. *If he had gone down, he'd have found you. If he kills me and AJ, Aaron and Cliff will get you out.*

From her hiding place in the hole Keegan heard the *whump* and felt the sudden change in air pressure. She snapped the cellphone light off to save the battery and started worming herself backwards into what she hoped and prayed had been LeClair and Diana's tunnel in and out of Stonehedge.

CHAPTER 43

"I told you to be careful around that," AJ scolded. "It was barely balancing there."

Faucon didn't buy the charade. He had seen Maryann push it over. "*Tres stupide*," he growled. "Now you must reopen it."

Maryann threw up her hands in a shrug. "Can't."

"You will." He advanced a step toward them.

"We really can't," AJ said, pointing at the cable. "The Come-Along—that's the hand winch that tightens the cable is down there—is on the other end of this." She tapped her toe on the taut cable. "We'll have to buy another one in town in the morning."

He stopped, his eyes narrowing as he stared at the cable. He glanced back up at Maryann, puzzled.

"*Porquoi?*" he asked.

Why? He doesn't know Keegan's down there.

"Because Luna's not here," she answered.

He looked puzzled again.

"What she's saying," AJ explained, "is that you didn't ask for our help. Luna did."

Le gargouille placed his hand under his chin and stood quietly for a moment.

He looks just like a person, Maryann thought, *contemplating, considering, weighing his options.*

He blinked his slow reptilian blink again, his red eyes dimming, and while the lid was down she didn't know if he was looking at the slab, the cable, or her and AJ. They opened again and glowed crimson.

"Shall we sit down and wait," she asked, "for Luna?"

Faucon took several more steps until he was directly over the place where the cable disappeared between roof slabs. He squatted, reached his hand down toward the cable, and hooked his thick fingers under it. He drew it up until the unseen Come-Along assembly hit the bottom of the slab, too big to pull through the narrow opening.

"Told you," AJ said.

He shot her a glance that froze her. When he saw her response, his thick lips curled into a faint sardonic smile.

"I meant," she said, finding her voice again, "I told you the winch was on the bottom end of the cable. Without it, we can't lift that roof piece. It weighs a few tons."

Faucon widened his stance, squatting like an Olympic weightlifter, his feet and toes perpendicular to the space between slabs. He wrapped the cable tightly around his hand, took a couple of deep breaths, and went as far down into his squat as he could. He straightened his spine and exerted pressure with his powerful legs, slowly straightening them.

AJ and Maryann kept their eyes on the slab. The edge closest to Faucon moved slightly, rising perhaps an inch, thanks solely to his sheer brute strength. He relaxed his grip for a moment.

Strong as he is, Maryann thought, *he can't lift it. There's no way he'll ever get it on its side again. Keegan, you're safe for a while.*

Faucon set himself again and repositioned the cable around both hands. But instead of trying a dead lift again, he unfurled his enormous upper glide wings, then extended the short wings below them. The short wings began to vibrate furiously, creating a loud hum, and the broad upper wings began to flap slowly, generating enough wind to force Maryann and AJ to their knees so they wouldn't blow off the roof. Faucon went into his squat lift, straightening up and channeling every other ounce of energy into the four wings. The slab lifted several inches, then several more, until the Come-Along housing shot out from under the slab, leaving the *gargouille* slightly off balance for a moment, something he corrected quickly with his wings. The giant slab *whumped* into place again where it had been a minute earlier.

Maryann and AJ stared open-mouthed.

The chamber was once again sealed as before, but the Come-Along itself was free and once again usable.

"No need to go to town for another," Faucon declared, breathing heavily as he folded in both sets of wings. "Hook it up."

☞ ☞ ☞

Keegan heard the *whump* for the second time and again felt the pressure change. It wasn't as loud or as close this time because she had backed farther into her hidey-hole beneath the four planks.

This must have been the tunnel LeClair and Diana used to get in and out of the granite cabin. They had no windows or doors for a reason: creatures that needed to avoid sunlight didn't want openings for it to get in.

What Keegan didn't know was whether the tunnel's 150-year-old supports had held up the dirt ceiling and held back the walls the whole time. Was there a collapse somewhere? She also had no way of knowing where the tunnel came out, or if the entrance was blocked. For all she knew, a towering pine could be smack dab in the middle of it.

She wished now that she'd slid in face first, because it was difficult finding her way with her feet. It would mean less knee pain if she could pull herself along rather than push. She had tried switching her cellphone flashlight back on, but it was hard to see ahead of her feet when she had to crook her head and shine the beam alongside her body. Besides, every yard of tunnel ahead was the same as the last. She had been contemplating crawling back to the planked-over entrance and starting over again—facing frontwards—when the second *whump* had come. It convinced her to keep advancing feet first.

After 20 feet she came to a corner, not an intersection but a turn of perhaps 60 degrees that was slightly wider than the straight-line section she'd come through. She was able to contort herself into a fetal ball and rotate her body 180 degrees—wincing through a long moment of excruciating knee pain—to unfold herself facing forward.

Thank God I haven't crossed paths with any rats or snakes.

She shone the phone flashlight ahead and saw there was another eight feet to go before the tunnel angled off again. The good news was: things were so far structurally intact. No collapse. No caved-in dirt blocking her way.

Her injured knee throbbed as she elbowed her way forward on her belly. The air felt like it was getting very thin and stale, hard to breathe. She reached the next turn—a 45-degree angle—and entered a long stretch that curved gradually. With all the underground twists and turns she had taken since leaving the chamber she had no mental map telling her where she was in relation to the Stonehedge structure. The only thing that seemed clear was that she passed under the granite wall and started angling back and forth in a gradual uphill climb. LeClair and Diana had apparently burrowed in from beyond the uphill side of the structure.

She negotiated a zigzag of six more straightaways before she had to stop and rest. Exhausted and sleepy, she was sweating profusely, jeans and shirt soaked through.

This is partly exertion, but it's also lousy air. I'm using it up, and there's no fresh air coming in on either end of the system. What if I reach the end and find it blocked? I'm so tired.

She put one palm on top of the other in front of her and rested her head sideways on the makeshift pillow and closed her eyes.

Don't fall asleep now, Dauphine. You'll never wake up.

Her eyes flew open and her head snapped up. Where had that voice come from? It had to have been in her head. Had she called herself Dauphine? No, she'd have called herself Keegan.

She pressed forward, her lungs straining like she was suffering an asthma attack. She yearned for a few lungsful of cool fresh air.

And then she saw the root system. It spread before her like a curtain of tentacles. The tree trunk they descended from was nine or ten feet above her. It had to be eight feet around at the base. With the root system, it spread over her like a gigantic umbrella. This was why there was so little air in the tunnel. All of what had seeped in had come down at the other end while the planks were off and Stonehedge's roof slab was tipped up. The first *whump* of the slab slamming shut had forced air into the tunnel. But none was getting in at the tree-covered end.

Keegan began to sob. She was trapped, and she wasn't sure she had the strength to reverse course and climb back out into Diana's death chamber. She tried desperately to think, but her mind was tired and her thoughts were scrambled.

Straight up, Dauphine. Dig. Tree trunks indicate ground level.

Keegan didn't question or argue. She couldn't afford to waste energy. She pulled out the last ceiling support where the tunnel came under the umbrella of roots. The ceiling didn't collapse. She pried at an overhead ceiling plank until it ripped loose. Most of the dirt stayed in place, but a few clods dropped in front of her. She wielded the plank with both hands, arms already weary from the maze, and began stabbing and poking at the dirt ceiling at the outer edges of the root umbrella because—as the voice had said—a tree trunk meant ground level.

Trunks don't grow underground. Straight up, Dauphine.

CHAPTER 44

F aucon watched AJ stretch and secure the Come-Along cable: the hook on one end around Keegan's original anchor tree, the hook on the other end biting into the tow chain that still encircled the slab. She took up the slack in the line, then cranked the lever handle until the cable was taut. From here on, the cranking of the handle would require strength. AJ was taller than Keegan, but not as strong—or perhaps she lacked the right leverage—and she couldn't pull hard enough to turn the take-up reel so the ratchet would click onto the next gear tooth.

Maryann tried to help, but it was awkward when the two of them tried to grip and pull together.

"We can't do it," AJ told Faucon.

"Or so you make it appear," he said.

They backed away as the *gargouille* approached and inspected the winch mechanism. He understood now how it worked and pulled the lever handle. *Click-click-click.* The cable tightened. He made it look effortless. *Click-click-click-click.* It tightened more, and the far edge of the slab began to lift, rising as if the inner edge was on a hinge.

Maryann and AJ watched from behind Faucon, standing next to the tree that was serving as the Come-Along's anchor. Maryann noticed Keegan's splitting wedge and the ax lying next to it. Faucon was four feet in front of them, his broad back exposed to them. She tried to picture herself scooping the ax up and swinging it windmill-fashion while covering the distance between her and Faucon, burying it in the center of his back between his upper wings.

Will an ax blade cut into his flesh or simply bounce off it? Is his back as leathery and armored as his helmet-like head?

Even if she could be guaranteed success—that her blow would kill or disable him—could she do that to another sentient being? She knew she could never do it to a human, but this was a *gargouille*. And she didn't know what value this *gargouille* placed on *her* life, or AJ's, or Luna's, or Keegan's.

What I do know is, Faucon isn't interested in saving Diana's eggs. He's here to destroy them.

❦ ❦ ❦

While Faucon peeled back the granite slab, Keegan was fighting her own battle. She needed to dislodge the packed dirt from the web of roots in front of and above her. The roots clung to the clods, only occasionally releasing their grip and letting small clumps and showers of loose soil rain down on her. The more she poked and jabbed with the plank, the more lightheaded she grew. The more she exerted herself, the more air—precious air—she was using up. She paused for several minutes, resting her weary arms and shoulders.

She steeled herself and renewed her attack, prodding and stabbing with the end of the plank, then switching to beating the roots with the flat side of it. More dirt fell and began to accumulate near her feet. There was now enough that it threatened to block the tunnel, so she dropped to her knees and scooped, pawed, and plowed it further behind her back into the tunnel. Her head pounded and her arms felt like they would drop from their shoulder sockets. Her lungs worked overtime like a vacuum cleaner straining to clean with a dust-clogged filter—an extraordinary effort sure to result in overheating.

She turned her efforts back to the roots above her and felt she was near collapse when a wide square of turf far overhead—not even a chunk she was working on—suddenly surrendered, as if some unseen ally had attacked it, and collapsed, breaking apart on its way down through the crosshatch of roots, shearing into smaller chunks and bits as it fell. Even sweeter, with it came cool air that struck Keegan's sweaty head and shoulders like a splash of cold water. The new air was rich with oxygen, and her starved lungs gulped it in greedily.

Tree trunks mean ground level, the almost familiar voice said in her head.

Keegan closed her eyes, her face and body caked with a paste of dust, dirt, and sweat. She was totally spent. She lay back on the mound of soil she had heaped behind her at the mouth of the tunnel and fell asleep.

CHAPTER 45

The slab was resting on its narrow edge again, with Faucon looking over it into the chamber below.

"Go around to the other side," he ordered, pointing across the yawning gap in the roof.

Maryann and AJ walked away from the tree anchoring the cable and stepped over the slab at the end, using the wall it had rested on as a stepping stone to get around the opening the slab had left.

Faucon used his short wings, rising straight up first, then moving forward over the opening before landing on the other side.

"Are you going down there?" Maryann asked.

"You are," he answered.

"Me?"

"You and the girl," he said.

"Why would we go down there?" AJ interrupted. "You said you were here for the bones—so you can bring them back to your grandfather. All you needed us for was to help you get in."

"I cannot leave you two up here while I go below. You say that you came to help, and so you shall. You will dig."

Maryann opened her mouth to protest, "But—"

"Sit down here," Faucon commanded, pointing at the opening to the room below. "On the edge, with your legs in the hole."

They didn't move.

"Would you prefer that I throw you down or lower you?" The question and his tone communicated both sensitivity and threat.

What choice did they have? They sat down and dangled their legs over the dark room below. Faucon came and stood directly behind them.

"Now raise your hands, *s'il vous plait*. Over your heads."

They raised their hands.

Faucon reached over AJ and hooked his thick fingers over hers then lifted her effortlessly as she gave a little chirp of surprise. He shuffled forward a step and held her suspended over the opening. He squatted and lowered his arms at the same time. AJ hung there, her curled fingers clinging to his hooked fingers, her shoulders and head even with the roof.

"Ready?" he asked.

She knew he wasn't going to lower her any further. Suspended over the dark floor, she wasn't sure how far the drop was.

"Don't!" she pleaded. "Please."

He straightened his fingers and let go.

AJ dropped through the stale air, somehow landing evenly on both feet, knees bent and absorbing the shock. She automatically relaxed, folding at the waist and landing on her butt with her hands to her sides where they pressed down into the soft top layer of soil, helping to cushion the impact.

"AJ, are you alright?" Maryann called down.

"I think so," she said, and stood up. Then she looked up at the opening and said, "*Monsieur Faucon*, when you lower my friend, please do not let go of her until I get my arms around her legs. If she breaks an arm or a leg in the fall, she will not be able to dig."

"*C'est vrai*," Faucon replied. "I will be careful. Are you ready?"

"I'm ready." AJ braced herself and looked up to see Maryann's body dangling from the *gargouille's* hands. She hugged her arms around Maryann's knees. A moment later gravity took over and Maryann's weight shifted onto AJ, who was almost prepared. The two of them fell down together in the soft dirt.

"Are you alright?" AJ asked as they sat up.

"No worse for wear. The question is: now what?"

Faucon heard Maryann. "Dig," he said.

"Where?" Maryann called up then spat out a series of questions. "And with what? We have no shovels. And how are we supposed to see what we're doing? You've got the lantern up there."

"*Un moment*," he said, and a minute later reached down to hand them the remaining lantern.

AJ, even though she was taller than Maryann, couldn't reach high enough to take it from Faucon's hand. So he dropped it, and she caught it carefully. It lit the room except for the shadowy corners. AJ saw the roots Keegan had mentioned. But she saw no sign of Keegan.

Where are the planks, Keegan, the ones you fell through, and the hole under them?

Maryann peppered Faucon with questions again. "Where do we start? How far down will her bones be? Was she buried in some kind of container? And remember, we have no shovels."

His answer was succinct. "You have four hands. Start at the center. She will not be deep."

☛☛☛

Keegan awoke disoriented, uncertain at first whether her eyes were open. Her right arm and shoulder felt sore and stiff. She glanced down and saw a glow by her side: the cellphone face-down in the dirt, its flashlight function still in use. She picked it up and noted first thing that it was 10:24. The second thing she noticed was the phone's battery level: under 25%. She'd have to use it sparingly. But first she needed the light to assess her situation.

The tunnel she had crawled through was narrow until it reached the big tree. Then it opened into a wider space that was too small to be called a room. It was circular like a cistern, an old well with hard-packed dirt walls and a diameter wider than a person spinning in circles with her arms out.

Nine or ten feet across. Hard to tell with all these roots hanging down like jellyfish tentacles.

Above the dangling roots was a thatch of roots that formed a natural ceiling.

They're what holds the dirt in place. The forest floor is right over them. I must have poked a hole in it and let some outside air down in here.

What she was looking at reminded her of a rope cargo net that soldiers might use to climb up the side of a ship.

Which is what I'm going to have to do if I'm going to get out of here without going back through the tunnel to Diana's room—which I'm pretty sure is sealed again. Up is the only way out. I'm going to have to thread my way through this maze with a knee that's killing me.

The canopy of roots was still too low for her to stand up, so she crab-walked forward a few steps, trying to ignore the screaming knee, and plopped down on her butt. She shone her light straight up. A shaft of cool air hit her upturned face and she saw, perhaps ten feet up, the hole—as big as her head—where the earth had caved under her relentless plank assault.

When I get to it I'll have to widen it to squeeze my shoulders through. But there it is: my escape hatch.

It wasn't like peering up an elevator shaft or the inside of a chimney—it wasn't clear, unencumbered space. It had to have been less root-bound in Diana's and LeClair's day—this had to have been their way in and out, and they would have kept it open and trimmed. But now it was like any yard or garden suffering a century of neglect. Dozens, perhaps hundreds or thousands of roots had effectively shut the door.

Keegan could see that making her way up through the tangle—*feeling* her way if the light died—wasn't going to be easy. But she couldn't wait for daylight. She had left her mother and AJ to deal with Faucon alone. She took off her running shoes, grabbed a root, and started to climb.

*Jack and the Beanstalk. I wonder if gargouilles say **fee, fie, foe, fum**.*

Section X

Faucon's Side
of the Story

CHAPTER 46

In Diana's chamber AJ removed her running shoes and slipped off her socks, whispering to Maryann, "Keegan put her socks on her hands. The idea of digging up a grave with my bare hands gives me the creeps."

Maryann removed her shoes and put her socks on like gloves.

"Dig!" Faucon commanded from above.

AJ and Maryann got on their hands and knees like field hands pulling potatoes and began pawing dirt.

"Where the hell is Luna?" Maryann muttered softly as they raked back loose soil.

"And where's my brother and Cliff?" AJ said, just as quietly. She slipped her cellphone out and saw there was no signal. If Aaron had heard her earlier message, it wasn't apparent. *Where's the cavalry?*

Maryann thought, *I need to know if Keegan's okay. Can the two of us disappear down that hidey-hole before Faucon grabs us?*

One at a time, said a voice in her head that wasn't her own, but sounded like her own. She hadn't heard it since the delivery room 17 years earlier, and she was sure it had to be a figment of her imagination. But it made her think.

She said to AJ in a voice Faucon could hear, "Yes, I know you have to go to the bathroom. I have to go, too. But it wouldn't be right to pee on *Monsieur Faucon's* uncle's wife's grave. Why don't you just go make yourself comfortable over there, *on that root?*" She nodded to the spot AJ had whispered was the place Keegan had hurt her knee when she broke through the planks. Then to Faucon she said, "*Monsieur*, can my friend take a minute from digging to pee?"

"*Rapidement,*" the *gargouille* replied.

"He said yes, but hurry," Maryann told AJ, adding, "Leave the seat up when you're done."

AJ made her way to the root, made like she was about to pull down her jeans, then looked up at the roof opening. "*Monsieur, s'il vous plait,* don't look."

Maryann said, "I'll give you a little privacy," and grabbed the lantern, repositioning it near her right knee so her body blocked it from shining on AJ. "I'll keep digging and you can let me know when you're done. Then it's my turn." She dug while AJ pried up a couple of planks in the dark.

"So, *Monsieur Faucon,*" Maryann said, continuing her digging motions. "Luna tells me your *pere* fought in the Great War."

"*C'est vrai.*" He hadn't expected this.

Need to give AJ time to get deep into the tunnel. Hopefully it'll be too narrow for him to follow.

"Would this be your *grandpere's* son? Is he still alive?"

"No. He died."

"Fighting the Germans?"

"*Oui.*"

"Luna said he was a hero."

"He died saving two comrades." Faucon revealed no more.

"I'm very sorry for your loss," Maryann said. "That must have been a very difficult time for you."

Le gargouille said nothing.

"I lost my younger sister—*ma soeur*—when she was twenty," Maryann said. "She was about to deliver her baby when something went wrong and she died. I think about her every day."

"What about the baby?" Faucon asked. "Was it lost also?"

"No. The doctor cut the baby out of her."

"He *cut* the baby out of her?"

"Yes," she said sadly.

"And the baby was raised by the father?" he asked.

"There was no father in the picture. I raised the baby as my own."

"And this baby is now the tall brown girl who is digging with you?" he asked.

"Yes," she lied.

"When you die," Faucon asked, "who will inherit?"

"You mean, who gets my estate?"

"You have a house, *n'est-ce pas*? And a bookstore? And an automobile? Maybe some money?"

Faucon didn't seem to notice that AJ hadn't finished her business. She hadn't returned to digging.

"I am leaving everything to her. My daughter."

"Your *adopted* daughter," he corrected.

"Yes."

He was silent for a moment.

"Why do you ask?" she said.

Faucon was quiet and took a moment before he replied. "*Mon pere* did not have to die in that war. He insisted on flying the *dauphin*, the crown prince of our *gargouille* race, to safety. That I can understand. But then he went back to save the other one. He had no obligation to do that. When he returned with him, he was mortally wounded by a German artillery shell. *Mon pere* may have been *un hero*, but he died days later, leaving me *un orphelin*."

"An orphan. I'm very sorry."

He ignored Maryann's condolences. "After the death of *mon pere* I should have been allowed to return to our clan. But *le dauphin*, in gratitude, promised he would care for me."

"That was very generous of him," she said.

"No, it was a curse. Instead of being raised by my own clan, *le dauphin's* promise made me a ward—*a servant*. He was sick, so I was forced to attend to his needs on the sea voyage home to America after the war. But he died on the ship, and his brother became next in line for the throne. I had no choice but to become the brother's servant."

"That was around 1920, when you were young. What happened after that?"

"Twenty years ago *le dauphin* adopted me as his son."

"So where do you and he stand now?"

"*Le dauphin—c'est le frere* who adopted me—died 20 years ago."

"What happened?" Maryann asked.

"He died in his sleep," Faucon said without emotion.

"So your adoptive *grandpere* lost two sons in that terrible war, and you lost your natural father. How terrible."

"The brothers—*le dauphin* and *le frere*—have died, but their *pere, mon grandpere* the king, is alive. For now. He is old and frail."

"So with both of his natural sons gone," she asked, "who is next in line?" She knew his answer before he spoke it.

"*C'est moi,*" Faucon hissed, his anger barely contained. "For nearly 80 years I was a servant. *Le dauphin* knew he was not well and finally agreed to adopt me shortly before his death. The throne is not only my sovereign right, *but it is owed to me*, for the princes cheated me out of my rightful place in my own clan."

"Were you the successor to your natural father?" Maryann asked.

"I was third in line after *mes freres.*"

Maryann steered the discussion away from Faucon's natural clan. "That is very helpful. Now I understand why you refer to the one buried here as your *uncle's wife* rather than your *aunt*. She was the mate of the first crown prince."

"*Oui. C'est vrai.*"

"But I do not understand. How will it help for you to bring her bones back to your *grandpere*, the king?"

Faucon didn't get to answer, because he heard the *whoosh, whoosh, whoosh* of wings far off and had to disappear fast.

CHAPTER 47

Luna spiraled slowly downward on her upper wings until she was 20 feet above the tallest trees. She pulled up short, at the same time extending her short wings and hovering as she folded the big wings onto her back. She moved cautiously from side to side, forward and backward, assessing the scene below. On her visit after dusk she had found Keegan's twin beacons, but was disappointed to find Stonehedge a virtual fortress, impregnable without crane or explosives.

This time, though, she saw that the light wasn't coming from lanterns at either end of the roof. Now it was emanating from the chamber, which lay open where a granite roof slab had been turned on its side. But there was no sign of activity: human or *gargouille*. Keegan's cryptic message to Brother Jerome had indicated she'd found a way to open it.

Did she open it and leave it for me?

"Anyone down there?" she called, but got no answer. "Keegan?"

Silence.

Something didn't feel right. She maneuvered lower, her eyes probing the shadows beyond the roof's perimeter.

No one.

The light faded for an instant—not flickering like a candle in the breeze, but as if something—a hand or a leg—passed in front of a lantern in the chamber. Someone was down there.

She descended further, alighting on the corner of the rooftop. She stilled her vibrating wings, the hum ceasing, but she kept them extended in case she had to react quickly. She slowly raised her hands and reached behind her head to grip a pair of hilts.

"Keegan?" she called out a second time. "Maryann?"

No answer. Then the realization.

"Faucon? Of course you are here. Faucon the pretender. Have you been digging, *monsieur*? Have you found them yet?"

A muffled sound—female.

Faucon has a hand around someone's mouth.

She tightened her grip on the hilts and very slowly and quietly unsheathed her sword and dagger, bringing them over her head and down in front of her body. Her senses were on high alert, her reptile awareness conscious of ever movement around her. The center of her eyes focused on the long, wide opening in the roof, but her peripheral vision took in everything else.

Champaigne, you trained me for battle, but I have never experienced it.

She stepped closer and looked directly into the chamber. As she did, she heard a faint but familiar sound, exactly the sound her weapons had made a moment earlier—the light hiss of two oiled blades being drawn out of leather scabbards. Faucon was below, and he was ready.

She leapt back a split second before his huge body shot past her out of the roof opening, his sword and dagger crossed in front of his chest, protecting his midsection.

Luna's eyes lifted skyward like she was watching a launch, eyes tracking her nemesis as he rocketed past her. An instant later he braked midflight and hovered 20 feet above the roof, sword and dagger out in attack stance now.

Champaigne's words returned to her.

Do not engage a larger opponent in the air if there is a choice. Anchor yourself so your legs add to your defense and to the strength of your blows. Being grounded means you do not have a vulnerable underside to defend.

"And I'll never be stabbed in the sole of my foot," she recalled jokingly saying to her mentor. She retracted her short wings so they wouldn't be damaged and took up a defensive stance.

"What have you done with my friends?" Luna demanded.

Faucon hung in the air like an angry hornet.

"Have you hurt them?"

"You are no match for me, Luna."

She wasn't, and she had no illusions about it. He was younger and stronger and would quickly wear her down. But she showed no fear.

"Did you find them?" she asked. "Diana's eggs?"

"I will. After you are . . . gone."

"Gone?" she asked. "You mean *mort*?"

"The choice is yours. Leave now and you live."

"I won't leave without the eggs."

"They cannot have survived," he said.

"If you are certain, why are you here?"

He didn't answer.

"If even one can be hatched—" she said.

Faucon's face grew ugly. He snarled, "I will not be denied."

She saw his body tense up.

"Last chance to leave alive," he warned.

"Not without the eggs," she said. "*En garde.*" She motioned with her sword.

She knew he would angle to her right side in a classic *en passe* move to see how well she blocked him and kept her balance. If he got lucky, he would uncover a vulnerability. He might even have a chance to make a reverse stabbing move with his *poignard* as he passed. It was also possible that her sword arm would cave right away under a series of heavy downward blows. She was confident she could deflect them on his first pass, but all her energy would have to go into defending herself. There would be little chance to wound him, and if she remained on defense there, he would quickly exhaust her.

Your best hope is to get away now, said a voice in her head that wasn't her own. *Or stall him, calm him down.* The voice reminded her of Maryann's. Or was it Keegan's. *Zelda?*

She lowered her weapons, allowing Faucon to see the change from defense, then gestured toward the open chamber with her dagger.

Talk to him, the voice said.

"When I was here earlier," she said, "I could not imagine a way to open this, so I left. How did you do it? It is quite ingenious."

Nothing inflammatory, just a simple compliment and a request for information.

Faucon relaxed slightly. "I also was here and left. When I returned, it was open. Two of your friends were here waiting. The older one saw me and pushed the stone back into place, but the younger one showed me how to pull it up again."

"The younger one showed you?" Luna echoed. *So at least two of them were here.* "And they left?"

"*Oui.*"

Liar, she thought. *I heard someone.*

"I was digging when I heard your wings," he said. "I did not expect you to return so soon."

Luna's ears picked up a soft groan below.

He doesn't have a hand over anyone's mouth now. Someone must be down there injured.

"Faucon, you say my friends left. I think they are still here. What have you done with them?"

Before Faucon could answer, a male voice asked, "Yeah, Faucon, where are they?"

Faucon's and Luna's eyes went to the low side of the roof where everyone had climbed on earlier. Standing on the ground, head even with the roof, was Aaron Stevenson in his patrol uniform. He had his hands raised in a shooter's stance, his flashlight and Taser pointed at Faucon where he hovered.

"Who are you?" Faucon demanded, looking more annoyed than afraid.

"Police," Aaron replied, hoping the *gargouille* didn't know the difference between a Taser and a pistol. "Drop your weapons and come down with your hands up, sir. Now."

Aaron knew that hitting Faucon with the Taser at this distance would literally be a longshot, and chances of it penetrating his reptilian skin were slim.

Faucon laughed.

"*Mon-sewer gargly*," called out another male voice, deeper than Aaron's. Cliff Bragdon, on one side of Stonehedge, had his pistol and flashlight trained on Faucon. "You, sir, are under arrest on suspicion of burglary, four counts."

"Ah, *le cavalerie*," Faucon said sarcastically. "Reinforcements with guns. This is very frightening." He laughed derisively.

Luna could see Faucon wasn't stationary, even though it appeared his arms and legs weren't moving. But his short wings were in play, and he tilted them slightly, easing backwards ever so slightly in slow motion—a sort of *gargouille* moonwalk that used a series of almost imperceptible movements.

"I will not *drop* my weapons, *monsieur gendarme*," he said to Aaron. "But I will put my weapons away if you and your comrade will do the same. After all, we do not want anyone to be hurt in the dark."

He turned the tips of his sword and dagger upward, making sure the two cops saw that his hand movements were exaggeratedly slow.

Aaron and Cliff didn't relax their guard. Luna maintained her defensive stance.

Then without looking, in what appeared to be a single fluid motion, Faucon sheathed both weapons at once. And with the speed and agility of a hummingbird leaving a blossom, he shot straight sideways and was out of sight before either cop could yell *freeze*.

CHAPTER 48

AJ escaped into the tunnel entrance headfirst, unlike Keegan who had backed in. This and the fact that AJ didn't have an injured knee would make her escape through the tunnel faster and easier.

The air was close and warm, and after two or three minutes with no sign of Maryann, she began crawling toward the unknown. She crept forward and, after many twists and turns, she came upon a roadblock, a pile of dirt nearly two-thirds the height of the tunnel.

Not a cave-in! Oh, please don't let Keegan be buried under it.

She aimed her light at the tunnel roof above the dirt pile. All the timbers were intact.

So if this dirt isn't from a cave-in, and there are no side tunnels, Keegan has to be on the other side of it. She piled it here.

AJ pawed and pushed the soil until she had room to squeeze over it. She found the tunnel widened but didn't go much farther because of a massive root system under a huge tree. She found the plank Keegan had used for poking the dirt loose above her.

"Keegan!" she called.

"Here," came the immediate answer.

AJ aimed her light up at the voice. She saw the curtain of root tentacles and above it a massive weave of more roots. But no Keegan.

"Where are you?" she called.

"Up here."

AJ shifted positions and shone her light at several different angles, trying to make sense of what she was seeing. The massive root system, much of it caked with dirt, had taken on the shape of a dome. At some time in the past, the space might have been free enough of roots to be considered a small, almost round room. Up near the roof of the dome was Keegan, resting among some roots like a rock climber in a cliff-side hammock. She had run out of gas and stretched her tired body across a weave of roots.

"I'm really glad to see you," Keegan said. "Where's Mom?"

"Back in the chamber. Faucon made us dig for the bones. Well, he said *bones*, but we know it's the eggs he's after. Your mom created a diversion while I slipped into your little hidey-hole. I'm glad it turned out to be a tunnel and not just some old well."

"So where is she?" Keegan asked again.

"I don't think she's found the right moment yet."

"So you just left her there?" Keegan asked accusingly.

"I had to. For now. She'd never have forgiven me if I wasted the chance. She also wanted me to see if you were okay."

"Well, I'm not dead," Keegan said. "But I am tired and cranky, and my knee is killing me."

"And?"

After a pause, "Thank you for coming."

"You're welcome. Now your mom was okay last I saw her. Faucon won't hurt her, because he needs her to dig while he keeps watch."

"That makes sense. You didn't say if you found anything. Bones? Eggs?"

"We barely got started," AJ said. "It takes a while to get through that loose stuff on top."

"Even if you found the eggs, Faucon would have them and it wouldn't help Luna, would it? Finders, keepers; losers, weepers."

"Like I said, we were just getting started. But what about you--are you resting or are you stuck?"

"Resting. It's been like climbing through a rat's nest. I did it in the dark and my knee hurts when I flex it. The good news is, if you look above me to my right, you can see an opening to the outside world. There's a little fresh air coming in, which is the only reason I'm alive and breathing right now. It opened up when I started whacking away at the roots, like one of those Florida sinkholes. Once I get to the top, I'll knock more dirt loose and both of us can get out."

"I'm okay here for the time being," AJ said. "I'll climb up in a minute. First thing you can do when you get out is call Aaron. I don't have a signal."

"My cellphone battery's had it. The flashlight drained it. We'll have to wait and use yours. We could sure use Aaron."

"He may know already," AJ said. "When Faucon showed up, I muted my phone and speed-dialed him so he could listen in. But I had to hide the phone in my back pocket, and I'm not sure he could make out any of it. He may have just assumed that I butt-dialed him. He hadn't arrived when I slipped into the tunnel. Wait there for me. I'll be right up."

CHAPTER 49

Aaron still had his flashlight and Taser pointed at the spot where Faucon had been hovering. He lowered the Taser and turned to the smaller *gargouille* on the roof.

"Luna, I presume? I'm Aaron, AJ's brother."

"*Excusez moi*," she said, and her short wings began to hum. "Somebody needs help." She sheathed the two blades behind her shoulders and disappeared through the roof opening.

Aaron rested his Taser on the roof and felt for finger and toe holds. "Cliff, keep watch in case that big one comes back."

"Got it," Cliff replied. "That was one big bumblebee."

Aaron climbed onto the roof. The first thing he saw was the upright slab and the long rectangular opening it had left in the roof. Lantern light came up from below. The second thing he saw was the toe chain and the tight-stretched Come-Along cable holding the slab in place.

Keegan's handiwork, I can tell.

He recalled a night the previous summer when Keegan had made him show her how to change the oil and filter in the Subaru.

Where are you, Keegan? AJ? Maryann? Tell me you're okay.

He peered into the chamber and saw Luna bent over by a wall, talking to someone. The lighting was dim and the *gargouille's* body partially blocked his view. He wasn't sure which of the three it might be.

"Talk to me, Luna," he called down. "What's the situation?"

"It's Maryann. It looks like she had the wind knocked out of her, but I think she'll be alright."

"What about AJ and Keegan?"

"*Un moment.* She is telling me."

Aaron worked his way behind the standing slab closer to Cliff and saw the ax and the splitting wedge next to the tree anchoring the Come-Along cable. He shook his head. *Tool girl.*

"You hear that, Aaron?" Cliff asked.

They listened.

Whoosh, whoosh, whoosh far above. They had not seen the long wings of either *gargouille* in action yet, only their short hummingbird wings. Faucon had shot out of the chamber like a bottle rocket, then a moment later hovered, reversed, and streaked away sideways before ascending. Luna had descended into the chamber like a helicopter on a jungle rescue.

No wonder Chamberlain went looking for them in the Allagash, Aaron thought.

"He's up there," Cliff said. "Circling. Waiting."

Aaron recalled the two dishwashers at the Maine Diner. They had not only *heard* the *whoosh whoosh whoosh,* they had *seen* the *gargouille.* One of them said it reminded him of a pterodactyl, and that its eyes had glowed red when it glared back at them.

This *whoosh whoosh* was what he'd heard at Toil & Trouble when he charged up the stairs and into Swett's second-floor office. He'd thought the sound had been a scrap of childhood memory: two geese taking off from the pond in front of his grandfather's camp. He'd tried to dismiss it as a memory. But the flapping sound had been real-time data. He'd heard it after Faucon leapt out the window. The *gargouille* had used the deacon's chair to clear out the double-sash window so he could take a short takeoff run and launch himself out the window. As soon as he cleared the frame he unfurled his upper pterodactyl wings in midair and flapped out and up—not down. That's why there were no ladder marks in the ground. He hadn't seen the *gargouille* that night, but now he had a close-up and knew what he was seeing, although he still didn't know what he was dealing with.

"You think your Taser would have taken him down?" Cliff asked.

"No way, not even at max."

"First you'd have to hit him. That sucker was fast."

"How about you?" Aaron asked.

"I switched from my Taser to my service piece last minute. I was lined up on his center mass, but what would have justified shooting? A couple of bookstore break-ins? Desecration of a cemetery? You don't shoot people—or gargoyles even—for that. The Stedman assault is in the past, but it wasn't lethal, maybe not even intentional.

"Hey, right now I'm not sure this is reality. I mean, just listen to me. A moment ago I used the word gargoyle in a sentence—the same way I'd use the word tomato or cowboy. Are we in some alternate reality? Here we are, battling gargoyles at some lost tomb none of us Wells kids ever heard about. It's like we're on the set of some weird horror movie."

"This is real, Cliff. We're not dreaming. We have a *gargouille* in the bunker under us and another one circling above it. We are awake and this is real. What worries me is, that big one looks like he knows how to use those swords."

"Should we call for backup?"

"Think about that, Cliff. That might be the worst thing we could do. You read *Night Hawks*. The Confederates called them banshees and harpies. They slashed the rebels to pieces after dark. If that one up there is half as dangerous as the Night Hawks were, calling backup into these woods at night would be like leading lambs to the slaughter. Right now there are two of us with guns and only one of him. Our priority is to get Maryann, AJ, and Keegan out."

"Should I walk out to the car for my shotgun? We'd have a better chance of hitting him with that than with pistols."

"I think it's too late for that, Cliff. You'd be a Confederate in the woods at night."

"Thanks for that image, Aaron. You could have just said I'd be a sitting duck."

Aaron walked around the slab and stood by the opening. Luna and Maryann were standing at the center of the chamber. He knelt down as they looked up.

"What happened?" he asked.

Maryann said, "We were waiting for Luna. AJ and I were on the roof, Keegan was down here exploring. She stepped through some old boards and hurt her leg. There was space under them. Before we could get her out, Faucon showed up. He didn't know there were three of us. We kept him talking while Keegan hid under the boards.

"Faucon set AJ and me down here and told us to dig for Luna's sister's bones. He stayed up there. We dug a while, then I distracted him so AJ could follow Keegan down the rabbit hole. I'd have gone, too, but didn't get the chance.

"When he heard Luna coming, he jumped down here with me and covered my mouth. He and Luna started talking and next thing I knew he slammed me against the wall to shut me up. It knocked the wind out of me."

"So Keegan and AJ are in the tunnel?" Aaron asked.

"Yes."

Luna said, "That explains how LeClair and Diana got in and out."

"Did you pull off the old boards to make sure?" Aaron asked.

"We just did that," Maryann answered. "Keegan and AJ aren't on this end."

"I'm coming down," Aaron said. "I'll go in after them. Hopefully nothing's caved in and they're at the other end."

From high up in the night sky, Faucon saw the brown-skinned policeman lower himself into the chamber. *A tactical mistake,* he thought, and began spiraling downward.

CHAPTER 50

Aaron shone his flashlight into the rabbit hole and called to AJ and Keegan.

No answer.

He walked back under the roof opening. "Cliff, can you hear me?"

"I hear you," Cliff answered. "Whatcha need?"

"I'm on duty now, you're not. I need you to report in for me."

"Why?"

"Because I'm going down into this tunnel. Let dispatch know I've gone into a cave after two hikers? Tell Marcy you're technically off duty but you're standing by."

"Will do."

"And Cliff, can you take up a position on the roof so we don't leave Maryann and Luna exposed. I don't want our guy to get down here."

"On my way. I know where to climb up."

Aaron went back to the rabbit hole and crawled in head-first.

"We may as well dig, Luna," Maryann said, and pointed to the place where she and AJ had been working earlier.

"Wait," Luna said. "There may be an easier way. See the roots coming in? They could be the feeders. If they are, they should come together at the eggs."

Luna found the root Keegan had first bumped. Maryann found the one she had gotten hung up on. They started brushing back dirt and following the two trails.

"Mine's nosediving and curling left," Maryann said.

"This one is turning downward and also to the left," Luna answered, "away from yours."

They kept at it, but the roots didn't look like they were going to intersect.

"I have another root crossing this one," Maryann said. "And another.

They all go in different directions."

"If two or more roots converge," Maryann observed, "it won't be in this new soil, it'll be down in that hard-packed ground that used to be the floor."

"*C'est vrai.* LeClair would have dug Diana a cradle a foot or two deep before she lay down with the eggs. He would have covered all of her body except her face."

Maryann shivered at the thought, then changed the subject. "You and Diana were sisters. Do you have brothers and sisters? If *gargouille* mothers laid six to twelve eggs, there must be more than two of you. Did others survive?"

Luna took her time answering. "Five of ten eggs survived: three of us were females."

"Three females? That would be Diana, you, and—"

"Irena, whose eggs were hatched about thirty years ago," Luna replied.

"So like Diana, she gave herself for the race."

"Not exactly. Irena gave herself for the race, Diana gave herself for the crown, to produce heirs."

Something's not right here, Maryann thought. "What about LeClair and Champaigne? They were called the twin princes. With humans, twins means two from the same egg. Was that true for them?"

"*Oui.*"

"Were there other eggs—brothers and sisters?"

"*Oui,*" Luna said again.

"Then why hasn't the next sibling in line been named the *dauphin* or *dauphine*?"

Luna was oddly silent. She turned and faced Maryann and said, "The others did not survive the hatching."

"They were stillborn?" Maryann blurted.

"In a manner of speaking," Luna said evasively.

"Meaning what?" Maryann pressed.

"They were terminated."

"Terminated?" Maryann looked confused. "You mean aborted?"

"Shortly after they were hatched they were … *eliminated.*"

"As in murdered?"

"From the line of succession, *oui,*" Luna said. "All of the eggs except the twin princes from the one egg were females."

Maryann gasped, horrified. *The females were aborted?*

"Had there been other males, Cyrus would have birthed them and brought them home alive."

"Wait. Because they were females? That's crazy. It's cruel. It's … murder."

Luna was at a loss for words.

"So Luna, let me get this straight. If Cyrus had fathered you and Diana and Irena, you wouldn't be alive now—but your brothers would?"

"*Exactement.* We were fortunate that we were not born to a king or a clan leader, for it is the same with both. It has always been so. The king and the clan leaders produce only males who will be in line for succession."

"That's coldblooded murder, Luna."

"It is called *culling.* At birth the father culls the females."

"Culling?" Maryann said. "That's horrible. It even sounds like killing. Culling. So Faucon's father Drago did this, too—culled his own daughters but saved his sons?"

"*Oui.* Faucon is the youngest of three brothers. The eldest is head of their clan."

"So Faucon—since all three are the same age—will never ascend to the throne there," Maryann said. "But as Champaigne's adopted son, he can see a way to a throne. He can even leapfrog over both of his brothers—because when Cyrus dies, he'll become king of the *gargouilles* kingdom."

"Which is why we must find the eggs," Luna said.

"But what happens once you find them? What if there are viable females as well as males? You know about culling."

Luna's face was stern, determined. "If the bloodline of Cyrus is to extend its rule, the kingdom will have no choice but to accept a queen."

"A queen?" Maryann asked, incredulous.

"Yes, a female," Luna replied.

"But what if some of the eggs are males?"

"It will be unfortunate."

"Wait. Luna, I thought you were here to birth all of your sister's children—LeClair's children, Cyrus's grandchildren—negating Faucon's claim to the throne. *Unfortunate* is all you can say? Unfortunate? You're talking about murdering Diana's male offspring."

"Maryann—"

"Don't *Maryann* me. You're telling me you will—by neglect or by direct action—slaughter your sister's sons, your blood nephews? That's premeditated murder, Luna. How is that different from Faucon smothering Champaigne in his sleep to steal the throne? Aren't you saying you're willing—no, *planning*—to use murder and manipulation for regime change—and that regime change in the name of equality or some sort of *gargouille* feminism?"

The two of them looked down at the dirt around their feet. Four of the roots they had uncovered now appeared likely to converge near one corner of Diana's chamber, four fingers pointing to her grave and nest.

"Luna, you led me and Keegan to believe you were here to be your sister's midwife, not her sons' assassin. Take it from one who knows, take it from one who watched your friend Zelda sacrifice herself, dying in childbirth, so a child—not a daughter or a son, but any child that came out of her—might breathe the air of this world and have a chance at life in it. I beg you, Luna, birth as many as you can, male and female, and rejoice in all those lives. Take them back to your clan, all of them, and when you do get home, argue forcefully and passionately that the first-born and second-born—whatever their gender—be accepted as the heirs apparent. But before anything, make sure that all of them that can, live."

Luna listened, then explained, "It is not that simple, Maryann. If I return with even one male, Cyrus will kill the females. If Cyrus does not kill them, the clan will do it. And if not them, then the other clans will come and do it. *Les gargouilles* will not break tradition. They will cull the females, no matter how long it has been since their birth. My only hope is to present the clan with all females, so they will be forced to choose between a female and Faucon."

Maryann had no answer to that, so she said, "Luna, as tempting as this is, it is not yours to decide. If you are to make any choice, let it be to birth them all and raise them all, even if it is away from the clan. If you cannot do that, don't ask me to help you."

CHAPTER 51

AJ threaded her way up through the root maze until she reached Keegan.

"Eleven minutes, AJ," Keegan said. "A new record for the obstacle course."

"How long did it take you?"

"At least triple that. But I had to feel my way in the dark—with a hurt knee."

"Which is only good for two pity points," AJ said. "Fact is, I was always a better climber." AJ flashed a smile that said *go on, admit it.*

"Okay, okay," Keegan admitted. "You're a better climber. Now can we get out of here?"

AJ used her flashlight beam to plot a course the rest of the way to the surface, then led the way. Five minutes later her head poked above ground like a prairie dog sniffing the air. She knocked dirt loose to widen the opening and worked her body up through it onto solid ground, then helped Keegan out.

"Where do you think we are?" AJ whispered.

"Not sure. Felt like the tunnel ran slightly uphill for a couple hundred yards."

"It must go through the heart of the hill."

"So Stonehedge is on the other side," Keegan said.

"Time for me to call Aaron?" AJ asked.

"Don't call. Text him. If he got your first message, he could be on the trail from the Elks Lodge. A call could give away his position to Faucon."

"Should I text Cliff, too? Your mother said he had to get his patrol car back and go off shift."

"Good idea," AJ said. "Make it a group text with Aaron, so we're all on the same page. Then we'll sneak over the top and see what's happening." They got to their feet.

"Wait a sec," Keegan said, and pulled one of the thumb-size flashers out of her pocket. She pressed the button once and a tiny yellow light came on, then she pressed it again so it switched to blinking yellow. Two more clicks and it through solid green to blinking green. She clipped it to one of the roots at the edge of the hole. "Should have at least ten hours of battery left to make it through the night."

AJ helped Keegan to her feet. "Going to have to change your name from Tool Girl to Gadget Girl."

As they started their quiet creep, AJ sent the text to Aaron and Cliff. Aaron's didn't reach him in the tunnel, but Cliff's pinged through.

CHAPTER 52

Cliff Bragdon pulled his big body onto the roof. "It's just me, ladies," he said into the chamber. "Buckingham Palace, changing of the guard." He stood up, holding his service piece in his right hand and his flashlight in his left.

"Cliff, this is my friend Luna," Maryann said. "She may look like the other *gargouille*, whose name is Faucon, but she is on our side. Or rather, we are on her side. Luna, this is Officer Bragdon."

"Protect and serve," Cliff said, and flipped them an overdone Boy Scout salute. "Nice to meet you, ma'am."

"Thank you for helping, Officer Bragdon," she replied.

"You're welcome. Not exactly sure what it is I'm helping with, but it seems like this Faucon wants something you've got down there."

"We haven't got anything yet," Maryann cut in. "But we're working on it. You be careful up there, Cliff." Then she added loudly, "And don't forget, we have Officer Stevenson down here with his gun, too."

Cliff caught on and answered loudly, "You're in good hands. Officer Stevenson's a good one to have with you. He's almost as good a shot as I am with a pistol. I'll be up here if you need me."

Luna turned to Maryann. "You have to get in the tunnel. Now. That policeman is very nice and well-meaning. But he is no match for Faucon."

"And if I do, what's *your* plan—I mean, if Faucon gets by Cliff?"

"Faucon will challenge me to come up and fight him. If I refuse, he will offer to fight me down here."

"And will he win? I don't know your level of expertise with those swords."

"I am technically as good as he is. He has size and strength on his side."

"So he'd beat you?"

"Luck favors those who are prepared."

Maryann thought for a minute. "How about this for a plan? Don't fight him up or down. Keep him in the middle. That opening in the roof is a bottleneck, a narrow pass. He can't swing his arms on the way down. So you take up a position under the opening. Every time he tries to come down, you slash at his feet and legs. How's that?"

Luna stood there, not fully grasping the plan.

"It's simple," Maryann said. "You defend, I dig." She turned away, got to her knees, and began digging.

⚜ ⚜ ⚜

Cliff had just taken up his position when his cellphone gave a silent burp in his pocket. *A text.* He gave a quick check of his surroundings, switched his weapon to his left hand, and reached for the phone. He pulled it out and held it at arm's length down near his thigh. *AJ Stevenson.* His eyes were downcast for only a few seconds and he was about to press the screen with his thumb when the roof in front of him darkened. He glanced up in time to see a pair of fierce red eyes coming at him fast, then a glint of metal as Faucon's sword arm slashed down, the long blade striking sideways across his chest with the force of a shotgun blast. There was no time to raise his arm, much less his pistol, in self-defense. Cliff, his weapon, and his cellphone tumbled off the wall and thumped onto the forest floor ten feet below.

⚜ ⚜ ⚜

Luna heard the *oof* of the blow that forced the air out of Cliff's lungs.

"It's Faucon," she said. "I think your policeman friend is down. The tunnel. Go, before it's too late."

"Only if you go, too."

Luna shook her head. "You know I cannot do that."

"Why not? Because he'll get the eggs? At least you'll be alive, and you can tell your people what happened. When they hear what Faucon's done to a legitimate crown prince's eggs, they won't let him near the throne."

"But they will. Sadly, Maryann, they will. Faucon has been lining up allies for years. You have no idea how devious and ruthless he is. If he cannot gain the crown through Champaigne's blood, he will find a way to seize it. He will not be denied."

Maryann didn't move.

"Maryann, please," Luna pleaded. "Go. You don't know Faucon. He plays on your sympathies, but make no mistake—if he gets past me, he will kill you, too, if you stand between him and the eggs."

"Luna, stick to the plan. You defend, I dig."

"Earlier when I told you what I would do with the eggs, you said you would not dig."

"That was then. Now, if I don't dig, none of them—males or females—will stand a chance. If I dig, maybe I can get one into the tunnel before he gets you." Without waiting for an answer, Maryann began digging furiously.

Luna gripped her sword and dagger and took up her position beneath the opening.

"Luna!" Faucon called down. "Leave your friends there and come out. I have no quarrel with them. I will not harm them. You have my word."

"Your word is worth nothing, Faucon."

"Come up now, Luna." Impatience frayed his voice. "We will settle this. I have Champaigne's weapons, you have LeClair's."

"You *stole* Champaigne's weapons, he did not give them willingly. You murdered him after he honored his brother's vow to raise you. You call him *pere* now only to gain what was *his* birthright: the crown of Cyrus."

"You are wrong," Faucon protested. "He wanted me to have it. Had he not adopted me, who would be next in line? He was going to die eventually—with no sons—because you, Luna, would not make the sacrifice.

You chose selfishly. Your sister Diana accepted responsibility, but you could not."

"You know nothing about it, Faucon. I loved Champaigne and he loved me, so deeply that he would not let me sacrifice myself at 50 or 100 like Diana did for LeClair. Champaigne wanted us to live the entire length of our lives together. Unlike you, he had no desire for the crown. He saw that it was a curse on his brother and Diana, who were obliged to produce an heir to Cyrus' throne. LeClair felt he had no choice but to surrender his beloved at that young age. It is the curse of *les gargouilles*, Faucon—a double curse. Not only must females suffer the sacrifice, but so must those who love them."

Unmoved, Faucon said, "So you have come to this place to birth your sister's sons. Why? So you can experience motherhood? Or is it to carry home a blood *dauphin* to King Cyrus?"

"Does my reason matter, Faucon?"

A pause, then, "It does not," and another pause. "The time for talk has passed, Luna. Come up."

"The choice is yours, Faucon. Leave now and you leave in peace. Go."

"Hah! You have no hope, Luna. If you do not come up, I will come down and bury you with your sister."

"I am not afraid, Faucon. This young policeman has additional officers *en route*. We will defend my sister's home until they arrive. LeClair's blade is still very sharp, and before you murdered him, Champaigne made sure I was skilled in its use. Come down if you must, but first choose which foot you will give up." She added, "Or you can leave while you still breathe."

Behind her, Maryann pawed back the last of the softer soil and broke a fingernail on the harder floor a foot down.

What is this stuff--cement? No, it's rock.

CHAPTER 53

Keegan and AJ crept quietly toward the crest of the hill.

"Neither one of them answered my text," AJ whispered.

Keegan stopped and reached a hand back, freezing AJ in place. They listened.

"Luna!" they heard a deep male voice say. "Leave your friends there and come out. I have no quarrel with them. I will not harm them. You have my word."

"That's Faucon," AJ whispered. "Sounds like he's on the roof and Luna is down below."

"They're just over this rise. If we can sneak up without making noise, maybe we can see what's happening."

They inched forward, dropping to a crouch and then getting down on their stomachs. They saw Faucon less than fifty yards off, alone on the roof, the soft light of the lantern emanating from the opening.

"Come down, if you must," they heard Luna say, "but first choose which foot you will give up. Or you can leave while you still breathe."

AJ said softly in Keegan's ear, "When I crawled into the tunnel, Faucon was on the roof and your mother was digging. I don't know how Luna got down there."

They watched Faucon pace the roof.

AJ cupped her hand to Keegan's ear again. "Should I call Aaron? Or at least 9-1-1?"

Keegan shook her head and held a finger to her lips.

Faucon stopped by the far edge of the roof and looked over it at the forest floor below.

"What's he doing?" AJ asked in a whisper.

Keegan shrugged an I-don't-know.

Faucon's short wings came out and started to vibrate. AJ and Keegan could hear them hum. A moment later the *gargouille* stepped off the roof, hovering mid-air, then descended.

"Where'd he go?" AJ said softly.

Keegan shrugged again and whispered, "If he was leaving, he'd fly up, not down."

The hum of wings grew louder, then louder still, like an engine having to work harder. Faucon's head appeared where he had stepped off, and as he rose they saw not his muscular *gargouille* chest but the face of Cliff Bragdon, head lolling to one side on his own shoulder. Keegan's and AJ's mouths fell open, but they let no sound out. Faucon had his arms around the big cop's chest like he was doing a Heimlich maneuver.

While Faucon's arms secured the limp cop's 250 pounds of dead weight, his wings strained to do the heavy lifting, hauling their human cargo fifteen feet above the ground. When all four feet, Faucon's and Cliff's, were level with the roof, Faucon stepped forward and the hum ceased. He worked his way closer to the opening, keeping Cliff in front of him like a shield. Then, supporting him with one massive arm across Cliff's chest, Faucon pulled out his thrusting dagger and laid it across Cliff's throat.

"Luna, come out or the *gendarme's* blood will be on your hands."

Luna could see Cliff's his head tipped toward one shoulder.

Is he unconscious or is Faucon using a dead man to draw me out?

"*Un moment*," she answered, and backed away from the opening.

"Now what do we do?" Maryann whispered. "You can't go up and fight him."

"Go find Aaron," Luna said very quietly.

"And do what—bring him back here? Faucon still has Cliff for leverage."

"I mean follow Aaron. Leave. I will deal with Faucon. It is the only way to save this other policeman's life—if he is still alive."

"What do you mean, *if* he's still alive?" Maryann croaked. "Do you think there's a chance he's not?"

"I cannot know from here. His body is limp. Faucon is playing on our emotions, using your friend to manipulate me."

Maryann called out, "Faucon, we need a guarantee that policeman is still alive."

"Shall I cut off his fingers so you can see that he still bleeds?" Faucon answered, giving a nasty little laugh. "Ah, but that would be vulgar, would it not? Perhaps I can make him speak. Would that satisfy you? Listen."

Luna and Maryann moved closer to the opening and glanced up.

Faucon sheathed his dagger and reached both arms around Cliff in a bear hug. Cliff's head, which had been on one shoulder, fell forward, chin on chest.

"Speak," Faucon commanded.

Cliff didn't respond.

Faucon dropped his arms lower, clasping his hands together under Cliff's diaphragm. "Your friends cannot hear you," Faucon mocked. "Louder." He tightened his grip, torqueing his arms tighter.

Cliff groaned but didn't open his eyes.

Faucon's breaking his ribs, Maryann thought, and cried, "Stop!"

The *gargouille* stopped. "Enough?" he asked, and smiled grotesquely. He returned to the one-armed grip, drew the dagger again, and placed it back across the unconscious Cliff's throat. "Your *gendarme* makes noise. Shall we see if he bleeds?"

"Stop!" Luna cried out. "I will come out." She said softly to Maryann, "Forget the eggs. Use the tunnel. Have Aaron call for more police. I will try to keep Faucon busy until they arrive. Tell them to destroy Faucon, if they can."

"But—"

"Maryann, go. Now."

Maryann's face bore a pained look. She reached out, gave Luna a quick hug, and whispered, "Good luck, Luna. You kick his big *gargouille* ass."

"I will do my best."

As soon as Maryann disappeared into the rabbit hole, Luna called out, "Faucon, move back. Give me room. I am coming out."

☛ ☛ ☛

Keegan and AJ watched Faucon dump Cliff off the high side of the roof.

"AJ," Keegan said. "We know why Cliff's not answering the text, but we don't know about Aaron. Sneak back to where we came out and call him. If you don't get him, call 9-1-1."

"And what are you going to do?" AJ asked.

"First thing, check on Cliff, see if he's breathing. And check for his gun and Taser. We'll need a weapon to help Luna."

"You said *first thing*. What's the second?"

Keegan pointed at the roof. "The slab is up. I've got to drop it back into place so Faucon can't reach the eggs."

"I did that once before," AJ said. "But Faucon winched it back up again. You knock it over, he'll just reopen it."

"Then I'll unhook it and throw it into the hole before I kick over the slab. He can't use it if he can't get to it."

"And where will that leave you?"

"Hopefully standing there with Cliff's gun, waiting for backup."

"Yeah," AJ said. "*Hopefully.*"

The two of them didn't move for a moment, until Keegan said, "You got a better plan?"

"Nope."

"Well, okay then. We're set. You go make some calls and I'll work my way around and check on Cliff."

"You be careful down there, Tool Girl," AJ said, eyes moist and lower lip quivering.

"You, too, BFF."

CHAPTER 54

AJ reached the green flasher and pulled out her cellphone to call Aaron. Before she could tap his number, she heard his voice, not on the phone but in the hole.

"AJ! Keegan! Is that you up there?"

She peered down, trying to make her brother out through the thicket of roots. She saw his flashlight beam.

"I can't see you, just your light," she said. "What are you doing down there?"

He used his light to illuminate his face and said, "I came through the tunnel. Is Keegan with you?"

"Yes and no. I just left her. She went to help Cliff. Faucon did a number on him."

"How bad is he hurt?"

"Don't know, but I'm guessing he's pretty bad. It looked like he was unconscious when Faucon stood him up and put a sword to his throat."

"He didn't—"

"No. He did that to force Luna out of the big room so he can fight her. He needs her out of the way so he can get at the eggs. She had no choice but to agree, and once she did, Faucon tossed Cliff off the roof. Do you still have your gun?"

"I do," Aaron answered.

"Good. You're going to need it."

"I've got to climb out," he said. "In the meantime, you call dispatch and tell Marcy we've got an officer down—but no shots fired. Tell her it's the sword guy from the Bear's Den cemetery call. We need backup. I'll confirm it with her when I get up there and my phone kicks in again."

Maryann scrambled through the tunnel as fast as her hands and knees would carry her. She came to the heap of dirt in the way and bellied her way over it to the place where things opened up. She saw that everything dead-ended and for a moment her heart sank.

Did I miss a side tunnel?

"Maryann?" Aaron's voice. Above her.

She aimed her light up into the root maze and saw a flashing green light.

""Here," Aaron said.

She dropped the beam a few feet below the flasher and saw a figure in a police uniform waving at her.

"Aaron?"

"Glad you made it. You'll have to climb up the roots to get to ground level. I'm almost there."

"As soon as I catch my breath," she said, and sat.

"AJ says Faucon used Cliff to draw Luna out."

"He did. She was still in down below when I dropped into the tunnel. She probably flew up when I was out of there. Any idea what's happening now?"

"Not sure," Aaron replied. "I had AJ call dispatch for backup. When I get up top and pick up a signal, I'll check in."

"Where are AJ and Keegan now?"

"AJ's right above me. AJ, you there?"

No answer.

"AJ?" Aaron called again.

Still no answer.

"Damn," he swore. "She went after Keegan."

"Get moving, Aaron," Maryann ordered, and started climbing.

With no flashlight to show her the terrain, Keegan felt her way down the hill while keeping her bearings on the light coming out of the Stonehedge roof opening. She checked the airspace above the treetops and saw the two *gargouilles* jockeying for position. *Keep him busy, Luna,* she thought, and tried to make a beeline for the spot where Cliff's limp body had been dropped from the roof.

Minutes later her hand touched cold granite, one of the wall blocks. She went right, the ground under her feet dropping slightly, and immediately came to a massive tree. As she rounded it her foot caught on something and she pitched forward on top of it—Cliff's unmoving body. He was face up, and she found herself lying across his stomach. She crawled off and sat up next to him. She placed a hand on his chest. He was breathing, but it was shallow.

Pat him down. Use your hands to see if anything's broken.

She did. Both legs were straight, and so was one arm. The other arm was hidden under his back, so she had no way of knowing how twisted it might be. She didn't dare press his ribs. There was nothing more to be done for him. EMTs would have to take over when they arrived.

She felt the buckle on his duty belt and worked her way around it to check for his pistol. Not there. Empty holster.

Where is it? Did Faucon take it or is it lying somewhere around here in the bushes?

Cliff's Taser was still there. It would be the same as Aaron's, which he had shown her and AJ when he first made the force. She was sure she could set it and fire it. She took it.

Cliff's rechargeable Mag Lite was missing, but in a pouch on his belt she found his smaller flashlight, the one he used for nighttime car searches. She also found the pepper spray.

Now to get around to the tree on the other side where the Come-Along's anchored. Maybe I'll get lucky and stumble over the pistol and Mag Lite. I'd feel better with a pistol than this Taser.

She continued downhill in the dark, not daring to use the flashlight, until she turned the corner and started feeling her way across the lowest side of the granite bunker containing Diana's bones.

Section XI

Swords and *Poignards* En Garde

CHAPTER 55

Luna's hands felt the heft of LeClair's sword and dagger. They were light, but right now they seemed heavier than she remembered. She hadn't swung them seriously in more than 20 years.

She recalled the night in 1995 when Champaigne gave her his brother's blades. It had been shortly before Champaigne's unexpected death. Even with his health and strength diminished, he had insisted the two of them fly to the outcropping where he and LeClair had saved Clayton Lussier from wolves in the 1850s. It had been the twin princes' favorite practice area, where they went to hone their weapons skills. It had been Lussier's good fortune they had been sparring near the river when he and his apprentice overturned their canoe.

Near the outcropping, Champaigne showed Luna a cave in which he had hidden a long flat wooden box. The case contained LeClair's sword, *poignard*, and a double leather sheath.

"I hid these here after the Great War," he told her. "I had no one to pass these on to." He held the case out on his palms.

"*Por moi?*" she recalled asking. "Why? Because I am Diana's sister?"

"Luna, this is not about my brother or his mate. It is not about inheritance. It is about having these blades in the hands of someone who can use them. Remember when the four of us were young—LeClair and Diana, you and I—and we practiced with them? We sparred nearly everywhere—on the ground, in secret among the trees—anywhere except the air, for fear that my father or someone from the clan would see us if we fought above the forest."

"You and LeClair were so easily manipulated. Diana and I talked two into not only teaching us to fight—but with your weapons."

"Because females have no weapons," he had replied.

"But we had them then," she had answered. "Do you not remember us disarming the two of you? We ended up with your swords and *poignards,* did we not?"

"I am not sure if it was your skills or your wiles that caused us to lower our guard," he said with a tired smile. Then he had placed the box on her upright palms, their fingers brushing.

"Why now?" she had asked.

"Because they need to be in the hands of someone who not only knows *how* to use them, but *when*. Against my better judgment I must pass my own weapons on to Faucon, who is already adept in their use. As an adopted son, he is entitled to them. That being said, I will tell you that I have never fully trusted him. He has ambitions, and I believe he is a plotter who sees me as feeble at a time when my own father nears the end of his life. It is becoming increasingly difficult for Faucon to wait for my life and my father's to end naturally."

Champaigne had withdrawn his hands then, and she had felt the weight of the case transfer fully to her hands. She carried it from the cave, laid it on the ground, and unhooked the catch. She opened it, lifted out the double sheath, and drew out the sword and dagger. The oiled blades glistened in the moonlight.

She and Champaigne had each taken a weapon and practiced in the clearing—he with dagger, she with sword, then the other way around—slashing, blocking, thrusting, stabbing, parrying. They never left the ground, stopping only when he was too tired to carry on. But he would not let her stop and handed her his weapon so she had the pair. He instructed her in how to fight with both at once. She practiced until she too was exhausted.

"I will keep them safe here in the cave," she had told him, "until I need them."

They had embraced then, and Champaigne's long upper glide wings had come out, spreading like an angel's and then gently closing around them both. They slumbered that way until dawn, safe in the cocoon of his wings. Then they had flown home.

Eight months later Champagne was dead, and she recalled his words: *Faucon has ambitions.*

She later returned to the clearing and the cave, where she retrieved the wooden case and carried it outside. She opened it and lifted free the sword and *poignard*. She held them up, saw them gleam and watched the moonlight glint off their blades. She practiced a few of the moves Champaigne had taught her before her grief overwhelmed her. Going through the moves alone brought back memories of their practice the night he presented her with his brother's weapons case.

She was about to close the wooden case when something about it caught her eye—the inside of the cover. Scratched there by hand—perhaps with the point of the dagger—were: *Prince LeClair, 1817-1919, American Civil War, mustard gas Great War France, died at sea, influenza.*

Her heart caught in her throat. Champaigne had to have written it there, perhaps on the sea voyage home. She felt the grief again, now doubled. She had loved both princes, as had Diana. All three of them were gone now, and only she was left.

Below Champaigne's epitaph for his brother she saw in smaller letters, probably LeClair's writing: *Diana, beloved mate of LeClair, 1817-1916.*

I was right, she had realized. *Diana didn't go to ground after the Civil War, not in 1865 or 1866. She and LeClair delayed their nesting until he was summoned by Cyrus to lead the Allagash unit with his brother. Diana lay down and he covered her, then returned home and went to France in 1917. He was planning to return to the nest in 2016. But the mustard gas and the influenza prevented him.*

Luna's chance discovery of Diana's epitaph inside the wooden lid that night in 1996 had become the seed of a plan. If she were to stop Faucon, she had 20 years to find her sister's bones and the attached eggs. But neither LeClair nor Champaigne was alive to tell her where the nest was. And she didn't want to arouse Faucon's suspicions 20 years early. Which was when she had come up with the idea of attending the University of Maine— the first *gargouille* to do so. She had told Cyrus, Faucon, and the clan it was about music, art, and literature—but it was really about genealogical research. It was about finding Diana.

That had led to her friendship with Zelda Keegan, the gifted student researcher—the same Zelda whose own sister, daughter and friends had now been drawn into something that put their lives in danger.

CHAPTER 56

Once Faucon got rid of Cliff, he launched himself skyward—not at Luna who was staying close to the treetops, but straight up. He passed by her, several body lengths away, and climbed another 200 yards before he stopped, a fat dot against the night sky.

Keep the sky at your back whenever possible, Drago had told him and his brothers when they were young, before the German armies swarmed over Europe like locusts. *Unlike the ground, the sky gives your opponent no reference points.* If he went at Luna with a blank sky behind him he would hold an advantage, for she would find it difficult to gauge his speed and distance.

In his mind Faucon saw that last night in 1917 before he and his father went off to war with their clansmen. Two dozen *gargouilles* equipped for battle had waited outside the cave while Drago said goodbye to his sons Lafayette and Fantome, Faucon's elder brothers. Both ached to join the fight, but their father insisted they stay behind, outlining his rationale.

"I am battle-hardened and still young enough to fight. As the clan leader I must lead this force. You three are too young and inexperienced.

"Lafayette, my son, you are the *dauphin* and must be protected, as must your brother Fantome, my reserve *dauphin.*

"Faucon, I would prefer to keep you safe here with your brothers, but we need another sword. You lack experience, but I will teach you as I can. You may have to develop skills in battle.

"Lafayette and Fantome, should the Germans reach this settlement, you will know that our force has failed in our mission and we have perished. From this night on it falls upon you to lead our clan—while we are away and later if I am lost in the fight. Begin preparing your defense now. *Au revoir, mes enfants.*"

Faucon also recalled his father later soaring over the glacier amid withering German artillery and rifle fire, carrying first Crown Prince LeClair to safety and then Prince Champaigne—only to be mortally wounded by a blast at the end of the second flight, when his tattered body shielded Champaigne's.

My father wasted his life. LeClair was near death and should have been left behind. Had he survived the influenza, he would have been a sickly king. Champaigne too was weak and fragile when he returned home and would have been a poor successor to Cyrus. My father's death may yet prove to be a lucky turn of events, for as Champagne's adopted son I will rise to the throne of les gargouilles, *surpassing Lafayette and Fantome.*

He raised his sword and dagger and slashed the air twice to loosen his shoulders.

"Luna," he yelled, "*en garde,*" and took off straight for her.

CHAPTER 57

Luna saw him barreling at her and knew he had no plan to pull up short so they could thrust and parry. He was hoping to use his weight and his downward momentum to deliver a single heavy crashing overhand—a cavalry move—in an effort to drive her back against the branches. He would not need his dagger, because he would pass too rapidly for a reverse thrust with it. Once he flashed by, he would circle back and see if the blow had stunned her. If it did, he could move in and pin her against the branches, giving her nowhere to retreat and leaving her in a space too restrictive for Luna to raise her sword over her shoulder. Then he could slash or stab her.

Luna placed her dagger between her teeth and gripped the sword hilt with both hands. She raised the blade in front of her face as if she planned to accept or deflect Faucon's passing overhand. His approach was straight and fast, but with only the sky behind him she couldn't tell quite how fast.

Now, a voice in her head ordered, and as Faucon's blade came down she flitted backward several feet, at the same time rotating upside down—all without moving her arms or changing her defensive stance. Instead of her blade being vertical and pointed upward, which would make it like an anvil absorbing a blacksmith's hammer blow, it was reversed, vertical but angling downward from the hilt. His sword came down and slid along her blade and past her forehead. It had been a risky maneuver, but it paid off for her. Faucon had been too heavily invested in the might of his downward blow—an anger fueled swing—but she had made her blade flexible, giving him no surface to absorb the blow. He tipped forward as if he had tripped, then spun off-balance so that he had to work hard to catch himself before crashing into the roof below. He was able to recover at the last second and looped back up to the top of an oak. He hovered there directly across 50 feet of open air from Luna.

"I underestimated you," Faucon said. "That will not happen again."

"I was lucky," Luna lied. "I am a female who has no experience with a sword. But I am smart enough to know that even the strongest carpenter can swing a hammer and miss the nail, crushing his own thumb."

"Do not mock the next king, Luna," he said threateningly.

Diana, I wish you were here to fight next to me as we did in our practices with LeClair and Champaigne. I remember those moves and I have my new learnings from my night with Champaigne at the outcroppin, when he taught me to fight two-handed. But everything was on the ground, not in the air. I am ill-prepared for this.

"I have not mocked the next king," she replied. "I have mocked you, Faucon."

He had no immediate response. Then out of nowhere he taunted her. "Champaigne didn't put up much of a fight."

She said nothing, knew he was goading her, trying to get her to act on emotion and make a mistake.

"Your beloved was, in the end, weak as a kitten."

She held her tongue though she seethed inside.

"Do you want to know the last thing he said to me?"

He wants you to lose control, to grow careless. He'll charge once he sees that he's got your blood boiling.

"The last thing he said was, 'When I am gone, Luna is yours. I give her to you, my son. Make her your queen.'"

Liar.

She took the dagger out of her teeth and assumed the two-handed fighting stance. Her jaw was tight and her nostrils flared with anger. Her fingers tightened and loosened, tightened and loosened around her weapons.

Take a deep breath, Champaigne's voice said in her head. She inhaled through her nose, then slowly exhaled out of her mouth.

"I just wanted you to know what his last words were," Faucon said, "before I smothered him."

Bastard.

"He died the same way LeClair died," he said, "aboard the ship."

Murderer.

She bit her thin bottom lip and tried to take another deep breath. But her chest heaved unevenly and it turned into an angry sob. The pain and anguish were for the moment too much to bear, and her transparent reptilian lids closed over her green eyes.

Faucon saw the slow blink and knew he had her off balance. The time had come to charge. He led with Champaigne's dagger in his left, the sword hand slightly ahead of his right shoulder so he could slash, deflect, or lower it to stab.

Luna saw him coming and raised her lids.

Not here, the voice in her head said. *The ground.*

She reversed and turned sideways in the air, flattening herself out, then pressed herself between two tiers of pine boughs on the tree behind her.

She knew she was momentarily exposed and shot through the branches just as Faucon's sword hacked down on something near her toes.

Let it be a branch, not my foot, not my leg.

There was no pain. But she understood shock. A body part might be severed without any accompanying pain right away. She used the dagger like a machete and slashed her way through the pine limbs, past the trunk, and out the other side. Behind her Faucon cursed. A moment later she came out on the towering pine's other side, deep in the woods where everything was closer together. She would have little room to maneuver, but the larger Faucon with his broader shoulders, longer wings, and longer reach, would have even less. Branches clawed at her lower wings, leaving her no choice but to retract them and tumble in a freefall. She struck branches in the dark as she fell, finally thudding onto the forest floor before tumbling forward in a somersault.

If I have to be run through, let it be by a sword and not a broken-off tree limb.

She came to a stop and lay on her back in the leaves and pine needles, catching her breath and collecting her thoughts.

Thanks to LeClair and Champaigne I know how to fight in close quarters. But how shall I draw Faucon here?

"Luna?" Faucon called from beyond the giant pine.

She heard no hum of wings. *He is on the ground.*

"Luna, it sounded like you suffered a terrible fall," he said, voice dripping with false concern. "I hope you are not hurt. I would hate to kill an injured female."

She didn't answer. If she stayed quiet and didn't move, he had no way of knowing exactly where she was. Would he come looking for her? Or would he go for the eggs, figuring she wouldn't dare attack him in the chamber?

He offered a compromise.

"Luna, we can finish this on the roof."

She had to think. *Where are my voices now?*

CHAPTER 58

Aaron was at ground level, finishing up his whispered call. Maryann was halfway up the ladder of roots.

AJ appeared next to Aaron, back from the crest of the hill. "What'd they say?" she quietly asked her brother.

"Marcy's sending two units. No SWAT. A whacko with a sword doesn't meet the guidelines. He should be within the capabilities of traditional law enforcement."

"But he's got *two* swords," she whispered. "And he flies. You're fighting him in the woods in the dark, Aaron. Don't let the uniform go to your head. He could kill you. I saw what he did to Cliff. He crushed his ribs. I don't want something to happen—"

"I know, AJ. I don't want anything to happen to you, either, or any of us. You didn't let me finish. The backup team is two of ours plus a Trooper, and a couple of EMTs. I need you to meet them up at the parking lot. Give them the picture then lead them in."

"And what are you going to do?"

"I've got Cliff and Keegan to worry about."

"And Luna," AJ added.

"I'll help her if I can, but Cliff and Keegan are my first priorities. And Maryann."

"What'll I tell them we're dealing with here?"

"Don't lead off with gargoyles if you want credibility. Maybe suggest two deranged Dungeons and Dragons reenactors—a big man and a small woman—*dressed* like gargoyles. Say they may have rubber costumes with wings hiding jet packs. But make it clear that the swords and daggers are real and they know how to use them. Be sure to emphasize that it's the big male who's dangerous. He's the one we need to neutralize."

"Neutralize? You mean eliminate?"

"Stun him, or bring him down, or drive him away. No guns unless he offers a direct threat to one of us. Last resort. Got it?"

"Got it," she replied shakily, and threw her arms around him in a hug. "You be careful, Aaron."

"You, too. Now go. Fast as you can but quietly."

☙☙☙

Keegan sat at the base of the wall below the anchor tree with the cable around it. She had heard the hum of wings when one of the *gargouilles* tumbled down through the branches and landed with a hollow thud. Then silence. Which one was it, Luna or Faucon? Probably her. And how far away out there, how far from the wall—20, 30, 50 feet? Hard to tell in the dark. Then she'd heard the hum of the other, descending, landing close to her before the wing noise ceased. Which one? Then the deep voice.

"Luna, it sounded like you suffered a terrible fall. I hope you are not hurt. I would hate to kill an injured female."

No response.

Is Luna injured? Unconscious? Dead?

A moment later, "Luna, we can finish this on the roof."

Got to move fast, Keegan thought, then straightened up quietly and reached up. *Can't do a pullup from this side. The roof is higher here.* She felt for footholds and toeholds, clenched her teeth against the knee pain, and climbed, pulling herself onto the roof. The balanced slab was there, held up by the cable. Lantern light came up on the other side of the slab. She also saw the Come-Along handle and take-up reel a yard from the slab.

Uh-oh. Maximum exposure. I'll be out in the open and backlit by the lantern light.

She listened but didn't hear Luna respond to Faucon. A voice in her head said, *Even if Luna's dead, we still need to protect those eggs from Faucon.* Had that been her voice or someone else's? It sounded strangely like her own but not exactly.

There was no hum of short wings, so Keegan made a quick check of the woods where she had last heard Faucon. She crept out to the Come-Along assembly, set her feet, and pulled the handle back half a notch, disengaging the tooth that locked the gear. The cable slacked and the slab stayed balanced without the support of the taut cable. She disconnected the hook from the chain that was still belted around the slab, then quietly laid the cable and winch apparatus down on the roof. Next she unwrapped the other end of the cable from the tree, then scooped up everything and dumped it over the slab into the hole. She put her shoulder to the slab and heaved. *Whump!* Over it went, back in its previous position with the chamber sealed. Keegan stood there on the roof in the dark.

"Luna?" called Faucon.

Keegan heard his wings hum. She had to get off the roof fast. She ran to the high side where Cliff lay below and turned around to back down.

"I'm here, Faucon!" Luna shouted. "Come and get me."

Luna, don't give away your position. She's trying to draw his attention away from me.

Keegan didn't waste the opportunity and disappeared over the edge, holding onto the roof slab by her fingers as her feet felt around in the darkness below her, expecting to come into contact with Cliff's unconscious body. Nothing. Just as she was about to let go and drop the rest of the way, she felt a pair of large hands grip her above the hips.

"Gotcha," a familiar voice said. Not Cliff. *Aaron.*

CHAPTER 59

"Where's Cliff?" Keegan whispered once she had her feet on solid ground.

"I carried him to the tunnel," Aaron whispered back. "He's still out. Your mother's with him."

"Where's AJ?"

"She's meeting the backup team at the parking lot. Cops and EMTs. I heard Faucon. Sounds like he's out past the other wall in the woods. I heard Luna, too. What's going on?"

"They squared off up in the treetops with their swords. I don't know what happened. I think she crashed down through the branches and hit hard. He must have landed so he could finish it. He called her out, but she didn't answer. He challenged her to a duel on the roof, so I pulled the Come-Along off and tossed it into the hole then slammed the lid. We can't let Faucon can't get to the eggs."

"You're lucky he didn't catch you in the open." He stepped away from the wall in the direction of the new tunnel opening. "Let's go."

"Go where?" she asked.

"Out of here. Time to withdraw. We go back and stay with your mother and Cliff and wait for the backup and EMTs. Everybody's safe, including Cliff, even if he's a little banged up. That was the goal."

"What do you mean *safe?* Luna's not. She's out there—maybe injured—with a psycho stalking her."

Aaron chose his words carefully. "I appreciate your concern for her, Keegan. As a person I'd like to help her, but as a cop my duty is to protect the public, to get the people . . . the humans . . . out of harm's way. That means Maryann, Cliff, AJ and you."

He started in the direction of the tunnel, then stopped, turned, and reached out a hand, palm up, like he was asking her to dance. "Please, Keegan, let's go."

She saw his gaze suddenly drawn to the roof behind her. His mouth fell open. Then he was eclipsed, blotted out by a huge dark form that dropped down, totally filling the space between them. She caught a sharp, fast movement—the *gargouille's* head snapping forward in a head butt. She heard it crunch against Aaron's forehead along with an *oof* as air exited his lungs. Then she heard his body crumple to the ground.

Faucon turned and faced her. He was a silhouette, the shadow of a towering hunchback. Her fingers refused to turn on Cliff's flashlight. She couldn't bear the thought of having to stare up at his terrifying countenance. He placed his hands heavily on her shoulders, and in his iron grip she fainted.

Section XII

The Universal Sisterhood Emerges

CHAPTER 60

"Leave the girl," a voice ordered.

Faucon glanced up at the roof and saw Luna towering over him, sword and dagger fanned in front of her. He held Keegan by her shoulders like he'd been hanging a shirt on a clothesline.

He can't draw his sword or dagger while he's holding her up.

He knew what she was thinking. "Back away, Luna, or I will snap her neck."

Luna stepped back from the edge of the roof, giving Faucon room to reach his weapons.

He released one shoulder, keeping Keegan suspended by the other, and reached behind his head, drawing his sword. He positioned it between himself and Luna then let go of Keegan. Before her limp body could hit the ground next to Aaron, he had the dagger out of its sheath. Now he was fully armed and battle-ready. His short wings vibrated and hummed, and he rose straight up like a man riding an invisible elevator, which he exited at roof level, sword and *poignard* at the ready, mirroring Luna's. Except he was two feet taller, and his arms were far longer than hers.

"The girl sealed Diana's chamber," Luna said. "You cannot destroy the eggs now."

"I do not have to. Once you are dead," he replied coldly, "your precious eggs will all rot naturally."

Champaigne's voice came back to her from their night in the clearing, their final training session.

I have watched Faucon practice. Do not expect a fencing match. He is formidable in the air but on the ground he is predictable. If he circles to his right he will spring like a tiger, coming at you with his sword up, slashing downward on you as he leaps over you. If he circles left he will lead with his sword, lowering like a charging rhinoceros. Either way expect him to engage suddenly in order to force you into a standing defense. He likes to occupy you with his sword so he can come under your belly with his dagger. Remember, right for tiger above, left for rhino below.

She extended her sword as if this were to be a classic fencing match with *epees*. Would he touch blades with her before engaging?

He took one tentative step to his right then came back and started circling to his left, backing slightly farther away from her as he moved.

Where are you going, rhino? Need a long run for your charge? This won't be as easy as smothering an invalid.

She knew what she had to do. Champaigne had taught her the risky maneuver, but she had never tried it in battle. How could she? The treetop skirmish 10 minutes earlier had been her first real trial, and it had nearly been the end of her. She watched Faucon extend his sword and almost imperceptibly lower the single horn on his forehead.

Rhino.

He charged, expecting her to resort to a defensive stance so she could deflect his blade to the side.

But instead of stepping back, she launched herself directly at him, diving between his thick legs like a base runner sliding headfirst into home plate. She kept the hilts of her weapons tight against her cheeks, the blades pointed straight up over her head like the masts on a schooner. If Faucon didn't do something to block Luna's twin blades, he would be a plank facing a sawmill blade, and his own forward motion would disembowel him.

His reflexes kicked in and he brought his thrusting dagger flat across his thighs so it pressed her blades back against her shoulders and upper wings. He made it safely past the twin blades but as he passed over her ankles she hooked his foot, throwing him off balance. He toppled forward and skidded along the roof on his barrel chest like a cargo plane touching down with its landing gear stuck up. He came to a stop at the roof's edge.

By then Luna was on her feet, watching him turn and get up.

Merci, Champaigne. It worked, though it did not wound him.

Faucon had underestimated her, not expecting the dive move that nearly gutted him.

Luna waited for him to make the next move.

"You might have become a queen," he said.

"*C'est vrai*, had Champaigne lived. But you murdered him, the very one who took you in."

"I did not mean *his* queen," Faucon corrected.

She looked puzzled for a moment, then got it and laughed disdainfully. "You cannot mean *yours*?"

His filmy reptilian eyelids closed slowly and the glowing red eyes appeared dull.

Got to him. Her words struck the blow that her sword and dagger had not. When his lids lifted again she saw that her rebuff had fanned two hot coals of anger.

"It is not too late," he said, not using her name. The bitterness in his voice promised revenge, not possibility.

Watch his feet for movement.

"Never, monsieur. I could not be queen to a murderer."

"And yet you would have been Champaigne's," he said tauntingly.

What does he mean by that?

He goads you, the voice warned. *Watch him.*

He stepped to his right and started to circle.

Springing tiger.

But she could not forget his taunt. "What are you saying, Faucon?"

"Did Champaigne not tell you about his beloved brother—what he did to him?"

He lies, Champaigne said in her head, *to steal your concentration. Watch for the tiger.*

She stalled. "His lungs were damaged by the gas and the influenza killed him. Champaigne's lung were also damaged, not as badly."

Faucon kept circling right.

Tiger. Be ready. She prepared to switch hands with her weapons.

"That is what Champaigne told the clan. Are you afraid to hear the truth?"

Luna kept silent and held her focus. Faucon was looking for the chink in her mental armor.

"What would you have done if LeClair had survived and asked you to be his queen? And what would your lover Champaigne have done?"

"LeClair loved my sister," Luna replied, as if it were a cold hard fact.

"But Diana is long gone. She was his *mate*, and she gave herself long ago. Yet a prince's desire for a queen lives on."

He wants me to make the first move toward him. The centers of her reptilian eyes stared straight at his face while taking in his foot movements.

"LeClair would never have asked me to be his queen. He knew how Champaigne and I felt about each other. Unlike you, LeClair was honorable."

"If that is true, then why did Champaigne smother his brother at sea? Could it be that *le dauphin*—in his fevered moments—confessed his desire for his younger brother's beloved Luna?"

Don't listen, she heard Champaigne say. *He twists the truth.*

But the seed of doubt had been planted. Had her lover Champaigne smothered his elder brother? Or had it been the influenza that took him, as was reported when Champaigne and Faucon got off the ship? She fought to make sense of it. There had to be an explanation other than what Faucon was suggesting.

Champaigne, if it was you who smothered him, tell me that your brother was near death and begged you to relieve him of his suffering. Then the cursed thought crept into her mind: *Or did you fear he would survive?*

Hush, my love, Champaigne's voice whispered in her mind. *The tiger will drop one foot back before he runs at you.*

"The influenza handed him a perfect opportunity," Faucon said. "He gave the dying *dauphin* what he yearned for—*la mort*—and at the same time stole his crown." Faucon paused for emphasis, then added, "And he made sure you were stolen by his brother."

Faucon waited to see if Luna would drop her guard and let out a little cry.

"If what you say is true," she said, "why did you not tell King Cyrus and the clan?"

"Two reasons. He threatened to kill me if I spoke of it. And he bought my silence by promising that in time he would adopt me."

She saw his foot drop back. *Ready.*

Faucon sprinted forward and sprang.

Luna swapped dagger and sword hands and at the same time dropped to her knees. The dagger hung she held in front of her face like a priest exorcising a demon—the hilt close enough to her mouth to kiss, the blade straight up in front of her eyes. She held the sword near her left hip, ready to slash.

Faucon had calculated the height of his spring and the down-stroke of his sword based on an upright opponent, not one on her knees and low to the ground. With nothing for his trailing dagger to stab at, he swung Luna's sword. But she leaned back on the hinges of her knees, her folded wings pressing the granite roof behind her, so that he sailed over her, his blow deflected sideways by her dagger. Before he was fully out of reach, she brought her own sword from her hip into an upward arc. She felt it connect and heard him yelp. From her bent-over-backwards position she saw his heavy body crunch onto the slab somewhere beyond her head. Like a gymnast she snapped to her feet and spun around before he could mount a fresh attack.

Faucon sat up and leaned against the tree that had anchored the Come-Along cable a half hour earlier. He clutched his right foot and cursed in French. On the granite slab between them Luna saw three fat sausages—the toes her sword had severed from Faucon's right foot.

She advanced on him cautiously, weapons in front of her.

Faucon pulled himself up and stood there, sword and dagger ready for an assault, his massive bulk disproportionately leaning on the intact left foot. The stubs of the right were still in shock, and no blood had started to run.

"It was not Champaigne who smothered LeClair on the ship," Luna spat out. "It was *you!* Just like you killed Champaigne after he adopted you. You would have inherited in time, but you could not wait, could you? You murdered the very one who called you his son." She swung her sword back and forth in a waist-high arc. "*You killed them both.*"

"Your twin princes killed my father," Faucon hissed, and hobbled toward her, leading with his dagger.

Luna had no choice but to meet it and deflect it, just in time to see his sword arm wind-mill toward her in a mighty overhand. She blocked with her own sword, taking it straight on. Faucon's blow was like a blacksmith's hammer pounding an anvil. It drove her to her knees in front of him. She looked like a prisoner about to place her head on a chopping block, with Faucon the executioner. She looked up and saw the fiery rage in his glowing red eyes.

"You may steal the throne, Faucon," she croaked, holding back his blade with hers, "but you will never have me."

He kept her pinned in place with the pressure of his sword and thrust at her with his dagger, but she turned her body at the last second. In that movement she slipped out from under his sword but could not avoid the dagger's thrust. She felt its blade pass through the meat of her right armpit and continue through the short wing. He pressed the blade in up to the hilt and kept it there, then twisted it to make her cry out. She clamped her teeth, refusing to give him the satisfaction of hearing her scream. He used the dagger to control her while he raised his sword and prepared for the kill, a slash across her throat that would be powerful enough to take her head off. Or halfway off.

But as his arm went back his head tipped and his mouth opened wide in surprise. He yowled and let go of the dagger hilt, leaving it jammed in Luna's armpit, the blade tip sticking out of her back past her short wing. He staggered slightly sideways, and Luna saw Keegan behind him, her hands still gripping the handle of the ax that she had buried in his right shoulder, the sword arm. She had swung it like she was splitting firewood at home, and the sharp blade had bit through one of his long wings before continuing on into the fleshy muscle and bone of his shoulder.

CHAPTER 61

Faucon thrashed, trying to get loose, so Keegan let go of the ax handle and stepped back. He turned and faced her, sword raised only slightly above his waist, his arm's range of motion limited by the buried ax head. Keegan still wasn't out of range, though, because even if he couldn't raise the sword for a down-strike, he could slash across. He drew it back a little as if to swing a horizontal arc that might slice her in half at the waist.

"Drop it, Faucon," a woman's voice yelled. "Or so help me God, I will turn you into Swiss cheese. This Beretta fires 10 rounds a second!"

"Mom!" Keegan cried.

Faucon froze and all eyes turned to see Maryann's face at roof level next to the trunk with the cable marks. Her hands were thrust forward in a shooter's stance, the pistol aimed at Faucon's torso.

"And in case you're wondering, Faucon, yes, the safety is off. And I'm set for semi-automatic fire. For the last time, *drop the sword.*"

He loosened his grip on the hilt and his sword clattered onto the stone roof.

"You leave now, you live," Maryann said. "Your choice."

Faucon glared first at Maryann, then at Keegan, then at Luna.

"You think you have won, Luna," he said, and reached behind his lower back with his good arm to grasp the very end of the ax handle. He grimaced in pain as he twisted and loosened the ax head, but he didn't cry out. He gave it one mighty yank forward across his hip, so that it came free of his wing and the shoulder underneath. He dropped the ax next to his sword with a clunk. "This is just beginning."

"Monsieur Faucon," Maryann said, "I think your dreams of a throne are dead. And when Luna's clan finds out that you murdered Champaigne— and LeClair, if I heard right—you may wind up dead, too. Everyone—the entire *gargouille* kingdom—will be looking for you."

Faucon's transparent lids drooped and his red eyes dimmed. When they lifted, his gaze shifted back over to Keegan then down at the ax at their feet. His searing look chilled her, declaring *I will not forget this.*

"You're done here, Faucon," Maryann said. "Find a deep cave and stay there. And don't even think about messing with our friend Luna again." She motioned upward with the gun barrel. "Now get out."

Faucon's short wings came out under his arms and began to hum. He rose slowly, the wound making it difficult to lift his bulky body. He ascended to the treetops and unsuccessfully tried his upper glide wings. The ax-damaged one was a problem. He gave up and instead of soaring high he made his way barely above the trees, then a moment later disappeared from sight.

Maryann climbed onto the roof, where she and Keegan carefully withdrew Faucon's dagger from Luna's short wing and armpit.

"You've got to get out of here fast," Maryann said. "AJ's coming with more cops and paramedics for Cliff and Aaron. We don't want them to see you. Can you make it back to our place?"

Luna nodded, still in obvious pain.

"Wait for us under the deck. When we get home, you can come inside and we'll patch you up as best we can."

Keegan added, "Pull the plastic tarp off the firewood and cover yourself with it. It will shield you from the sun if we get in after dawn. We don't know how long any reports may take."

With her good arm Luna sheathed her sword and her dagger.

"What about Faucon's weapons?" Keegan asked.

"Hand me his dagger," Luna said. "I can fly with it in my left hand."

"What about his sword?" Maryann asked.

Keegan picked it up and threw it far out into the woods. "We'll come back for it. Nobody will find it tonight." Then she threw the ax out after it.

"We'll figure out our story later," Maryann said. "At home."

Keegan pointed down and asked, "What about those?"

Luna picked up Faucon's three severed toes. She held them out to Keegan.

"I'm not taking those," Keegan said. "No way."

"There's a pocket on the side of my scabbard," Luna said. "Put them in it."

Keegan made a face.

"Oh, for crying out loud," Maryann said, and held out her hand. She took the toes from Luna. "This from somebody who just buried an ax in Faucon's back?" She slipped them into the pocket on Luna's back.

"We'll see you at the house," Keegan said.

Luna got a short running start and catapulted herself off the roof, shifting quickly to her long glide wings in midair.

Whoosh, whoosh, whoosh.

Maryann turned to Keegan. "If they ask why we were here: you came across Zelda's interview with Byron Littlefield, and we came looking for Stonehedge."

They heard AJ call from the brook trail. "Coming up the hill. Everybody okay?"

"We're okay, AJ," Maryann yelled back, then spelled it out. "Cliff and Aaron are out cold and need the EMTs. Keegan and I are fine. *Everybody's accounted for.* Relax." She exhaled a sigh of relief and exhaustion.

"Before they get here, Mom, let me ask you something," Keegan said.

"What?"

"Did you get that line from an old movie?"

"What line?" Maryann asked.

"*I'll turn you into Swiss cheese.*"

Maryann laughed. "Probably an old gangster movie. I'm not sure. But I haven't used it since I put it in a short story I wrote in junior high English. I got an A+ and my teacher wrote next to that sentence: *great image.* Why? Did it sound corny?"

"It did. But it worked. And how about that *10 rounds per second, set on semi-automatic*? Where'd you get that?"

"I made that up on the spot, Keegan. Why?"

"Because that thing in your hand doesn't look anything like a Beretta. It's a Taser."

Maryann held the stun gun up and stared at it. "Well, Faucon didn't know that. I grabbed the first thing I could find on Aaron's duty belt."

CHAPTER 62

AJ arrived with two male EMTs, two Wells patrolmen, and Officer Alicia "Smitty" Smith, the State Trooper who had responded with Aaron on the Toil & Trouble call a week earlier.

The EMTs had left their wheeled gurneys in the truck and lugged along two military cot-type stretchers. With Cliff and Aaron both unconscious, they were forced to conscript the Wells cops to act as stretcher-bearers. The four of them—a paramedic and a cop for each litter—had no choice but to make the downed officers a priority and left immediately for the Elks lot. AJ insisted on riding to the hospital with Aaron.

"Call us from the hospital," Maryann said to AJ.

Which left Smitty to take the report. She could see Keegan and Maryann were tired and dirty, so she didn't press them for details, just listened and jotted down their basic story.

They had heard about Stonehedge on Zelda Keegan's 1990s historical society interview and thought they were learning of a previously undiscovered Wells cemetery. They hiked in after work and found it. They returned later with AJ, Aaron, and Cliff. Cliff and Aaron climbed onto the roof while three of them checked for windows, doors, or secret entrances in the granite walls. None of them saw what happened to Aaron or Cliff. They made no mention of a tunnel.

"I twisted my knee," Keegan said. "Can't wait to get home and ice it then soak it."

Smitty strung crime scene tape around Stonehedge and escorted Maryann and Keegan back to their car.

The two of them climbed in and as they drove off, Keegan asked her mother, "Any idea how to treat a gargoyle with a stab wound?"

"About the same as you would if it was one of us, I'm guessing," Maryann answered.

Section XIII
Emptyhanded

CHAPTER 63

It was after 3 a.m. when they got home. They found Luna under the deck, squatting by the plywood kindling box. She hadn't taken the tarp off the firewood.

Maryann knelt down next to her. "How's the bleeding?"

Luna extended her arm and put her short wing out to the side so Maryann could inspect. "It bled a bit while I was flying, which wasn't long. Looks like it stopped after I landed and sat still."

Maryann checked the wound. "The armpit is clotting nicely. I can't tell about the wing. Let's go inside and I'll clean and dress it. I've got hydrogen peroxide to flush it, antibiotic cream for infection, and gauze bandages and tape to cover it. We'll get you patched up and put you in the guest bedroom."

Maryann and Keegan helped Luna up the deck stairs and into the kitchen.

"You two wait in the living room," Maryann said. "I'll get the medical stuff." She disappeared upstairs.

"The sun will be up soon," Keegan said. "You'll have to stay here in the house while we go to work. It's Saturday, our busiest day."

"But the eggs," Luna protested.

"I know you need to find them," Keegan said. "But even if you weren't wounded, you couldn't go back now. The police are probably still out there."

Maryann interrupted from the top of the stairs, "We'll go after lunch."

"What?" Keegan asked dismissively, glancing up the stairs her mother. "Seriously? It'll be daylight."

"Exactly," Maryann said, and started down the steps. "That'll take Faucon out of the equation. If I thought he was still a threat to you, Keegan, I wouldn't suggest this. But he's badly injured—that ax did some real damage—and he's got no weapons. And it'll be broad daylight. I'm not saying he won't be a problem for Luna in the future, but I don't believe he's going to bother us today."

"So what's the plan?" Keegan asked.

"You and I work the morning while AJ goes to the monastery and picks up Luna's stuff from Brother Jerome. Luna can call him after breakfast. At noon we slap a note on the door of the bookstore—something about a family commitment—and head home. Luna slips into her habit and we take the car and get there by 1 p.m. Luna, are you okay with walking the path to Stonehedge in the robe?"

"I will be very slow. You saw me walk when I came in to make the book order."

"I have the solution for that," Keegan said.

Maryann and Luna turned to her and stared, waiting.

"The wheelbarrow," Keegan said. "It's only got a single wheel. If I can move firewood in it, I can move Luna. It'll be faster than her walking in that robe."

Maryann appeared to ponder this, then said, "Okay. Good idea."

"Also," Keegan said, "we'll take along our garden tools from the garage for digging. We've got small spades, hand rakes, and claws out there."

Maryann set the hydrogen peroxide, gauze, and antibiotic cream on the coffee table and set about the task of patching Luna up.

"*Merci*," Luna said softly.

Maryann's cellphone rang. Keegan picked it up.

"AJ, hi," she said, then whispered *hospital* loudly enough for Maryann and Luna to hear. Then she mouthed *AJ's mother and father are there*. She repeated what AJ was reporting. *Cliff is conscious. Broken ribs. Aaron's still out but should come around soon. Broken nose. Concussion. Doctor says he'll have a wicked headache for a couple of days.*

"Are you on speaker now?" Keegan asked AJ.

"No," she answered, then, "I'm walking out to the hallway."

Keegan fed AJ the basic story she and Maryann had used with Trooper Smitty. "Can you pass it on to Cliff? And to Aaron when he wakes up?"

"I will," AJ replied. "And I wouldn't worry. I'm pretty sure neither of them plan to mention *gargouilles*."

Keegan told AJ the plan for Saturday.

"Count me in. I'll bring my mother's garden trowel. I think she's got one of those claw things, too."

"Great," Keegan said. "See you at the store in a couple of hours."

AJ groaned.

Section XIV

Persistence

CHAPTER 64

They couldn't wait until noon. At 11:15 Maryann put the note on the door, locked up, and the three of them went home. While Maryann helped Luna into her habit, Keegan and AJ loaded the wheelbarrow and two cloth bags of garden tools into the back of the Subaru. They grabbed sandwiches on the way out the door and were unloading at the Elks lot by 12:30. They helped Luna into the wheelbarrow and started down the trail. Twenty minutes later they were at the base of the hill below Stonehedge. There was no sign of any police presence, only the crime scene tape Smitty had strung around it.

AJ and Maryann helped Luna out of the wheelbarrow while Keegan retrieved Faucon's sword and the ax from where she had flung them in the woods.

"Got 'em," Keegan said when she got back. "Now let's get to the new entrance."

They traipsed up and over the hill, the three of them supporting Luna and pushing her. Keegan spotted the still flashing jogger light they had clipped to a root.

"With that wound, how is Luna going to get down there?" Keegan asked. "And once she does, crawling through the tunnel is sure to open up that wound."

"She doesn't have to," Maryann said. "The eggs aren't in the chamber."

The others turned and stared at her.

"What do you mean they're not in the chamber?" Keegan asked, incredulous.

"They're probably down there," Maryann answered. "But they can't be in the chamber. When we were digging last night, I broke my fingernail—because underneath that soft sediment I hit solid rock—not just in one place but in several. It took me this long to figure out why. The floor is bedrock—a ledge. When Joshua Chamberlain ordered Stonehedge built, the quarry workers here in Wells did it the easy way: they located a fairly level ledge that made a natural floor. All they had to do was stack their wall blocks on it in a rectangle then top it with roof slabs. In essence Stonehedge is a manmade *gargouille* cave. Today that floor is hidden under a foot or two of composted vegetation that smells like potting soil. LeClair couldn't have covered up Diana and their eggs in that chamber if he wanted to. The only opening in that floor is where the tunnel comes up."

"Then where are the eggs?" AJ asked.

"Directly below us," Luna answered.

"Correct," Maryann said. "Near the base of this big tree. That maze of roots? They're the feeder lines."

⟐⟐⟐

Luna's injury kept her above ground. The narrowness of the opening and the density of the root system made it impossible for her to fly or climb down.

AJ volunteered to stay with her. "I've got this ball of twine I can use to lower stuff down or haul it up."

Maryann backed down into the hole, found roots strong enough for footing, and with AJ shining her flashlight from above she began making her way to the bottom. Climbing down now was easier than climbing up the night before. Keegan followed, grimacing each time the knee pain shot through her. But she managed.

Ten minutes later the two of them were on their knees on the dirt floor where the tunnel widened under the tree.

AJ tied the twine to the handles of two cloth shopping bags and lowered them to Keegan, who dumped out the digging tools and a battery powered Coleman lantern. When she snapped it on, the little space was far brighter than it had been when they saw it by flashlight.

"Wow," Maryann said. "It looks a lot different than it did last night."

"We weren't looking around much then," Keegan said. "We were intent on getting up and out. You had your flashlight when you came through here, and I had my dying cellphone light, neither of which penetrated these roots."

They glanced around.

"If all these roots weren't clogging the space," Maryann observed, "it'd look like a little bell-shaped room. Maybe seven or eight feet in diameter and seven or eight high."

"The base of the tree is a natural roof," Keegan said. "The trunk is probably a foot or two into the ground and has to be three or four feet in diameter. Everything to the side of that or below that is roots or soil."

"I heard you mention roots," AJ called down. "Do you want me to lower the ax?"

"No," Maryann answered. "Keep it up there for now."

Keegan picked up a digging claw and handed Maryann a hand spade. Neither of them moved.

"Ready?" Maryann asked.

Keegan whispered back, "This gives me the creeps. Part of me hopes she's not here."

"I know. But we have to do this. Zelda's watching."

Keegan rested her digging claw on the dirt in front of them and gave a perfunctory pull. "The dirt's harder here, firmer than that top layer in the chamber. She won't be very deep. I hope we find her feet before her head. We don't know which way he buried her, which direction she's facing. I'd hate to hook her skull and pull it off her shoulders."

"You know, Keegan, you've always chattered like this when you're uncomfortable."

"I know, I know. But it's understandable, Mom. We're digging up the dead. It's creepy."

"I know," Maryann said. "So let's do it reverently. Let's take our time and do it right. Work slowly. We don't know how delicate the eggs are."

They started, scraping and pulling and sifting their way forward over the six by ten plot as if they were excavating an archaeological dig site. The further they advanced, the greater the curtain of roots got.

"You seeing what I'm seeing?" Maryann asked, after they'd been at it 20 minutes. She placed the camping lamp between them and slightly ahead.

"You mean the curve of the roots?" Keegan replied. "Or the fact that they're making a lower ceiling here? As I move forward, they're forcing me lower and lower. I can feel the stress in my back."

"I was talking about the way they curve—sort of like looking at a skeleton's ribs. The right side curves one way, the left the other, but they're fairly symmetrical, and you get a clear sense of where the middle is. These roots are converging from two sides—like Mother Nature's GPS. Diana's where they meet."

"Problem is," Keegan said, "all these smaller roots are getting so close together it's like a curtain—one of those strung-bead curtains."

"Then we must be close to the body. And the eggs."

"Mom, I don't think we can dig much further forward with the roots blocking us. We're going to have to cut them."

"Which—if they really are the feeders for the eggs—will be like cutting a baby's umbilical cord *before* it's born."

"If they're even alive," Keegan said.

"Assume that they are," Maryann said. "At least one."

They stared at the tapestry of feeder roots blocking their progress—dozens, scores, hundreds of roots.

"AJ," Keegan yelled skyward. "Lower Faucon's sword."

"Faucon's sword? Why?" AJ responded.

"Just lower it, AJ," Maryann said.

AJ did, and Keegan untied it from the rope. Maryann tied the two fabric shopping bags on instead.

"Don't pull the bags up until we tell you," Maryann called up. Then she and Keegan faced the curtain of roots that was blocking their way forward.

Keegan pulled the camp lamp back out of the way. Maryann gripped the digging claw in one hand and the hand spade in the other.

"Ready?" Keegan asked. "We've got to be fast."

"Ready," Maryann answered, and stepped back out of the way of Keegan's swing.

From her kneeling position Keegan drew Faucon's sword behind her right hip, preparing to swing it in an arc that would rely on her leg, hip, shoulder, and arm strength. She leaned into it and came around fast, the blade singing and sizzling through the air, biting, cutting, and slicing through a dozen delicate roots before its forward movement stopped. She pulled it free and drew it back behind her again, then swung it sideways like a woodsman felling an oak--again and again, six times. By then she was exhausted and fell back away from her target.

"Your turn, Mom," she panted, and Maryann lunged past her, pushing aside the cut and bleeding roots so she could get to the ground they had been attached to.

A moment later Keegan was beside her, and the two of them scooped and raked and hoed, no longer timid about disturbing Diana's moldering body. They were in a frantic race to reach the eggs and whatever might be left inside them.

Maryann uncovered the first one. It was the size and shape of a football without the pointed ends, the stems of five or six severed feeder roots still attached as if with suction cups. It had been very close to the surface, and Keegan's horizontal sword swing had chopped the roots off barely eight inches above the rubbery shell. Maryann rolled the egg out between her legs and kept digging for others.

Keegan found the second and third eggs on the opposite side of the little mound that was Diana's rib cage. Some of the feeders were severed, but a couple were still attached, so she could free the two eggs without cutting the intact feeders. She had no room to swing the sword again, and the blade wasn't helpful for sawing in close quarters, so she pulled out her Swiss army knife, opened the largest blade, and cut the cords. She rolled first one egg then the other alongside her leg and behind her, then returned to digging. She felt her way up—or was it down—the string of pearls Luna had described, wondering if Diana's skull was in front of her or under her feet.

Maryann found another, but it was leathery and deflated like an old airless basketball at a dump, so she left it and moved on. The next two were like it. Had the first one, the one she had rolled out between her legs, survived by feeding off the three lifeless ones? Was the first one even still alive? She backed away.

"Let's go, Keegan," she said. "I got one."

"A flat one here," Keegan answered. Then, "Make that two. No, three."

"Any live ones?" Maryann asked.

"Yep, the first two. They're back by my feet."

"So we've got three. Let's go. Fast."

They backed away from the mound that had once been Diana, then placed the three eggs in the shopping bags.

"Pull them up carefully, AJ," Maryann ordered. "We don't want them to catch on a root and dump out. Give them to Luna as soon as you get them up."

AJ lifted the first bag—two eggs—hand over hand, until she had it at ground level. She gave the bag to Luna. Then she pulled up the second bag with the third egg and held it tight against her.

Maryann and Keegan left the tools and the sword. They climbed, Maryann powered by surging adrenalin, Keegan taking deep breaths to stay with the task at hand, not the screaming knee.

Section XV

Midwives

CHAPTER 65

"Where are they?" Maryann asked, as AJ helped her onto solid ground.

"Luna's got them," AJ said, and pointed to some bushes less than ten feet away.

Maryann squinted and spotted a silhouette that reminded her of a crèche—the Virgin Mary leaning reverently over a manger crib. Behind her she heard Keegan ask AJ for a hand up, which AJ offered. Maryann edged toward the hunched figure and saw the cloth bags on the ground halfway between them, empty, discarded.

"Luna?" she asked softly and approached.

Luna didn't answer, so Maryann placed a hand on her shoulder, hand brushing the top of the glide wing, which felt thin and rubbery like a bat's. She could feel her *gargouille* friend's shoulder trembling, shuddering, and knew Luna's chest was convulsing with sobs.

Oh, no, Luna, not the eggs. What did you do to them?

"Luna?" Maryann asked. "The eggs?"

Luna seemed frozen and speechless.

Keegan came up behind Maryann and shone her light in front of Luna. Spread on the ground was a beach towel Maryann had packed, and on it lay the three eggs looking like eggplants with long broken stems. They were still whole, not deflated like those they had left below in the grave dirt.

One of the eggs moved, wobbling slightly like a giant Mexican jumping bean. Something inside it was kicking, struggling to get out.

"Luna," Maryann said. "You have to do something. Now."

But Luna didn't move. She was still sobbing.

Maryann thought, *she doesn't dare hatch them, because she'll have to kill the males. Or would she kill the females?*

"What are we waiting for, Mom?" Keegan asked, unaware of Maryann and Luna's earlier conversation about females in the royal succession.

A second egg moved.

"Luna!" Maryann said sharply. "Make a decision."

Keegan pushed past her mother and fell to her knees by the cloth robe. Pain roared up and down her leg. She leaned over and placed her hands around one of the eggs.

"It's kicking," she said, and began to weep. "It's pulsing."

Maryann pressed on Luna's shoulder forcing her forward over what was left of Diana's nest.

"Luna!" Keegan said, lifting her egg the way a priest raised the Eucharist. "We don't know what to do."

Luna dumbly stretched out her hands and let Keegan hand her the egg. She took it and kept her arms away from her body like she was receiving a casserole.

Keegan picked up another egg and handed it to Maryann, then slipped her hands under the third egg and drew it close to her body.

Luna stood like a statue.

"Luna, please," Maryann begged. "They're suffocating."

The three closed ranks and faced each other as if in a small prayer circle, tiny Luna standing with Maryann and Keegan on their knees. As the circle closed, each of them instinctively drew her egg to her midsection and held it close. An observer might have mistaken them for three pregnant mothers waiting for a childbirth class to start.

AJ's voice startled them. "Will they hatch on their own like sea turtles or chickens? Will they peck their way out of the shells?"

Keegan and Maryann knew the answer. These shells were nothing like hen's eggs. They felt like Vitamin A fish oil pills, squishy but relatively firm, except a hundred times the size of the little gelatin capsules. *Gargouille* eggs clearly needed to be birthed.

"What do we do, Luna?" Maryann asked, voice pleading. "Help us. If you can't do it yourself, tell us how."

"Mine's kicking, Mom," Keegan said.

"Mine, too," Maryann answered.

"Not mine," Luna said. She stepped back from the circle and said, "AJ, hold the egg a moment."

AJ accepted it.

Luna stepped into a bit of shade, brought her right hand in front of her and removed the black glove. Then she straightened her thick index finger. Maryann and Keegan stared at the stubby fingertip as a single curved talon unfolded from its end like the can opener blade on a jackknife. It appeared only at the tip of the index finger, not on any of the others.

"What are you going to do?" Keegan asked.

Luna ignored her and told AJ, "Hold the egg on your palms." She placed hooked fingertip on the egg where the largest of four feeder roots had been attached and pressed the sharp tip against the rubbery egg covering. She drew her finger across the shell, piercing it with a slight pop. Then she pulled out the talon tip and took back the egg. A thin greenish fluid seeped out.

"Is it—" Maryann started to ask.

"Green is good," Luna said, and cradled the punctured egg in one hand against her hip. With her free hand she reinserted the talon in the same hole and drew her finger lengthwise along the egg as if tracing the seam of a football. She slit the shell end to end, slicing through only the outer membrane, taking care to not harm whatever was curled inside. More green fluid seeped out along the cutline. She retracted the talon and set the egg down on the towel. It looked like a small watermelon that had split after falling off the back of a truck.

"Hand me another," Luna said.

"Is that one dead?" Keegan asked.

"No," Luna answered. "It has air now. But we have to hurry."

Maryann passed the second egg to her and Luna repeated the slitting procedure. As soon as the green fluid began leaking out, she placed it on the towel next to the first egg.

Keegan handed her the third egg. Luna cut it open and set it down with the others. They all had their oozing slit sides up.

"Now we turn them over," Luna said, "and separate the halves with our fingers. The liquid will gush out and the baby will fall into the puddle. Scoop up the liquid and coat them with it—completely. It will help them build immunities."

All three eggs rocked on their own like they were in cradles. Their occupants wanted to get out.

"Then what?" Keegan asked.

"Mother them," Luna answered. "Ready?"

Luna reached for the first egg, and Maryann and Keegan leaned forward for theirs. They all turned their eggs upside down and used their fingertips to pry them apart. The fluid gushed, as Luna had said, and two of the hatchlings plopped out of their shells into the puddle of green fluid pooling on the robe.

"They look like Ninja turtles," AJ exclaimed from behind them.

Luna and Keegan used their hands to coat the little *gargouille* bodies with the green liquid.

Maryann's hatchling didn't drop out of the shell. "It's stuck," she said. "Either it's too big or it's like a human breech birth."

"Can you pull the shell wider?" AJ asked, and tried to give Maryann a hand. The shell would only stretch so far.

They heard what sounded like a honk, so Maryann held up the egg and looked under it. Fluid was seeping, not gushing, out of the crack, where a tiny *gargouille* head was sticking down. It hadn't been honking, though, it had been gasping, choking on the fluid. *Drowning.*

"The shoulders—or maybe it's the wings—are too big," Maryann said. "They won't fit through."

"Take this one, AJ," Luna said, and handed her the first baby.

Then she said to Maryann, "I'll separate the shell while you pull it out."

Luna stood over Maryann's egg and reached her hands around it so her fingers were in the slit seam underneath. "Now," she said, and pulled, feeling the pain under her right arm where the sword had pierced her and Maryann had patched her. She let out a mighty cry as Maryann gripped the head of the choking baby and exerted a steady downward pull.

"Once more," Maryann urged.

Luna clamped her knees around the two ends of the egg and became a vise, squeezing and groaning as her finger pulled at the seam she had ripped, straining to separate it. Maryann pulled steadily until—with a plop—the baby shot out. Luna kept the empty egg above it, letting the green fluid drip down as Maryann coated its skin and scalp. It began to cry, sounding like a human baby, and the other two newborns on the towel joined in.

Keegan and AJ picked up the first two and cuddled them. Maryann picked up the large baby, held it and kissed it on its forehead. Then she handed it to Luna, who did the same. All four adults were weeping.

"Are they males or females?" AJ asked, and Maryann couldn't help but cringe.

"How do we tell?" Keegan asked.

"Eye color," Luna replied.

AJ looked down into the eyes of hers. "Green."

Keegan checked hers. "Also green. Like Luna's eyes. Females."

AJ turned her light toward Luna.

"Luna?" Maryann asked.

Luna had the third *gargouille* pressed against her chest, where she could feel its tiny heart beating. She turned the baby slightly away from her chest so its eyes could be seen.

"Red," AJ said, and Luna began to sob.

CHAPTER 66

"We've got to get them back to the house," Maryann said.

It was 3:10 and they were still next to the hole that led down to the tunnel. All three newborns were crying. Rocking them wasn't enough.

"They're hungry," Keegan said, remembering from their first encounter on the deck that Luna had no breasts. "What do we feed them?"

Luna set the large male down on his back on the sticky towel and raised Faucon's sword the way a king's executioner might.

"Luna, no!" Maryann cried out and reached to restrain her.

Luna's blade hissed through the night air in a deadly arc, striking the largest of the newly vacated shells. The blade cleaved neatly through it, dividing it into two halves, each coming to rest on its rounded end, each of the pieces resembling a deviled egg on an *hors d'oeuvres* tray. Luna raised the sword and struck again, this time cutting both pieces in the same blow, then did it several more times—whack, whack, whack—leaving the rubbery egg in more than a dozen small chunks. She picked up three pieces and handed them to Keegan, AJ, and Maryann.

"Let them suck on these for now," she said. "Gather up the extra pieces and the other two shells and put them in the cloth bags. We will take them back to your house."

They gathered the cut-up egg pieces and used them as pacifiers, except these pacifiers had nutrients. The three babies, as soon as they began sucking on them, quieted down. They walked Luna downhill, juggling newborns as they went, then loaded her into the wheelbarrow where they had left it on the path. Maryann took two babies and handed the oversized male to Luna. AJ and Keegan took turns pushing the heavy wheelbarrow uphill to the car.

It was 4:50 when the Subaru pulled into the driveway and carried the three new *gargouilles* inside. They gave Maryann's food processor a workout, blending nuts, berries, and vegetables into a pasty substance that Gerber and Beech Nut would gladly have sold on grocery shelves.

Section XVI

Homeward Bound

CHAPTER 67

With the bookstore closed on Sunday, they swaddled the newborns in beach towels and, with Luna in her habit, set out at 6 a.m. for the Allagash Wilderness, an eight hour drive. There were no car seats, so they hid the babies under a blanket in the way-back cargo area. State Troopers were few and far between on Sunday mornings in rural Maine.

The plan worked. They arrived at 2:30. Luna had Maryann drive another hour on a back road. A while later they parked partway up an isolated logging trail and waited—walking and rocking the babies, and feeding them in the four hours until it was dusk.

"It will be dark very soon," Luna said, "and I will be able to remove my robe and use my glide wings. Wait here with the babies. I have two friends I can trust to help me. I will return with them in two hours."

A while later they got out of the car and Luna took off the heavy robe.

"I will say *au revoir et merci* now," Luna said. "I am thankful for everything you have done. I could not have done it without you. I am sorry that AJ's brother Aaron and your friend Cliff and the other policeman—his name was Stedman, *n'est-ce pas*—were hurt."

"You're coming back here, right?" Keegan asked. "For these babies? All of them?"

"*Oui*. As I said—in two hours." She handed the robe to Maryann. "Leave the babies in the towels, but also leave them wrapped in my robe—over there." She pointed to a rock outcropping with an overhang that formed a natural but shallow cave. "Place them there in an hour and a half and return to the car. We will come for them. Two hours. Do not approach us."

She hugged the three of them. They were all in tears.

"You say we helped you, Luna," Maryann said. "But it was you who helped us. You gave us—especially Keegan and me—a gift. I was privileged to help you do something I did not get to do 20 years ago with

Zelda—deliver a baby. It was an amazing, wonderful gift that has helped heal my broken heart."

"And mine," Keegan added. "I did not even know my heart was hurting, and so deep down. Thank you, Luna." She kissed the *gargouille* on the forehead.

Luna stepped back and looked Keegan in the eyes. "Zelda would have been so proud of you." She reached up to Keegan's temple and touched the shock of white hair there. "So would your father."

"My father?" Keegan gasped.

"You know who he is?" Maryann asked, equally shocked.

"I had no idea you did not know."

"Zelda never told me," Maryann said.

"He was a graduate teaching assistant, perhaps 30 years older than Zelda. He was from Holland and had come to Maine for his teacher certification. I have forgotten his family name, but Zelda called him *Yon*—that's how it was pronounced—but it's spelled spelled *J A N*. It is one of the most common Dutch names. I saw him but I never met him or talked to him. He had the same shock of white hair."

"J-A-N?" Keegan spelled out, remembering the letters *Jan—not a month but a name*—scrawled above the name *Dauphine* on the back of Zelda's little yellow notebook. "Does he know about me?"

"I have no idea," Luna replied. "He was only in the United States for your mother's senior year and then went back to Holland."

Keegan and Maryann had a few more questions like *is he still alive?* But Luna had no more answers.

"Two hours," *la gargouille* said. "Remember. Leave the babies in the cave shortly before that and stay in the car. Do not approach us."

"Two hours," Maryann echoed. "You take care."

Luna took a long run across the hardscrabble and flapped her long upper wings.

Whoosh, whoosh, whoosh.

An hour and forty-five minutes later they carried the three baby *gargouilles*—snugly swaddled in their colorful beach towels—to the outcropping, where they spread Luna's black habit out under the overhanging ledge. They hugged the babies close and kissed them, passing them back and forth. Then somewhat reluctantly they lined them up together on the robe like three egg rolls in a Chinese restaurant and folded it over them. They walked glumly back to the Subaru, zipped down the windows, and waited, eyes on the outcropping.

Ten minutes later they heard them coming overhead.

Whoosh. Whoosh. Whoosh.

But they couldn't make them out. They were shadows gliding in on wide bats' wings. Their wings pulled up, slowing them so they skidded in like geese landing on a moonlit pond. The three of them made no other sounds and spoke no words that could be heard through the open car windows. They moved like ghosts—or maybe harpies—disappearing beneath the overhang and reappearing a moment later, each *gargouille* hugging a precious package against its chest.

And then Keegan, Maryann, and AJ saw the universal silhouette—the stance of joy—as all three raised the swaddled babes before their faces at arm's length and slightly overhead, then wiggling them before once again drawing them close.

The trio's wings came out and they broke into a short run—exactly the same for all three—then lifted off—*whoosh, whoosh, whoosh.* When the sound of air rushing beneath their wings ceased, they watched from the Subaru as the three ghosts—*night hawks* described them perfectly—ascended up and across the face of the moon and out of sight.

In Keegan's head the wheels were already turning. *Tomorrow is Monday. Call UMO about Jan. Check airfares Boston to Amsterdam.*

Maryann was thinking the same thing.

THE END

AUTHOR'S NOTES

Only the following paragraph of *The Bookseller's Daughter* was actually written by Joshua Chamberlain:

"It was a cold night. Bitter, raw north winds swept the stark slopes. The men, heated by their energetic and exciting work, felt keenly the chilling change. Many of them had neither overcoat nor blanket, having left them with the discarded knapsacks. They roamed about to find some garment not needed by the dead. Mounted officers all lacked outer covering. This had gone back with the horses, strapped to the saddles. So we joined the uncanny quest. Necessity compels strange uses. For myself it seemed best to bestow my body between two dead men among the many left there by earlier assaults, and to draw another crosswise for a pillow out of the trampled, blood-soaked sod, pulling the flap of his coat over my face to fend off the chilling winds..."

The rest of the Chamberlain journal entries, the (fictional creation) Clayton Lussier journal entries, and the Civil War letters or reports from both sides (e.g. letters home) were pastiches that I created for this novel.

Wells, Maine does in fact boast 201 cemeteries in its roughly 60 square miles. I have visited more than half of them. I see the little one at Bear's Den RV Park on Bear's Den Road nearly every day from mid-May to mid-October when I'm at our Wells summer camp. Stonehedge is probably a fictional one.

Annie's Book Stop is a local gem that sits one block south of the traffic light where Route 1 meets Route 9W (Littlefield Road). Annie's has been around for decades and is a great place to shop for used paperbacks. The staff (who are not the staff in this novel) are booklovers themselves and are always friendly and helpful. While Arrington's, Douglas Harding's, and Mainely Murder are real bookstores, Toil & Trouble is made up.

What I referred to as the *Wells Town History* was based loosely on town historian Hope M. Shelley's 2002 book, *Town History of Wells*. It was an invaluable resource for information about quarries, cemeteries, and historical characters like Reverend Burroughs.

Millennium Granite is a real place on Quarry Road in Wells. Owner Richard Bois gave me a quick tour, answered my questions, and let me walk the property alone. The water-filled quarry pit has been off-limits as a swimming hole for 30 years. One of the You Tube videos I describe in the book exists, but the one with the Keegan sisters does not.

The two cemeteries books and the *Night Hawks* book were made up for this novel.

Mike's Fish Market at the corner of Chapel and Post Road is real and is a wonderful place to get fresh, reasonably-priced seafood you can cook at home.

———————

Here's a chance to sample the opening chapter of Steve Burt's *FreeK Camp,* the opening novel in the FreeKs psychic teen detectives series:

FreeK Camp, FreeK Show, and *FreeK Week*

Available in paperback, ebook, and audio book.

Chapter 1

NO ONE SUSPECTED there was a camp for kids with paranormal powers in the backwoods of Maine—or that its past would put their lives at risk.

The five "different" 13- and 14-year-olds took their seats in the battered pale blue van marked Free Camp #2 which—thanks to someone wielding a red Magic Marker two years earlier—had become FreeK Camp #2. Not only had no one felt the need to erase or paint over the added K, but whenever it faded, it was magically freshened up by someone under cover of darkness. Beneath the camp name someone had added a Smiley face with a third eye—like the CBS eye—in the center of its forehead. It was what Free Camp kids called the mind's eye.

Once they were in, the driver, a tiny man with curly red hair, reached up and closed the side doors, reassuring the parents and siblings in the parking lot, "Don't worry. Never lost a summer camper yet. I'll get them there in one piece." Then, with the families trying not to stare, he opened the driver's door and climbed up onto a child's booster seat. With the door still open so they could see, he strapped a pair of leg-extenders onto his calves. "Got to reach the pedals, you know!" He flashed them an impish grin. "Seatbelts, everybody," he called back to the kids behind him, and buckled his own. He slammed the door once, twice, and finally a third time. "Some days it doesn't want to latch," he said to the families. "But everything else works fine. See you back here in a week."

The odd little man eased the van out of the parking lot into the flow of traffic, encouraging his passengers to show genuine enthusiasm in waving goodbye to their families. They were off, though to where, the kids weren't exactly sure. Free Camp's mailing address had been a post office box in rural Bridgton, Maine, in the state's western lakes region. But the actual camp, according to the brochure, was pretty far from town, more than a long hike. Still, even if it was a few miles away from civilization, a free week at summer camp in July would be a welcome change from their hometowns.

The front passenger seat was empty. It wasn't that they felt uncomfortable sitting next to the midget, as they'd begun referring to him in their parking lot whispers—he seemed nice enough—but he'd neither invited nor instructed anyone to sit there. Once they'd stowed their backpacks, suitcases, and sleeping bags in the way-back cargo area, he'd motioned them through the double side door.

The Hispanic-looking brother and sister had grabbed the comfortable captain's chairs, leaving the third-row bench seat for the other three. The first in was a slight boy with long blond hair and wire-rimmed glasses. Wedged between himself and his armrest was a book, the spine imprinted with the title, *Encyclopaedia of Psychic Science*, and the author's name, Nandor Fodor. In the middle sat another boy—pudgy, pale-skinned, and freckle-faced, a raised brown Mohawk tuft spanning his shaved scalp front-to-back like the Great Wall of China. The last in was a frizzy-haired brunette in wrap-around sunglasses, dangly turquoise pierced earrings, and carved-wood peace-symbol necklace. She held a Free Camp brochure on her lap, an index finger resting on the words "those unique, special, and unusual children who, because their gifts are so very different, may feel strange or alienated from other kids."

The five weren't yet a group, a team. But they'd become one soon, and not in the usual summer-camp way. No, for this group it would happen differently. Fate—and the biggest challenge of their young lives—would draw them closer, soon. At the moment, as they rode peacefully along on a sunny July morning, they had no way of knowing just how lucky they were—for in an hour they would arrive at Free Camp safe and sound. Safe.

The other van, Free Camp #1, which had picked up another five "different" kids two hours earlier, would not. That van had been carjacked by a madman.

www.SteveBurtBooks.com

CPSIA information can be obtained
at www.ICGtesting.com
Printed in the USA
FSHW012132100919
61860FS